BROCKTON PUBLIC LIBRARY
W9-ATD-873

Who Steals My Name . . . ?

By James Fraser

WHO STEALS MY NAME . . . ?
A WREATH OF LORDS AND LADIES
THE EVERGREEN DEATH
THE COCK-PIT OF ROSES
DEADLY NIGHTSHADE
DEATH IN A PHEASANT'S EYE
BLOOD ON A WIDOW'S CROSS
THE FIVE-LEAFED CLOVER

Who Steals My Name...?

★

JAMES FRASER

PUBLISHED FOR THE CRIME CLUB BY
DOUBLEDAY & COMPANY, INC.
GARDEN CITY, NEW YORK
1976

All of the characters in this book
are fictitious, and any resemblance
to actual persons, living or dead,
is purely coincidental.

ISBN: 0-385-11589-X
Library of Congress Catalog Card Number 75-40724

Printed in the United States of America
First Edition in the United States of America

Who steals my purse steals trash;
'tis something, nothing; . . .
But he that filches from me my good name
Robs me of that which not enriches him,
And makes me poor indeed.

Othello

Who Steals My Name . . . ?

CHAPTER 1

Lord Mawsley shifted uncomfortably on the chair in his study in Mawsley Hall, feeling a twinge of pain in his back that told him he would have no more comfort that night. Dammit, he knew he'd walked too far that afternoon but the air had been so tempting, the sky so clear, the trees and birds of the estate had beckoned so undeniably. It was a long time since he had walked as far as Willow Copse and the lake beyond it. How he remembered the wonderful times he'd had as a young boy, swimming daringly in the lake without clothes, escaping the stifling tweed knickerbockers, woollen hose that came to his knees, a Norfolk jacket, and the cap that had been the uniform without which Peabody would not permit him to leave the premises. Of course, the willows had not been planted then and the copse had been ringed with elms. One by one the elms had died, almost as if they were marking the passage of the years of his life. It was the last elm that had been responsible for the injury to his back only eight years ago. The last elm had succumbed to a night of storm. Lord Mawsley had ridden Thundering Cloud III round the estate to see the extent of the damage. Thundering Cloud had a heart like a lion and a foolish ambition to match and when Lord Mawsley, in a capricious moment, put him to the six-foot jump over the fallen tree, Thundering Cloud III went at it like a three-year-old. Neither one of them had seen until it was too late that in falling the trunk of the diseased elm had split and on the other side of the jump a stake extended towards them on which Thundering Cloud III impaled himself. The horse died, mercifully instantly. Lord Mawsley was flung fifteen feet through the air, somersaulting to land with his back against a branch of the same tree that had killed his horse. For six months he'd been in agony, the lower part of his body encased in plaster, but finally tiring of the encumbrance he ordered it cut away and went to see a chiropractor no one respected at Leicester. The chiropractor worked wonders, as on so many other occasions, and enabled Lord Mawsley to walk again if not to ride. Now the man in Leicester was dead and no one could take his place to relieve Lord Mawsley of the pain that came whenever he was impetuous enough to prolong a walk too far. He got out of his chair, crossed to the fireplace, and drew on the velvet cord that dangled there. Although it was approaching ten o'clock, he felt no tiredness and knew that many waking hours lay ahead of him. He turned his back to the open log fire and felt the gentle warmth seeping through his clothing. Wood burns tender, not fierce like coal or harsh like gas. A tap came on the door and he called "Come in" in his deep mellifluous voice. The door opened and Peabody stood there, tall, thin almost to a point of emaciation, white haired, stooping slightly, the same Peabody, who all those years ago as second footman charged with the responsibility of "the young master," had forbidden those deliciously wicked, naked immersions in the waters of the lake. In his hands Peabody carried a silver tray on which was a small silver box, a decanter of whisky, and a syphon of soda.

"Is our back acheing, your Lordship?" Peabody asked, unable to resist the inner smile that, had Peabody been so impertinent, would have said, "I told you so."

"You were right, dammit, Peabody," Lord Mawsley said, "but then over the last fifty years you've never done me the kindness of being wrong, have you? I ought to have taken the ride home in the Land Rover."

Peabody forebore to reply. He placed the tray on the round-topped mahogany table beside the leather-covered wing armchair in which Lord Mawsley sat. He opened the silver box, which dated back to Georgian times, and in it revealed two red-coloured plastic capsules which looked out of place in such an elegant surrounding. One felt they should have been small, pink, and round and have smelled of violets. He poured a generous measure of the whisky into the heavy cut-crystal goblet and into it deftly squirted a large quantity of soda water.

"Don't *drown* the damn stuff," Lord Mawsley said testily, but Peabody looked at him. "I thought the doctor insisted the whisky be diluted when we take our pills," he said.

"I *know* what the doctor said." To Lord Mawsley, it was sufficient of an offence that the good whisky be contaminated with soda water, without the offence being compounded by the use of such a large quantity. But Peabody, of course, was right again. On the one occasion he'd taken the pills, and had guiltily refilled his glass with neat whisky after Peabody had left, he'd had a dreadful night with high temperatures and nausea, tossing and turning in his nightmare-raddled sleep.

Peabody held the tray carrying the pillbox; Lord Mawsley took both pills and washed them down with a gulp of the whisky-soda Peabody next offered. "I shan't want anything else," Lord Mawsley said, "but you'd better leave the whisky and the siphon. That young fellow, Baron, said he might pop in to see me, a bit later."

"I do hope Mr. Baron won't be staying too late," Peabody said, a frown of distaste crossing his face. In his day the people of the village came when they were commanded; they didn't ever "pop in." That was another of the modern crazes to which he could not accustom himself. Like Lord Mawsley walking about the Hall of an evening wearing a polo-necked cashmere sweater. Ever since Lady Mawsley had died fifteen years previously, Peabody had noticed a certain laxity in Lord Mawsley's manner, almost as if the old customs, the old traditions, had died with her Ladyship. He could not remember any man being permitted to walk inside the Hall at any time of day or evening without a tie, unless he should just happen to be passing through, suitably clad of course for a game of cricket or tennis; even then some sort of cravat at the throat would be required. He sighed. To hear Peabody sigh was in itself an experience.

"Oh, go on with you," Lord Mawsley said. "Get off to bed. You're becoming crotchety in your old age. I've a good mind to put you out to grass!" It was a threat to which Peabody was quite accustomed, and evoked from him his customary smile and shake of his head. "I think if you will pardon me saying so, my Lord, we shall both take to the pasture together." He walked from the room with the dignity of Black Rod about to summon Parliament, and the heavy door closed behind him without a sound.

Left to his own devices, Lord Mawsley prowled the bookshelves of his study seeking a suitable volume with which to while away the time until Baron should appear. He stopped in front of the curtain and pulled the cord that drew them back. He opened the window and let in the night air, glancing guiltily over his shoulder as if expecting Peabody to reappear and chide him for such folly. He looked out over the rose gardens to the terrace beyond them and the woods that lay below. The tops of the trees showed like a growth of hair at the level of the stone balustrade. He looked up at the sky, saw the clouds which scudded across in the unusually high wind. It was coming up to full moon and the scene before his eyes changed rapidly, sliding swiftly from dark black to stark silver as if some giant shutter were flicking across the face of the moon. He remembered an occasion the previous year when he permitted Cedric, his son, to take over the small ballroom of the Hall for a discotheque. Electricians had swarmed over the Hall for days previously and had installed all manner of most curious lighting effects. He'd walked into the ballroom during the playing of one of the tunes by a group his son had brought from London, paying them what seemed to Lord Mawsley the outrageous sum of two hundred pounds to come. When Lord Mawsley had gone into the ballroom he had thought for the moment that he had lost his senses. The young couples appeared to be standing adjacent to each other and moving with a curious puppetlike jerk as somewhere the source of the light flickered. It was rather like that toy he had as a young boy where you turned a handle and picture cards moved around the edge of a circle. The continuous flicking of the picture cards produced an illusion of actual movement in the figures on the cards. Cedric had later explained that this type of lighting was what he described as a "rave up," which left Lord Mawsley no wiser.

For some reason, Challenger was cantering across the paddock to the right of the rose garden and as the long ribbon of cloud moved across the face of the moon the light appeared to be alternately switched on and off, and Challenger appeared to be flying not cantering, his tail floating out behind him, his head lifted high, a moonlit Pegasus. For some reason, Lord Mawsley shivered, stepped back, closed the window, and pulled the curtain close again, as if to shut out some intangible evil. The movement of pulling the curtain taut caused a twitch of pain in the base of his spine and he turned and looked over at the clock above the fireplace. Twenty-five minutes past ten. "Oh dear, was Baron coming or wasn't he?" Lord Mawsley regretted having placed himself at Baron's disposal but such was his nature, such his relationship with the people of the village that he could not change the habit of a lifetime. To Peabody's frequent distress, he always made a point of being available when a member of the village of Mawsley should require him, though, at times like the present, it was deuced inconvenient. He longed to go to his bedroom and lie flat along the horsehair-mattress-covered board on which he'd slept for years, gradually allowing the pills to take effect, to relieve the tightness of the muscles which caused this intense stabbing pain. What was it Baron had said? "I'm having a meeting in the clubroom and may need to come and see your Lordship later. Would it be all right for me to do so? If I do come, it will be an official matter." Lord Mawsley was used to official matters. Though his appointment as Lord Lieutenant of the County was considered by some to be largely an honorary one, it did possess certain responsibilities. Besides living in Mawsley, young Baron was a member of the Birton Police Force; Lord Mawsley had stood referee for him. For a long time Lord Mawsley had hoped that Baron was going to look after the stables. The stable block had been built in the fifteenth century and was now scheduled, as was the Hall itself, as a Building of Historic Importance. In the old days, of course, it contained twenty hunters and Lord Mawsley had practically been born on a horse. It was said that his mother came back from the Easter Meet, dismounted, went up to her room and immediately into labour. Young Bobby Baron had appeared very crestfallen one day and had confessed that though he loved horses and had always anticipated a lifetime working with them, of late he'd conceived an intense passion to join the Police Force. Would Lord Mawsley consider it a breach of honour if Baron were to resign his position as head groom and apply for admittance to the Police Constabulary? Of course, Lord Mawsley agreed instantly, especially since Baron had promised to devote his off-duty hours to helping with the riding school that had been established in the stables now the hunters were gone. Lord Mawsley had bought a half-dozen good ponies and young Marilyn Combes had been delighted to teach such of the village children as wanted to ride. Bobby Baron turned up during his off-duty hours and helped with the riding instruction and the grooming, establishing a sort of Pony Club which used the former large tack room as its premises. He even married Marilyn's sister, Betty Combes, and took her to live in the cottage rented from Lord Mawsley.

"I'm going to have an official meeting tonight," Baron had said, "in the clubroom. I may need to come and see you afterwards. I know it will be rather late but it's official business and I'd be very grateful if your Lordship could help me. There is no one else I can turn to." Well, of course, in that circumstance, there had been nothing else but for Lord Mawsley to agree, though he had not anticipated he would be in agony with his back. "I don't think young

Baron will mind," he said to himself. He left the study and went into the hall. Quite unusually, the stables had been built onto the side of Mawsley Hall and Lord Mawsley used the door that led via a short corridor directly into what was now the clubroom. He listened at the door for a moment to see if he could hear any sounds of the meeting in progress, but the door was thick, solidly constructed of three-inch oak, and no sound could penetrate it. He tapped gently on the door and then put his hand on the handle and allowed it to swing forward open away from him. The clubroom was twenty feet square and all around the walls it carried the wooden pegs and shoulders on which individual saddles and tack had been hung. Ranged against the wall were a number of wooden saddle horses. In the centre of the room was a cluster of four armchairs. In one of the armchairs his son, Cedric, was sitting, his eyes open but his gaze unfocused. He was snapping his thumb and third finger together in an endless continuous echo of some inner rhythm. The snap of his fingers was the only sound to be heard in that brightly lit room. In the chair next to Lord Mawsley's son, Cedric, Constable Baron was slumped, his head forward, cradled along the inside of his right arm. From the base of Baron's skull the thin stream of blood ran down his neck and under his collar, along which the fresh red stain had spread for three inches or more.

Constable Baron was dead; that much Lord Mawsley could immediately discern. He closed the door, turned round, and walked back to his study. He pulled the cord, placed his back to the comfort of the log fire, and waited. Peabody appeared within two minutes; in his hand he carried the silver tray from which he was almost inseparable, the tray that symbolised order and dignity.

"Yes, my Lord," he said.

"Be a good fellow, Peabody," Lord Mawsley said, "and telephone the police. It appears that Mr. Baron is dead, in the clubroom. Mr. Cedric is with him, and I fear he might be responsible."

"Very good, my Lord," Peabody said. "I presume we'll be requiring a couple more of the pills. For our back, I mean."

"Yes, Peabody. A couple more pills. I imagine it will be a long and painful night."

CHAPTER 2

Detective Superintendent Aveyard staggered up the steps of the Police Headquarters in the park just outside Birton beneath the weight of six planks, each two metres long twenty-five centimetres wide and three centimetres thick. He had reached the door of his office with his burden when a police constable came out of the radio room further down the corridor, looked guiltily about him, and then scurried to where the Superintendent was bent, trying to fumble the key into his office door.

"Let me give you a hand, Superintendent," the constable said.

Aveyard's look could have dropped him in his tracks. "You're supposed to be on the front door, Birkett," he said, "not chatting up the birds in the radio room. Just because it's late at night and you don't think anybody's about. . . ."

Birkett sprang to attention, "Yes, Superintendent," he said.

"But since you're up here, you can give me a hand in with this lot."

Birkett held one end of the planks while Aveyard opened the door and they carried the heavy load through into Aveyard's office. "Right, now you can get back to the desk," Aveyard said. He shut the door and turned on the overhead light. He immediately checked that the carpenter had installed the brackets where he had marked the wall. He tested them with his hand; they had been put in firmly, a solid craftsman job of work but then, he thought, the man who'd done them was a civilian. Six months ago he'd asked the Police Department Maintenance men to install a set of shelves for him; for six months the paperwork had passed backwards and forwards. In desperation he had brought in his own craftsman, bought the wood out of his own pocket, and now planned to occupy the peace of a late evening with its installation, working at a time when the telephone wouldn't be constantly ringing, when the dynamo of a police headquarters was temporarily stilled. There's not much crime about at that time of the evening; wise coppers snatch a rest between eight o'clock and eleven. Later, the layabouts come roaring out of pubs with a skinful of booze and the radio room springs into life, despatching police cars like scurrying ants over the face of the city. Most of the incidents would be small ones the radio cars could deal with. Any man arrested would be taken to Divisional cells for the night. Serious crime would come into Headquarters, of course, but mostly it would be handled at Divisional level. Aveyard had reckoned on at least an hour in which to put in the twelve screws that would hold his shelving firm. He looked at the files which littered his side desk. Soon he'd be able to stack them in an orderly manner. Though Aveyard spent little time in this office, he liked to keep it tidy where everything he needed could easily be found. A couple of desks, three telephones, a filing cabinet, a set of shelves, and his favourite chair were all he needed.

He had finished the third shelf when a loud knock came on the door. He shouted "Wait" but was too late. The door opened quickly, the plank which had been resting against it swung over and toppled down, landing, before he could move, square on the top of his head.

Through the mists of pain he heard the voice of the Chief Superintendent. "What on earth are you doing down there, wrestling with that piece of wood?"

Aveyard got to his feet, rubbing the top of his head. "Thank you very much," he said. "I think you've just cracked my skull."

The Chief looked at the top of Aveyard's head, scrabbled about with his fingers in Aveyard's hair. "There's no blood," he said. "I can't see any blood."

Aveyard staggered across the room and sat in his chair. The Chief looked around, selected the only place he could find to sit and promptly put his weight on the end of one of the planks.

Aveyard started to shout, but once again was too late. That plank had not yet been screwed to its support. The Chief went down, the end of the plank came up, dislodged the one resting on the supports above it, which slid down at an angle, thudding on to the top of the Chief's head.

"Bloody hell!" he said.

Aveyard grinned mercilessly. "Now you know how I feel," he said.

The Chief rose slowly and staggered about rubbing his head. Aveyard got up too, came round the desk and scrabbled about in the

Chief's hair. "You're all right too," he said. "I can't see any blood on you either."

The Chief began to laugh. "A right comic pair we are," he said. "Laurel and Hardy. We ought to go on the Halls!" Now it was the Chief's turn to sit in Aveyard's chair.

"What are you doing here at this time of night?" Aveyard asked.

The Chief was rubbing his head. "I was at that Grocer's dinner," he said. "Deadly boring. I made an excuse and came away. When the constable on the door told me you were in, I thought I'd come up and have a word about that Crime Prevention thing. We never get the chance to talk much during the daytime. I didn't know the first thing you'd do was to hit me with a plank of wood!"

Aveyard scowled. The last thing he wanted to discuss was Crime Prevention. The Chief wanted him to take over the responsibility for all the Crime Prevention work in the Birton Force. It would mean appointing a whole new squad of officers, setting up training routines for them, working from behind a desk. Superintendent MacNally had been in charge of Crime Prevention for the last five years but the Chief felt he'd gone stale on the job. Now MacNally was due for retirement and the Chief wanted Aveyard to look at the problem again, co-ordinating the activities of the Records Office and the Statistical Department, trying to devise new ways in which the computer link could be used, talking to the boffins, the crime psychologists, the psychiatrists, the crime statisticians. Bill Aveyard preferred the constant activity of crime investigation. He considered himself too young to settle down yet behind a desk.

"Do we have to talk about that tonight, Chief?" he asked. "I really would like to finish these shelves. Let's face it, the most useful thing for a Crime Prevention Officer is a set of shelves."

The Chief's look admonished him. "Look, Bill," he said, "one day you're going to have to settle down. I've put you up for this job in Worcester, along with Superintendent Colby, and if you get that you'll need to settle down. You can't be a teararse all your life!" Any decision was postponed when the telephone rang. Aveyard picked it up and heard the voice of the girl in the radio room. "I believe the Chief Superintendent's there?" the girl said.

"Yes, he's here!" He handed the receiver to the Chief Superintendent who took it and listened without interrupting the person at the other end. "Righto," he said, "leave it with me." He put the telephone down and looked at Aveyard. "I've got a very delicate one for you," he said. "That was Constable Semple of B-Division speaking from his car. It sounds like an odd one. They've found a police Constable dead in the stables at Mawsley Hall. Young Cedric Mawsley, that'll be the Honorable Cedric Mawsley, was also found, sitting on a chair next to the body. The Honorable appears to be stoned out of his mind. They were discovered by Lord Mawsley himself, but it was his butler who reported it. I'd better handle it until Superintendent Colby gets his case wrapped up, tomorrow. . . ."

"What's wrong with me? I can look after it!"

"I thought you might be too busy, putting up your shelves, making your office pretty. . . ."

★

It took Detective Superintendent Aveyard ten minutes to drive to the village of Mawsley; he arrived at the same time as Sergeant Bruton, the doctor, and the "murder" team, all of whom had been called out by the Chief Superintendent.

Three radio cars were parked in the centre of the stable block, each with a driver. When the Superintendent arrived, the drivers got out of the cars and stood beside them, waiting. One driver spoke to the Superintendent. "Constable Jones, sir. Constable Witchett is by the door here, Constable James inside, keeping an eye on the door that communicates with the house, and Constable Frobisher is at the back."

"Good man. Anybody been in the room where the body is?"

"No, Superintendent. We could see all we wanted from the doorway. There's no doubt that Constable Baron is dead, and the man with him, they say is Cedric Mawsley, is obviously under the influence of drugs. Witchett is near enough that if Mawsley wakes up or stirs, Witchett can jump him, but we thought it was best to keep out of the room."

"Good man," Aveyard said. "That's good thinking."

There is nothing worse than to arrive on the scene of a crime and find well-meaning police officers trampling all over the place, often concealing vital evidence of footprints, fingerprints, positions of the body. The first responsibility of the man who arrives at the scene of the crime is to ensure that no other crime takes place, to ascertain if a death has taken place, to "control" the scene while his partner radios for additional specialist help.

Dr. Samson grunted when he saw Aveyard. "Whenever I get a late night call," he said, "I usually discover you there . . ." Aveyard smiled; he'd worked with Samson many times, knew him to be a meticulously efficient doctor with a large practice of patients, a man to whom police work was a hobby he tackled with cool professionalism, enjoying the academic side of forensic pathology as distinct from the frequently emotional and social aspects of a large General Practice. They walked to the door of the tack room together, stood at the threshold looking in.

"Is he dead?" Aveyard asked.

The doctor grunted. "No doctor can certify death at ten paces," he said.

"Could you delay a minute while I get a picture of the room? It isn't often we find an undisturbed scene-of-the-crime!"

"There's no hurry for me to go in there," Samson said.

Aveyard beckoned the forensic men forward. "Can you set up a camera here," he said, "and give me a panorama of the whole of that room? Something big, so we can blow it up if necessary. It isn't often we get a scene-of-the-crime so undisturbed. Might as well take advantage of it."

The forensic photographer used his 35-mm camera first, taking a series of pictures sweeping from left to right, providing a good overlap on each frame. Then he produced a large plate camera and repeated the process, in black and white. The final sequence he took with a Hasselblad, tripod mounted, in colour to be enlarged if necessary. He took two series, one using the existing light within the room, another bouncing a sharp photoflood along the room at floor level. That would reveal any floor prints, making them stand out in bold relief. When the photographer had finished, another man came forward and rolled a "carpet" of polythene sheeting across the room, backing along it so that his feet never touched the wooden floor beneath it. The doctor walked along the polythene sheet until he came to the two chairs. He examined Constable Baron's neck without touching the body, bent low and listened for a sound of breathing. He reached out and touched Constable Baron's wrist, feeling for a pulse. Then he stood up and shook his head. "He's dead, poor chap," he said.

Aveyard had walked along the polythene carpet.

"See that hole?" Dr. Samson said. "Someone has driven something in there, with violence. You can see the bruising around the side of the hole. Whatever it was, it was thin, like a nail."

". . . or a bullet?"

"I can't tell yet."

"At least, it wasn't the proverbial blunt instrument."

Dr. Samson had turned his attention to Cedric Mawsley, who was sitting in the other chair with his eyes open, his body rigid. Cedric looked about twenty-five years old, a blond-haired boy with a sharp aquiline nose, a full mouth with thickish lips that seemed to imply a strong sensuality. He was wearing a navy blue blazer, "pepper and salt" wide-bottomed checked trousers, a stone-coloured shirt with a long pointed collar and a wide tie, black-and-brown shoes with half-inch platform soles. The top button of his shirt was undone, and his tie had been pulled loose. On the fingers of the hand which lay along the arm of the chair were two rings, one a skull in gold, the other a large flat diamond that must have cost a year of Aveyard's wages. Dr. Samson looked closely into the pupils of Cedric Mawsley's eyes and grunted. He took hold of Cedric's wrist and held it for a full minute. "He'll be out for at least another couple of hours or so."

"Was he a patient of yours?" Aveyard asked.

Dr. Samson shook his head. "I treated him once, about ten years ago, for a stomach disorder. I haven't seen him since. I'm not sorry. I've enough to do with people who are really ill."

"Hypochondriac . . . ?"

"I wouldn't make a statement like that. You know me better. Let's say, he didn't want to return to public school after his holiday, and was ingenious in trying to prolong a medical excuse."

"What's wrong with him now?"

"Official, or not?"

"No. Not yet."

"He's under narcosis. What the young people call, blown out of his mind. What shall I do? Leave him while I get on with the preliminaries? I'd like to get a body temperature soon."

"Can you give me two more minutes?"

"More pictures. When will you chaps learn that an early medical examination is worth more to you than all your pictures!" Dr. Samson stepped back, reluctantly, and again Aveyard beckoned the photographer forward. Whatever the doctor may say, a picture's worth a thousand words, he thought, as he turned on his heels, careful to walk on the plastic sheet, and left the room. The forensic men knew what he wanted; Dr. Samson was an experienced forensic man; Aveyard could safely leave the "scene" to them.

Sergeant Bruton was waiting for him. "Inspector Roberts is Incidents Officer, Superintendent," he said, "and he's setting up an Incidents Room, pro tem, in the Parish Hall. I've had a quick word with the butler, the man who telephoned, and he's waiting in the Hall. Lord Mawsley, who found the bodies, is waiting in his study. The butler will get him when we want him. Nobody else in the house."

"No family? No servants?"

"None of the servants lives in any more, except the butler. They'll be back at half-past seven in the morning. A housekeeper, a couple of cleaning women, a cook, a maid, two gardeners, and a handyman. They all live in the village, except when there are houseguests."

"That's unusual."

"Apparently Mr. Cedric, as the butler calls him, wanted it that way. What are you going to do with Mr. Cedric, by the way?"

"I'm going to let Dr. Samson finish his examination of Baron, and then I'm going to waken him, rather rudely. I want to see his reaction when he sees the body of Baron."

"I hope his nerves are good, Superintendent."

"If they're not, he shouldn't be using drugs, should he?"

★

"You'll want to see Lord Mawsley," Sergeant Bruton said, "since he discovered the body." It was written that way in the Book, wasn't it? The Investigating Officer should interview the man responsible for the discovery of the crime at the earliest possible opportunity. But the Book said nothing about the discoverer being the prime suspect's father and the prime suspect being blown out of his mind.

"No," Aveyard said, "*you* would go and see Lord Mawsley first because that's the correct thing to do, Jim. But you know me! I don't have your self-discipline and sometimes I seem to find more interest in doing the incorrect thing first. Peabody—did you say that was the butler's name?— Peabody is an old family retainer; normally you wouldn't open that trap of a mouth of his with a crowbar. But he's in shock, too, and who knows, ten minutes' gossip might give us a lot of useful data for when we talk more seriously with his Lordship."

Peabody led them into a small room off the main Hall, simply but elegantly furnished, most of the chairs functional rather than relaxing. The heavy curtains were still drawn. "Where does this window overlook?" Aveyard asked.

"The front of the stable block, sir. This room was always the one used by the Agent when interviewing the Staff. I've no doubt Lord Mawsley will wish to see you in his study, but I thought it more suitable if you and I held our conversations here."

"Very fitting," Aveyard said, easing into the style of the butler with a chameleonlike facility. "I just thought I'd like to have a few informal words with you before I saw his Lordship. I thought you might be able, so to speak, to prepare the ground for me. We don't wish to waste his Lordship's time in this tragic hour, do we?"

"Indeed we do not, sir," the butler said vehemently. "Anything we can do to assist his Lordship is our bounden duty. In what way can I be of assistance?"

"Can you tell me if there was any relationship between Mr. Cedric and Police Constable Baron?" Seeing the look on Peabody's face, he quickly added to his question. "I mean were they engaged together in any sort of enterprise?" The look did not go away.

"You understand, sir, that Mr. Cedric was a member of the younger generation and, though it is not for me to criticise, sometimes the relationships he formed were not ones that would have been considered suitable in previous generations. However, sir, I need not tell you the times are changing. In answer to your question, I do not know of any enterprise in which Mr. Cedric and Mr. Bobby — I'm sorry, sir, but it's very hard for me to remember young Mr. Bobby's rank as a police constable; I knew him as a very young boy— were engaged together."

This was a lode of pure gold that Aveyard had come upon unexpectedly. "I'm very pleased to hear that," he said. "Your knowledge of 'young Mr. Bobby' will be invaluable to me when I start the investigation of his death. In the meanwhile, I wonder if you could give me some indication as to the type of man Mr. Cedric had become."

"Oh dear," Peabody said, "you no doubt wish me to speak my mind! This is a tragic time, a tragic time for us all. You'll have to bear with me, sir. I do not find it comes easy to me to express opinions about the family I have served for so many years. I do not even think it correct for me to have 'opinions.'"

"You're a gentleman of the old school!" Aveyard said.

"Begging your pardon, sir, I am a *servant* of the old school. I would not presume to think of myself as a *gentleman*."

"But as you yourself said, Peabody, times are changing. It must be quite inconceivable to you that a man of my age should bear the responsibility for an investigation of crime. But I do, you know, and I do have the obligation to press you to give me your opinion, something I would not normally do, please believe me! Please believe me also that not a word of what you say will be repeated outside this room."

Bruton's way of coughing contained its own eloquence. He coughed now. Aveyard knew Bruton had a strong constitution and an unblemished throat, and reacted to his cue with alacrity. "Sergeant Bruton," he said, "I wonder if you'd be good enough to see how Dr. Samson is getting along?" Bruton smiled with a look that seemed to say "Yes, my Lord; well done, my Lord," but he excused himself quietly and left the room. Jim Bruton was right, of course! It was inconceivable that Peabody would discuss his masters in front of a mere sergeant.

"Mr. Cedric has always been a very forward young man," Peabody started, speaking slowly, weighing each word as if it were a grain of gold dust, determined that each adjective would reflect the correctness of his thoughts. "One might almost say," he continued, "that he was somewhat *progressive*. Of course I suspected something amiss when he grew up without that love of the gun and the horse that has so characterised his ancestors, including his own father. I might even be so indiscreet since indiscretion seems to be the order of the day, as to reveal that the matter has sorely troubled his Lordship, and gave her late Ladyship, God rest her soul, so much pause for thought. Mr. Cedric is a wilful young man, restless, unsettled. Nothing has caught his attention and held it for very long. It is my opinion"—here Peabody pressed his fingers together as if praying for forgiveness for possessing such a thing—"that Mr. Cedric perfectly exemplifies the truth of the maxim 'Spare the rod and spoil the child.'"

"Can you tell me any reason for a meeting between Police Constable Baron and Mr. Cedric at this time of night, in what I believe is called the clubroom?"

"I can*not*, sir!" Here Peabody spoke vehemently again. "I had occasion recently to reprimand young Bobby—even though he was Police Constable Baron—for some indiscreet and quite outrageous remarks he made in my hearing about young Mr. Cedric."

"Will you tell me what those remarks were?" Aveyard asked. Seeing the closed look on Peabody's face he went on, pressing home. "Come on now, Peabody, you and I understand each other. You have my confidence but I must have your trust."

"Very good, sir, though I had never thought to be induced to repeat such things. Young Bobby said 'That Mr. Cedric will come to a bad end, you mark my words, and it may well be that I will be the one responsible.' What a thing to say! What a threat to make gainst a member of the family that had nourished young Bobby during the whole of his life."

"If it's any comfort to you," Aveyard said, "I suspect that those remarks were made, not by young Bobby, but by Police Constable Baron. What, if anything, do you know of drugs, Peabody?"

"A great uncle of Lord Mawsley who worked for the East India Company accustomed himself to the use of drugs, sir. In fact he died of an excess of what in my young day we used to call 'laudanum.' I know that the indiscriminate use of narcotics has become a problem among the younger generation and I've even heard the opinion expressed that narcotic cigarettes should be made freely available."

"Do you know if Mr. Cedric was a habitual user of drugs?"

"I'm afraid that's the sort of knowledge which I do not feel I have any right to acquire, sir," Peabody said.

Aveyard knew the line had been drawn. He would get no information from Peabody on that subject.

"It only remains for me to thank you, Peabody, for your frankness and sincerity."

"The sincerity, sir, if I may say so, is no more than my duty; the frankness is an indiscretion for which I can only pray for forgiveness. May I take you to Lord Mawsley, sir? He has asked that you be brought as soon as you wish to see him."

"That would be most kind, Peabody, most kind."

CHAPTER 3

"Of course I knew the young devil was on drugs," Lord Mawsley said. "I threatened many times to cut off his allowance, to write him out of my will. But I had no other heir and he knew I couldn't see the line suffer. I had a word with Sir John Molton in Harley Street. I value his opinion highly. He told me lots of the young 'uns are at it but that it's a passing fancy. I made Cedric see him a couple of times. Apparently, or so Sir John told me, there are two kinds of drugs and Cedric wasn't using any of the really bad ones."

Bill Aveyard knew of Sir John Molton, had seen him on television, had read his articles in the paper, and despised him for his liberality and lack of reality. If Sir John could spend a little more time in some of the cells at the back of police stations and less time in what was doubtless a swish office in Harley Street and under the bright lights of the television studios, he might change his opinions about what were "the really bad ones." Aveyard was strictly an anti-drug realist. He didn't agree with the move to legalize the sale of marijuana—any chemical substance that could cause euphoria was a poison; any abuse of the mind or the body by taking or smoking chemical substances was a horror. His feelings were further strengthened by a knowledge of his own weaknesses in that direction. Far too often when troubled in mind Aveyard himself succumbed to the temptation of pulling the cork on a bottle. His hangover was always greatly increased by his contempt of himself.

"Your son is under the influence of drugs at this moment, Lord Mawsley," he said. "I cannot pretend to give you a medical opinion but it may well be that in his present state he could have committed certain acts of which he will later have no knowledge."

"You mean that under drugs he could have killed Constable Baron?"

"That's exactly what I do mean." Lord Mawsley was standing with his back to the fire. He turned and bent stiffly to pick a log out of the brass basket by the fireside; when he turned back again, Aveyard could see his eyes were moist. "I haven't stopped thinking about that possibility since I saw them together. All I can say is that you must do as you think fit. You must not let any consideration impede your investigation and subsequent action. I shall, of course, resign all my official duties as soon as possible tomorrow, though, as you may know, it's a fairly lengthy process to renounce my Lord Lieutenancy of the County. I shall get on to the Palace first thing in the morning."

"I'm sure we understand each other, Lord Mawsley," Aveyard said, admiring the quiet dignity of this man, the iron discipline with which he could change the course of his life. "Can you tell me of any relationship between your son and Constable Baron?" he asked quietly.

Lord Mawsley, in obvious pain, had lowered himself into his armchair. "Forgive me," he said. "Damn back bothers me a bit sometimes." He took a large white handkerchief from his sleeve and used it to wipe his eyes. He blew his nose vigorously. "Beg your pardon," he said. "I'll be all right in a minute! Trumpeting here like an old warhorse."

Aveyard was content to wait until he could compose himself.

"No," he said finally, "I can't think of anything they had in common. Cedric wasn't the least bit interested in the horses and Baron, well, until he got this passion for the Police Force, had no time for anything else. Except that pretty girl he married of course."

"There is one connection we can safely make," Aveyard said. "Your son used drugs. It would not have been difficult for Constable Baron to discover that fact. Possibly Constable Baron met Mr. Cedric on that account."

"Could be," Lord Mawsley said. "Baron was that sort. I mean, it would be his way to have a word quietly with Cedric. Baron never did anything quickly or impetuously. He'd think the thing out. Dammit, it took him well over a year to tell me he wanted to join the Police Force. Mind you, he was stubborn. Once Bobby Baron had made up his mind not a thing in the world would shift him. I remember we were at odds for a year about what sort of bit I should use on one of my horses. I could never change him. Damn thing was, he turned out to be right most of the time."

"That room, Lord Mawsley, that clubroom? Assuming Constable

Baron wanted to have a quiet word with your son, is that where they would meet?"

"There's something I haven't told you," Lord Mawsley said. "Earlier today, young Baron came to me and said he was going to have a meeting in the clubroom. Later, he said, he might want to see me on what he described as official business. I can see it quite clearly now. He was going to have a word, I imagine, with my son about the drugs and, if the interview didn't go off too well, he was going to come and see me and do the decent thing by informing me he was going to put my son under arrest."

"That would certainly seem to be the case," Aveyard said, "but now we must determine what happened at that interview."

Lord Mawsley struggled to his feet, hobbled over to the fireplace, and pulled the velvet cord. When Peabody appeared, Lord Mawsley was standing erect with his back to the fireplace looking every inch the aristocratic gentleman.

"Superintendent Aveyard will be investigating the death of young Mr. Baron. You're to give him and his men all the assistance you can, do you hear?" he said. "You must permit them to come and go as they need. Do you hear me, Peabody?"

"I understand, my Lord," Peabody said. "Shall we be going to bed now, sir?"

"Yes, Peabody, we shall be going to bed."

Aveyard knew in his heart that it was a sleep from which a lesser man than Lord Mawsley would hope never to awaken.

★

The sight that greeted Aveyard's eyes as he re-entered the clubroom was macabre in the extreme; the body of Police Constable Baron was still lying where it had been discovered, and Dr. Samson was conducting a medical examination on the still-sleeping form of Cedric Mawsley, whose tie he had removed and whose shirt he had opened to the waist. He'd even pulled one arm out of the shirt and was examining it, doubtless for the telltale signs of a hypodermic needle.

"I finished my examination of Baron," Dr. Samson said. "He hasn't been dead long; in fact, for once you'll be happy to hear I can even speculate as to the time of death. I'd put it at about ten o'clock. The cause of death seems to be that cavity in the back of the head. Whatever was introduced, and we'll be able to tell you more about that when we conduct the post-mortem, went straight into the brain. There's no sign of a struggle or a fight and I would guess he was sitting in that chair when it happened. For example, the underside of his fingernails is quite clean. I thought I had better turn my attention to this young devil while I was waiting for you. Of course, I can't give you full information without a pathological examination but there are one or two confusing medical details. First of all, he's taken some form of drug, secondly, he's drunk some alcohol, thirdly, he's walked a distance since he did so, I would say at least a couple of miles or more; fourthly, although he's not a nail-biter by habit, he has bitten three of his fingernails. He's also bitten his lip. And lastly, his fingernails are not clean and there are skin lacerations on his skull. We shall quite easily be able to compare the underside of his fingernails with his skull and I think we'll find he was scratching his head. Does that tell you anything?"

Aveyard thought for a moment and the picture the doctor had painted emerged clearly. "Yes, it does," he said. "Let me try it out on you since you're the expert. Cedric Mawsley had run out of drugs. He was suffering some sort of withdrawal symptoms in which he bit his fingernails and scratched his head. He was nervous, couldn't settle down, so he went walking. He came back. He still had no drugs but needed to give himself some sort of a high. He took possibly a couple of these so-called headache pills some of you chaps prescribe instead of telling your patients to breathe deeply and get some fresh air, and then he drank some alcohol. It's a well-known fact that alcohol and drugs don't mix and can produce a high. He set off walking again, still biting his fingernails, still scratching his head, and eventually—we don't know how—he got himself here. At this stage I won't speculate as to what happened when he got here, but one thing we do know, the pills and the alcohol worked together in him and knocked him out."

"I can see you've had a lot of experience with drugs."

"I'm up to my neck with them. I can't tell you how angry the mere mention of drugs makes me, and, Dr. Samson, I regret to say in large measure I hold your profession partially responsible."

"My dear fellow," Samson said, "no need for regrets. I quite agree with you! However our major problem at this moment is, what do you want done with Constable Baron and Cedric Mawsley?"

"Is he in any medical danger?"

"I can't tell until I've examined him more thoroughly than is possible here."

"Right. We'll put him into a private ward in the General Hospital with a policeman at his bedside. Can you examine him there or does the hospital staff have to do it?"

"Oh, I can do the preliminaries. I may need to call on Forbes or someone like Paisley for a second opinion."

Aveyard turned to Bruton.

"Can I leave you to fix that, Jim?"

Bruton nodded. "What about Constable Baron?" he said.

"I don't want him removed yet," Aveyard said. "Let's get this idiot out of the way first so that I can look around a bit."

The police ambulance was waiting in the centre of the stable block. Cedric Mawsley was picked up gently as a baby and carried out of the clubroom and into the back of the ambulance. "Come back when you've delivered him," Bruton said to the driver. "And you, Witchett, ride with him and stay by the bedside. Jones can look after your car until you're relieved." Quietly, deftly, with a minimum of fuss, Sergeant Bruton organized the departure of Cedric Mawsley from the scene of the crime, mentally noting the details, the times, the people involved, for entry into the Inspector Roberts' Incidents Book.

Aveyard was standing inside the clubroom, looking around, seeking to fix the scene in his mind, trying to establish the nature and relationships of all the objects he could see, not yet knowing which of them might later assume a deeper forensic significance. The forensic team waited in the stable yard, standing together in small groups, chatting in low voices, a quiet murmur in the night air. Someone had found the light switch and the whole of the centre of the stable yard was illuminated. All the ponies must have woken and six heads looked curiously over the tops of stable doors. A couple of the forensic men were stroking one of the horses which had a long white blaze down its nose. Aveyard's eyes swept across the clean wooden floor of the clubroom, saw the way all the tack was clean with the well-rubbed look of leather that is constantly used and cared for. The floor itself had recently been swept. That would be a help, though he could have wished for a layer of dust to reproduce any footprints Baron and Mawsley might have made. The air held the pungent smells of horse manure, sweat, and saddle soap, but above it, or this could have been his imagination, he thought, was the acrid odour of spilled blood, the sour taste of sudden death.

He beckoned one of the forensic men forward. "Dr. Samson thinks the murderer might have stood behind that chair, so I want the whole of the chair dusted for prints. The wound was on the left side of Baron's head and it could well be that whoever did it rested their hand on the top of the chair back."

The forensic man looked at the chair itself which was covered in old red leather. "We should be able to pick up something from that," he said.

"A lot of people use this room, so you better get yourself a set of comparison prints from those saddles. Tomorrow we can get a list of the people who normally use this room and print them, but for the time being see what you can get off the saddles. I don't think you'll get a lot off the floor but it'll be worth a try. Anyway I'd like a low-level picture, just in case there is anything."

"Can we start now?" the forensic man asked.

"Yes," Aveyard said. "I've finished for the moment." The forensic man went to the door and beckoned his team forward.

Aveyard left the clubroom and walked across to the car in which Constable Jones was sitting. "Can you get me the Chief Superintendent on the line."

Constable Jones spoke into his microphone, received a "wait" instruction from the radio room, and within a couple of minutes there was a click on the loudspeaker and the voice of the Chief Superintendent came through. "Yes, Bill," he said, "how does it look?" Aveyard gave him a brief description of the scene of the crime and told him he'd sent Cedric Mawsley to the General Hospital.

"Best place for him," the Chief said. "Do you need any help out there?"

"No, Chief, I think we can manage."

"I'll be here if you want me."

The high wind had blown all the clouds from the sky and the moon now shone unimpeded across the landscape, etching each tree, each bush, grey green. Aveyard touched Bruton's arm and they walked slowly down the gravel path that led from the stable block past the edge of the exercise paddock alongside a quickthorn hedge to the back gate of Mawsley Hall. Both men were silent with the companionship that comes from a knowledge of each other. In his mind Bruton was setting up the administration of the investigation, thinking of the prosaic recording and reproducing of the reams of information they would need to assemble before the case could be completed. A murder gathers about itself a mountain of paperwork; the successful organization of detail was Sergeant Bruton's strong point. Aveyard, as yet, was not thinking of the routine details. His mind was freewheeling over what he knew of the people so far involved, trying to fix each in place and time. Cedric Mawsley for example. A young, spoilt, immature boy who had lacked discipline in his life, a boy who had turned his back on everything dear to his family and fallen victim to the modern disease of self-indulgence. Police Constable Bobby Baron too had turned his back on the past, hadn't he, and renounced the comfortable life of groom to Lord Mawsley in favour of the far from orderly, far from routine life of a police constable. What a metamorphosis it must have been when young Bobby Baron took off his riding britches and put on his blue serge, exchanged his riding crop for a truncheon, his flat cap for a policeman's helmet! What was it Lord Mawsley had said?—young Bobby had had a *passionate* desire to become a policeman and the obstinacy to fulfill that desire. In what way could these two dissimilar creatures be linked except by crime, the crime of Cedric Mawsley possessing and using drugs, the crime of young Bobby Baron being murdered? It was a temptation to connect the two crimes but Aveyard was too experienced a policeman to do that yet; he'd need tangible evidence and it was his job to secure that. A five-bar gate stood closed at the bottom of the gravel drive; Aveyard could see where the hooves of horses had scuffed the gravel as the riders stooped over to open the gate. The top rail was made of oak and smooth.

"It might be well worth looking at that rail," Aveyard said. He took a handkerchief from his pocket, rolled it into a sort of cord, and used it to open the gate catch, so placed with an extension that it would come easily to the hand of a mounted horseman. He drew the gate open and they went through.

"Come to think of it," he said, "we've had three police cars and an ambulance through there!"

On the opposite side of the village street a small cottage stood on its own. The living quarters appeared to be on the first floor above what must at one time have been a blacksmith's shop. Several ploughs had been abandoned to rust on the ground beside the cottage, and lengths of metal tube. To the right of the smithy, a small door doubtless led upstairs. In the open shed which formed the smithy, three anvils stood and a blackened coke fire under a hood with a rusted air-pumping mechanism beside it, two large bellows, a handle, and a foot strap. It didn't look as if the smithy had been used for years. Two lights were on upstairs, one at each end of the building. Aveyard placed his back to the smithy and looked across the gate through which they had come. The quickthorn hedge curved to the left and behind it a stand of tall trees hid the Hall from view. The trees were moving vigorously in the high wind but the moon was so strong, Aveyard could see every leaf.

"We might as well start here," he said. He knocked on the street door and after a very short time heard footsteps behind it. The door opened and a large fat woman stood on the bottom step of a flight of steps looking down at them. She was wearing a black skirt and above it a black cardigan over a white blouse. Her hair was iron grey and dragged back from her forehead.

"Good evening," she said. "Who are you?"

"We're policemen," Aveyard replied. "I'm sorry we come so late, but would it be convenient to have a couple of words with you?"

She backed slowly up the stairs, the wooden treads creaking beneath her weight. They followed her slowly. At the top she turned, a difficult manoeuvre considering her bulk and the narrowness of the tiny hall in which they found themselves, one door to the left and one to the right both open. She was wheezing with the effort of climbing the stairs, and chuckling.

"I've been expecting you," she said, "considering everything that's been going on! All them police cars, and an ambulance an' all. I'll tell you, it's been quite exciting, like watching the television. I shan't get to sleep at all, tonight!"

She eased her bulk into a chair in the sitting room to which she showed them. Aveyard noticed that the chair was by the window and a quick twitch of the curtain would expose everything that happened in the street and in the drive of the Hall to her vantage point. With her weight and the difficulty she'd shown in climbing the stairs she wouldn't go out much, would she? He saw the large television in the corner. Yes, watching that would be her chief source of excitement. That, and the events in the street below.

"You don't come from these parts, Mrs . . . ?"

"Jones is my name and you're quite right. Born and bred in Cardiff I was," she said, putting on a thick stage Welsh accent, "but since I've been living here for twenty years I've lost most of it. My husband was Tom Jones, you know. Not the singer, of course. Thomas Jones, Master Blacksmith. But we didn't like Cardiff. A worker my Tom was, and left me well provided."

Aveyard glanced at the television which, he guessed, any other evening would have been still switched on.

"With a good life insurance, eh?"

"Oh yes, very well provided I am. Little bit in the bank, a nice annuity, and my widow's pension."

"It must be comforting to be left well provided," Jim Bruton said, "to be able to take it easy and watch what's going on about you." Jim had recognized the type instinctively and knew that sometimes Bill Aveyard was too tolerant. They'd be here all night if Mrs. Jones had her say.

"Oh yes," she said, "my Tom always said I had a sharp eye."

"And being nicely placed here, you'd see most of what went on in the street below, especially around the gate to the Hall. It's just down below here, isn't it?"

"Oh yes. This used to be a Lodge House, one time, before they brought the road through and made it into the smithy. My Tom said finding this place was a Godsend."

"And so you'd be able to tell us everybody who used that gate this evening, wouldn't you?" Jim Bruton persisted.

"Yes, I suppose I would. My Tom hung that gate there; he made that opening catch with his own hands. Quite an inventor, he was . . ."

Aveyard cut in. "Can you give us a list of all the people who've used that gate this evening? My sergeant will write it down."

Bruton had taken the pad from his pocket and sat with his pencil poised over it to forestall any further references to "my Tom."

"Oh dear," she said, "that's a tall order. Well now, let me see. There's been nobody after the horses came back at seven o'clock, and they closed the stables at half-past eight."

"Nobody at all, Mrs. Jones?"

"Well, nobody to speak of."

"Mr. Cedric Mawsley? Is he someone to speak of."

"Oh well, there's him, but he lives there, don't he?"

"Yes, he does live there, Mrs. Jones. But has he used that gate this evening?"

"Oh yes, I suppose he has."

"*Suppose*, Mrs. Jones . . . ?"

"Well, if this is an interrogation . . ."

Aveyard could hear a note of antagonism creeping into her voice. "Not at all, Mrs. Jones," he said. "We're merely asking a few questions. I'm sure my sergeant agrees that you're being very helpful to us. In police work, as you must know from the television, we have to be quite precise, you know."

Mrs. Jones giggled. It was a monstrous sound that began from somewhere in the lower regions of that quivering mass of flesh and eventually reached her mouth with a young girl's high-pitched note. Tears welled into her eyes and she wiped them away, laughing. "You're far too young to be Barlow," she said. "Yes, I can see what you're after. You want evidence, don't you? You want me to give you a few clues. Have you seen that Sherlock Holmes series? My Tom used to read all of Sherlock Holmes."

"Did Mr. Cedric Mawsley go through that gate tonight?"

"Yes."

"At what time?"

"Well, that's where you've got me. I remember I watched the ten o'clock news. Now was it before the news or after the news?"

"I don't know Mrs. Jones. That's what I want you to tell me."

"Well, it was either before or after the news. But I can't remember exactly. That Richard Baker, the news reader, there's a fellow I could go for. Not like Cedric Mawsley. He's not my cup of tea at all."

"Before or after the news? Try to think. It's very important."

"One thing I can tell you," she said. "It was about ten minutes after Ted Roper."

"Ted Roper, Mrs. Jones? You haven't mentioned him before."

"Oh, haven't I? He was the first one who went up after they'd closed the stables. Ted Roper. And then, about ten minutes later, Mr. Cedric. But I can't for the life of me remember was it before or after the news . . . ?"

★

When they came out of Mrs. Jones's house, Jim Bruton was figuratively speaking mopping his brow. "All that," he said, "and for what?"

"For some very valuable information," Aveyard said. "You can't expect everyone to have your precision-built mind, Jim. At least now we know that Mrs. Jones only saw two people come through that gate after the stables were closed for the night. A man called Ted Roper and Cedric Mawsley. There's no other way into that stable block except via the house. Ted Roper went first and Cedric Mawsley followed him about ten minutes later. We've set the time as being somewhere before or after the ten o'clock news. We know that Mrs. Jones identified them in the bright moonlight and that there were clouds about at the time. For example, she didn't know it was Ted Roper going through the gate until he was five or so paces up the drive, the clouds blew back and the moonlight revealed him."

"But she'd be seeing him from the back, wouldn't she?"

"Back or front, it wouldn't matter, Jim. Don't forget she knows these people. She's lived in this village for twenty years and probably spent most of that time sitting in that window looking out."

"What a life," Jim Bruton said. "What do we do now?"

"We find Ted Roper."

★

It was midnight when they came out of Mrs. Jones's house and turned left to walk up the extension to the High Street. Bill Aveyard could not remember when he'd seen a brighter moon. A couple of men walked down the pavement, looked curiously at them as they passed. "Good night," one of them said in the cheerful way of country people. "Good night," Jim Bruton replied. There were few lights in the houses of the village as they walked through it and apart from the two men they saw no one. The village was in the process of going to sleep, not knowing that in the morning their quiet orderly life would be disrupted by scandal. The following day the press would descend, local reporters and photographers, stringers for the national dailies. At first light the police would start combing the village, going from house to house with questions, seeking to locate each of the two hundred or so people who lived in Mawsley in time and place. Where were you last night? At around ten o'clock? Somewhere in the village, in the General Hospital in Birton, or anywhere he had fled, the murderer of Police Constable Baron was remembering the moment of death. So many murders are discovered only because the man responsible cannot live with that memory. The police cannot wait for confessions. From a long and painstaking series of small interviews and interrogations and investigations, the gravel of knowledge is quarried to be sifted slowly and painstakingly for the grains of significant truth. Aveyard shivered as they walked along the street, not so much with cold but because of an ability to see the events of the past through the eyes of the people concerned. It was obvious that Baron had not known he was going to die or he would have put up a fight. But the murderer had known he was going to kill, hadn't he? He had known that spasm of hatred or fear, the indescribable moment at which the decision to take another person's life had been made.

"This must be where she told us to turn right," Bruton said. They turned down the street. "I've been wondering when we are going to tell Baron's wife?"

"Not until we've moved the body," Aveyard said. "She might want to see it and I'd rather spare her the sight of her husband sitting dead in the chair."

"You're a very understanding fellow for your age," Jim Bruton said. "You never fail to amaze me. I wouldn't have thought of that. I'd have popped around there right away and broken the news to her as gently as I could. There's always time for bad news, isn't there? And you're quite right, it need never be hurried."

"This is different from our usual cases," Aveyard said. "Baron was a copper and I have the feeling that even though he was found in his civilian clothes in his civilian environment, he was killed because he was a copper."

They had arrived at the cottage Mrs. Jones had described to them. It was typical of many of the other cottages Aveyard had already seen in the village, built about a hundred and fifty years ago to accommodate one of the estate workers. It was surrounded by what once had been, no doubt, a productive vegetable garden but now had regressed entirely to grass. A rusting mowing machine stood where it had been abandoned. The front door was set in the middle of the cottage with a small slate-covered porch over which at one time clematis, honeysuckle, or a rose would have rambled. The rose was still there but its crudely chopped stems hung from the wall ties in haphazard fashion without trace of a bloom. No light shone from the cottage.

Jim Bruton put his hand on Bill Aveyard's arm. "Keep on walking," he whispered. In the silence that followed Jim Bruton's words, Bill Aveyard heard the shuffling footsteps coming along the street behind them. Without turning his head too obviously, he glanced as far backwards as he could. Fifteen paces after the cottage wall he stopped, bent down, and fumbled with his shoelace. A man walking along the street behind them had stopped at the gate of the cottage.

"Mr. Roper?" Aveyard called out.

The man stopped with his hand on the catch of the gate. "Yes," he said, "that's me. What do you want? Who the hell are you anyway?"

Aveyard hurried back and stopped in front of the man. "Ted Roper?" he asked.

"What's the police doing in Mawsley at this time of night?"

Aveyard knew the type, felt the antagonism that always possessed him when he had to deal with such a man, an obvious layabout. "Could I have a word?" he asked.

"What about?"

Aveyard looked towards the door of the cottage.

"We can talk out here," Roper said. "My mam will be asleep and I don't want to waken her. Not for a copper."

"Maybe they'll have to waken her, to tell her we've got you inside . . . ?"

"Bollocks, copper! You've got nothing to take me inside for. I haven't done anything. I can tell you where I've been, what I've been doing. I can account for every minute. . . ."

"Including the time you were at the Hall?"

"I was never there. . . ."

"Come off it. You were seen going in."

Roper laughed. "Oh, that fat bitch Jonesy. Bloody spy. Sees everything. Well, you want to get your facts right, copper. Jonesy saw me go through the gate all right. I saw her curtain waving like a bloody flag. But I turned right round, and came right back out again. I was never in the clubroom, not tonight."

"You can prove that . . . ?"

Sergeant Bruton had placed himself to the side, ready to pounce if Ted Roper should make a move. Roper looked at him and laughed. "You can call the dogs off," he said. "I don't have to prove it. I know that much. You come with evidence that I was there, and then we'll talk. Sure, I went through the gate. I know Jonesy saw me. But then I came right out again. So, put that in your pipe and smoke it!"

Aveyard looked at Jim Bruton. "A right little tear-away, isn't he?"

Jim Bruton nodded and chuckled. "And a lawyer, as well."

"If we hang on a bit," Aveyard said, "he'll be quoting that bit about his rights, and police brutality. You'd better be careful not to hit him."

"I wouldn't dirty my hands," Jim Bruton said.

"Very funny, copper. And now, unless you have any objections, I'm going to bed. That's unless you want to arrest me. . . ."

"Who said anything about arresting you, Ted? I came here to ask you a few civil questions, and get a few civil answers. You don't want it that way. All right. We have more important things to do, but we'll get round to you. When we do, I won't bother coming round here. We'll pull you in, and sit you in a chair, and eventually, you'll tell us what we want to know without all this tough-boy stuff."

Aveyard turned on his heel to go. "I didn't go up to the clubroom," Ted Roper said.

Aveyard called over his houlder. "I don't give a damn what you say, lad. If you were there, you'll have left some sort of evidence behind you. We'll find it, if it's there. And then, we'll talk to you again. When you're not feeling so tough."

"I won't leave the village," Ted Roper said. "I'll be here, if you want to talk to me again."

Aveyard stopped, turned round, and looked at Ted Roper up and down as if he were a particularly obnoxious species of some unpleasant animal. "Ted, you've had your chance. I don't give a damn what you do or where you go. When I want to talk to you again, I'll find you, no matter where you may be. Only this time, you'll be answering questions."

Bruton and Aveyard turned their backs and walked away.

"He might skip," Jim Bruton whispered.

"He might," Aveyard said, "but somehow I don't think so. Anyway, even if he does skip, we can always find him. Lads like that don't have the intelligence to skip very far, or vanish very effectively. Next time I talk to him, I'd like to have a little more background knowledge about him. See what you can dig up in Records when you got a moment."

They walked back down the High Street together, meeting no one. When they went through the back gate of the Hall, they saw Mrs. Jones's curtain twitch, and her hand wave at them. The gate swung shut behind them, and the moon disappeared behind a heavy cloud and the night became black as pitch. From the darkness, sounds came more strongly at them. Some sort of bird caw from the trees behind the quickthorn hedge, the snuffle of a horse in the paddock to their right, down the terrace. Suddenly the night seemed to draw in on them.

"I'm tired," Bill Aveyard said.

"So am I," Jim Bruton said.

The forensic men had finished their examination when Aveyard arrived back at the clubroom. "We've struck gold," the sergeant said. "A footprint. On the boards behind the chair. And I think it was made this evening."

"Has somebody saved one of Cedric Mawsley's shoes?" Aveyard asked quickly, cursing himself. He ought to have thought of that earlier. The sergeant smiled. Both shoes had been taken from Mr. Mawsley's feet before he was put in the ambulance. The sergeant held each of them, stored separately in polythene bags. "They don't fit," he said. He bent down and showed the Superintendent a square on the floor that had been outlined in chalk. Aveyard could see a purple pattern on the floor. "Gentian violet," the sergeant said. "Come over here, Superintendent."

Aveyard followed him across to the corner of the room, by the door. On the floor were the squashed remains of what looked like a soft mint toffee, from the end of which a purple substance had been squirted.

"Unless I miss my guess," the sergeant said, "that's a pessary of the type they use on horses. Dr. Samson had already left when I found it, but I bet he could tell us. I haven't shifted it, but we've taken a photograph. If you'll look, you'll see a pattern here, and here and here." He pointed to squares drawn on the floor with chalk. In each one Aveyard could see the dark purple stain, the outlines of a part of a footprint, the markings of the pattern of a rubber sole. "He came in that door," the sergeant said, "walked round the room here, across to this door that leads into the house, then to the chair, behind it, and finally out of the same door through which he'd come in."

Aveyard examined the path the footprints took. "If he came in here," he said, "he would have been in sight of anyone sitting in that chair. He walked round this wall, across to that door, then to the chair always in sight, then round the back of the chair."

"And then out of the door."

Aveyard turned to Jim Bruton. "Send a car and a constable," he said, "to Ted Roper's house. Tell the constable to bring back the boots Ted Roper was wearing tonight. He'll recognize them because there's a heart-shaped drop of paint on the left-hand boot, where the toecap is stitched to the upper."

Jim Bruton wasn't surprised by the Superintendent's keen eye. He hadn't noticed the paint when they saw Ted Roper. "A *constable?*" he asked. "You wouldn't like me to go myself?"

"No, Jim. Send a copper. And if Ted Roper makes any difficulty, tell the copper to kick him all the way from Mawsley to the station in Birton."

CHAPTER 4

It was half-past three in the morning when Mr. Partridge, the forensic pathologist, called Superintendent Aveyard.

"You've got a funny one here," he said. "A very funny one."

"I suspected that. Can you give me the cause of death without the medical terms?"

"Yes, but it's a funny one. Somebody fired into his brain through the back of his neck."

"A shot."

"Yes, point-blank range. They held the gun against the back of his neck and pulled the trigger."

"I didn't see any powder marks," Aveyard said mystified.

"There weren't any. There wasn't any powder. It was an air pistol. We've picked a piece of lead out of him. I'll tell you something else very interesting. It had gone a long way in. Anywhere else and it would have bounced off the bone and wouldn't even have given him a headache. But this was a skilled job. It looks as if whoever did it knew exactly where to put that pistol. Fascinating, really! You know I'm not given to speculation but as far as I'm aware only two kinds of people know how to do that. Well, three if you add the medical profession."

"The other two?"

"The hit men of the Mafia and Secret Agents of the Russian KGB."

"Come off it," Aveyard said. "The Mafia and the KGB, in the village of Mawsley." He heard a chuckle at the other end of the line. "I thought that would fascinate you," Partridge said. "Shall I waken the Chief Superintendent and tell him?"

Now it was Aveyard's turn to chuckle. "That's as much as your life is worth," he said. "I'll tell him in the morning when he's had his breakfast!"

It was four o'clock by the time the Superintendent got home to bed but, nevertheless, he was up again by eight. He breakfasted off coffee, black with sugar the way he liked it, and two slices of buttered toast. He even made himself sit down and read the *Telegraph* quickly and skim through his mail before ringing Jim Bruton. "He's left," Mrs. Bruton said. Next he phoned the Chief Superintendent who was already in his office. "Hold on to your chair, Chief," he said. "You won't believe what I'm going to tell you."

"We have the Mafia and the KGB in Mawsley. Shall I get on to Interpol?"

"You've heard?"

"These pathology boys . . . I wouldn't waste any sleepless nights over it. I can't somehow see Police Constable Baron being the subject of a contract for a hit murder, or a member of MI 6. Whoever put that gun at the back of his head was just lucky to find the right spot. Too much of this Sherlock Holmes business is creeping into crime work. Find a motive and you'll find a killer. That's the way I was brought up. That's why I think you'll do well in Crime Prevention because you'll be looking for motives before crimes are actually committed."

"We might have a possible suspect in Cedric Mawsley," Aveyard said, in a hurry to change the subject. "We've also found a set of prints that looks interesting."

"I've heard about them," the Chief said. "Gentian violet. You're lucky. It's hell to wash off."

"I've sent a pair of boots for examination."

"That lad, Ted Roper?"

"I can't tell you anything, can I, Chief?"

"I keep myself informed. Some of you lads are a bit sparing with information. That's something for you to look into when you take over Crime Prevention."

"I'm a bit wary about the footprints, and about Ted Roper, too. Murder seems right outside his league."

"He has form. All for violence of one sort or another."

"I'm not suprised. But this doesn't look, at first sight, like a violent crime."

"You can never tell. Keep an open mind, Bill, until all the facts are in. Incidentally, Colby finishes today. He'd be quite happy to take on the Mawsley case, if you want to hand it over and get on with Crime Prevention. I'd even have a word with maintenance for you, and get them to fit those shelves so they won't fall down every time a Chief Superintendent breathes on them. . . ."

"No thank you," Aveyard said. "It's my case and I'll see it through."

Before Aveyard had left Mawsley the previous night, he'd written down the questions he wanted answered. The night-duty officer had printed the questions on sheets of paper, and had issued them to the constables borrowed from D-Division who were already walking from door to door. At this stage, they were only interested in discovering who had seen who doing what and where. Later, the replies would be sifted, and interesting people seen by a sergeant or an inspector for a deeper interview.

"I have two things to interest you, Superintendent," Jim Bruton said. Aveyard noticed that Jim had brought his favourite chair from his office and had placed it behind a desk in the Parish Hall they were using as an Incidents Room.

"Two things . . . ?"

"Yes. First, this cup of coffee! Second, a man called Westmacott, lives in the village, was seen by several people, went home, went out again, hasn't been back." He placed the questionnaire on the Superintendent's desk, but Aveyard didn't trouble to read the constable's spidery handwriting. He knew Jim would "interpret" the replies for him.

"Source, Mrs. Westmacott and others. Husband spent last evening in the pub. She'd gone to bed when he came in at half-past ten. Heard him pottering about in his room—apparently, they don't sleep together because he snores—then go downstairs again, and out. She heard him take his car."

"He didn't say good-bye?"

"I suspect he hasn't said good-bye, good night, or good morning for a long time, to judge by her expression. No, he just left. And hasn't come back."

"What's her theory? Another woman?"

"He's a technical rep for a firm of boiler manufacturers. He covers the entire Midlands. She thinks he's on a job."

"How long do these 'jobs' usually last?"

"Usually one night. Sometimes more."

"Has he any form?"

"None, not even a motoring offence."

"What do you think?"

"It's not up to me to think, Superintendent. I'm just trying to give you the facts. . . ."

"Like the 'fact' they don't sleep together anymore. Come on, Jim you must have formed an opinion. . . ."

"I'd say, another woman. Spent the evening at the pub, got a bit —well, you know the way some men are after an evening on the beer —and took off for the night."

"Are we getting on to his firm?"

"Yes. They're up in Liverpool but so far, we can't raise anybody up there who knows anything. We're still trying."

"Good man." Aveyard sat back, looked around the room. It didn't take long for an Incidents Room to take on the busy bustle of a crime investigation. Inspector Roberts, bending over his book and his papers, with his box and card index files, the tools of his trade. Three constables sitting round the walls typing. Why, when typing constables were shown in fiction, he thought, were they always portrayed tapping reluctantly with one finger? So many coppers had done touch-typing courses; the three men against the wall were rattling away faster than any girl secretary.

Copying machine in the corner, and a coffee/tea/soup dispenser, though Aveyard's cup, he knew, had come from a kettle and a Melitta filter. A constant flow of constables in, constables out, each carrying the inevitable aluminium clipboard and a stack of forms. Each reported to Inspector Roberts without so much as a glance at the Superintendent; each stood in front of the Inspector's desk like a schoolboy submitting a homework essay, while the Inspector skimmed through the reports, looking for words he couldn't read, phrases he couldn't understand. Mostly the answers were simple, and tendency to ramble removed by the precision of the questions asked. Aveyard could tell the questionnaire was a good one, well composed, since the Inspector rarely had to seek supplementary answers from the constables. Mostly, he knew from experience, the answers would be negative. How few people really see what's going on about them. How many people would, could, walk down a village street and say they'd seen no one, when a half a dozen people had been on the same street at the same time. The mind's a self-protecting mechanism, and often doesn't accept information that is not of immediate and selfish use. The mind can reject, too, and refuses to store information that might be potentially dangerous. With luck, when the questionnaires were sifted, a picture would be formed revealing where everyone was in the village, or where they said they were. But sometimes, an anomaly was revealed. Someone would say three people were on a street, and someone else would say four, and the fact of the "extra man" would become important. It might not constitute evidence that would help in the solution of the crime, but it would create a pattern of orderliness in which the truly significant "disorders" could be identified and traced. And from them, evidence might come.

"Pathology report in yet?" Aveyard asked, but Jim Bruton shook his head.

"Ted Roper's boots?"

Again, Jim Bruton shook his head. "They've been to the clubroom and have taken a cast of the first mark, the one involving the pessary."

Bill Aveyard groaned. Often the forensic men found a piece of evidence, but spent so much time "legally" verifying it, that the evidence itself became well-nigh useless. Especially when the forensic men suspected the piece of evidence would be produced in court. "They wouldn't have taken a cast if they didn't think it was good," he said, as he picked up the telephone.

Sam Grade was on duty in the lab. "It looks promising, Superintendent," he said. "Now we're making a cast of the boot."

"You've identified gentian violet on the boot sole, have you?"

"It's too early to say. We're waiting until Robbins comes in to do the chemical conformation on it. I mean, it won't help you if it was just any old gentian violet. You'll want the chemical geography to conform, won't you . . . ?"

Chemical geography. Conform. "All I want you to do," he said, "is tell me in non-technical language if Ted Roper's boot made that footprint or not!"

"Hang on, Superintendent, that's Mr. Partridge's job, you know. He signs the reports. Robbins and me, well, we're just a couple of lab technicians."

"I'm not concerned about the report. Come on, you're experienced in this kind of thing. Somebody down there must have worked it out! Is it Ted Roper's footprint or not? You can dress it up in all the legal crap later on."

Sam would not be drawn. "Mr. Partridge is in Court at the moment," he said. "They're going to put him on first. I'll ask him to give you a ring as soon as he comes in."

Jim Bruton was smiling wickedly when Aveyard put the phone down. "You'll never get anything out of Sam Grade," he said, "or Robbins, for that matter. I had a word with Sophie. You remember Sophie. I got her that job in the lab washing out the test tubes. Sophie has a sharp pair of ears. They're just being a bit cagey, that's all. They think that Ted Roper stepped into some lime somewhere and apparently lime destroys gentian violet. They think the outline matches but they are bothered about the chemistry. Let's face it, if they go into Court with a standard production sole and a chemistry that doesn't match, they'll be in trouble. Any smart barrister will make capital out of the fact that a hundred thousand soles are manufactured every year and a million gentian violet pessaries sold. That's why they want the casting, to relate the boot exactly to the print. I'm afraid it's going to take some time the way they are going about it."

Aveyard groaned. "Thank God for Sophie," he said.

"We could pull Ted Roper in?" Jim Bruton suggested, but Aveyard shook his head. "I don't want to see that lad again until I have a handful of trumps and a joker or two."

"Well, what is today's programme?" Jim Bruton asked.

"Let's take a look at Cedric Mawsley's room."

They were about to leave the Incidents Room when the telephone rang. The Inspector called across the room. "It's for you, Superintendent," he said. "Dr. Samson."

"It was touch and go for a while," Dr. Samson said, his voice soft and blurred with tiredness. "If we hadn't got him into the General when we did we'd have had another death."

"What had he taken? Was it a suicide attempt?"

"I don't think so," Dr. Samson said. "He'd taken three different kinds of amphetamines and drunk a bottle of brandy. Fortunately the amphetamines were the slow-acting kind but they were building an effect inside him; in another hour he'd have been dead without ever knowing what hit him. Damn fool. I think it confirms your theory of what happened last night. I think he took *three* separate amphetamines because he didn't have the drug he normally takes."

"And what is that?"

"Heroin."

"You didn't find any syringe marks, so he's not injecting it yet."

"No. So far he's only sniffing it. Injecting it comes next. . . ."

"Right," Aveyard said with no trace of pity in his voice. "When he's fit to move we'll throw him into St. Wilfred's and lock him up."

Bruton was waiting for him at the door. "He's been sniffing heroin," Aveyard said, "but he ran out. He nearly killed himself with booze and amphetamines. Come on, let's go and find out a bit more about Cedric Mawsley. Let's go and find out what makes a young man with all those seeming advantages turn himself into a walking chemist's shop."

★

Lord Mawsley himself took them up to Cedric's quarters. "I find this very hard to understand, Superintendent," he'd said when Aveyard told him about the drugs.

"So do the rest of us, Lord Mawsley. There isn't any single common factor to drug addiction unless it be lack of parental control and discipline. I blame the new liberals, but I won't trouble you with my theories."

"Can you keep him in confinement?" Lord Mawsley asked.

"We can do, but he's twenty-five and if he gets himself a good solicitor he'll come out on bail. Unless we charge him with murder."

The night had left its terrible toll on Lord Mawsley and his face was grey with fatigue and physical pain. Only his eyes, sunk deep into their sockets, revealed the effect of that other pain, the disappointment, the intense sorrow caused by the knowledge of his son's activities. "I shall speak to him and for once he will listen to me. He will stay in such care as is needed to remove this drug habit and addiction."

"The charge of using drugs may be the least of his problems, my Lord," Aveyard gently reminded him. "We may be booking him for something much more serious."

"I'm perfectly aware of that. That thought hasn't left my mind during this entire night. Come with me; I'll take you to his room."

Cedric Mawsley's *room* was a set of quarters on the first floor. He had his own sitting room, his own bedroom, his own bathroom. Lord Mawsley stood at the door and pointed the quarters out to them. "I won't come in," he said. "I've made it a practice to give my son privacy here. I don't think I've been in these rooms for ten years."

"If you'll forgive me saying so, Lord Mawsley, it might have been better if you had been in these rooms from time to time, but, however, you don't need me to tell you that now."

Lord Mawsley turned and left them without a word. Aveyard and Bruton stood still in the centre of the sitting room and looked about them. The first thing that caught both their eyes was a display that occupied twelve square feet; Aveyard walked forward, Jim Bruton at his side as they looked at the air pistols hanging on the wall.

"It would be interesting to know if Cedric Mawsley has ever studied anatomy," Aveyard said, "or ever started training in medicine. I'd also like to find out if he has any books dealing with the technical methods of the Mafia or the KGB!"

Jim Bruton was looking at a set of golf clubs standing on a lightweight trolley in a corner of the sitting room next to a half dozen tennis rackets in frames, three squash rackets, a half a dozen table-tennis bats, two shotguns, three fishing rods, two cricket bats, and a set of pads in a long bag.

"He was right-handed," Jim Bruton said, "and would appear to have been something of a sportsman."

"He may have been right-handed, but he was a dilettante. Look, the golf clubs are immaculate; so are the tennis rackets and the squash rackets. Everything! He bought everything and used nothing."

"Unless he used one of these guns in the clubroom that night," Jim Bruton said.

They walked around the room, into the bathroom, the bedroom. Everywhere they found evidence of self-indulgence, of a mind that refused to settle to anything.

"Typical," Aveyard said when they looked into the bathroom. On the shelf beside the sink were ten different aftershave lotions and toilet-water bottles. "He couldn't even decide how he wanted to smell!"

Jim Bruton wore a sorrowful look. "It's enough to make you want to be a communist, isn't it?" he said. "All this money wasted, all thrown away . . ." Bill Aveyard looked at him, remembering how Jim Bruton had always been about money. He'd married late, determined not to offer his wife less than a paid-for house with furniture, a settled way of life. Jim and his wife had waited too long for financial security; as a result, they'd missed the chance to have children of their own. Mrs. Bruton would have been a good mother, and Jim, Bill thought, would have been a good father. Bill couldn't see Jim indulging his son in this way, lavishing material things on him and neglecting his "spiritual" welfare as Lord Mawsley had so blatantly done.

"I don't think anything here is of value to us," Bill Aveyard said. "We'll let the Drugs people turn the place over. I'm certain they'll find traces of something, somewhere. I'm interested in a murder, not a young man's morals."

"And I'll get forensic to check those guns, shall I?"

"I'll give you a fiver if anyone of them turns out not to have dust in the barrel."

"I won't take the bet. . . ."

★

The newspaper reporters flooded the Incidents Room just before lunch, spilling over into the clubroom and the pub. Aveyard gave them a brief story. Yes, Police Constable Baron had been found dead in the clubroom. Yes, he did appear to have been shot in the back of the head. No, Cedric Mawsley had not been arrested. Yes, he was in hospital. Aveyard had no medical knowledge and couldn't therefore give them any information about his ailment; for that they'd have to see Dr. Samson who was treating him. Yes, Cedric Mawsley was helping them with their enquiries, or rather, he would be, when he was able to do so. No, there were no suspects. Yes, the police were pursuing the matter vigorously, with Superintendent Bill Aveyard in charge of the enquiries, under the direction of Chief Superintendent Batty, from whom any further information could be obtained. Yes, Superintendent Aveyard would pose outside the clubroom for one, and only one, photograph. No, Superintendent Aveyard didn't necessarily think the murderer was someone from the village of Mawsley. It could be someone from outside the village, couldn't it? It could be someone from Birton.

MAWSLEY MURDERER COULD BE BIRTON RESIDENT, SAYS SUPERINTENDENT BILL AVEYARD, the headline from the early edition of the *Evening Chronical* read.

That headline was to cause Bill Aveyard more anguish than any other single factor in his entire career.

CHAPTER 5

During the next forty-eight hours, the investigation of the Mawsley Murder languished. Cedric Mawsley was removed to St. Wilfred's under tight security, unable to speak, unable to be interviewed. Lord Mawsley arranged for him to be examined by specialists in drug addiction; all agreed it was too early to assess his condition, but there was a possibility of brain damage resulting from the particular combination of the amphetamines he had mixed with alcohol.

Meanwhile, a dispute flourished within the forensic laboratory. Partridge and his chemist were at odds. The chemist had proved to his own satisfaction that the particular combination of lime, earth, and gentian violet on the sole of Ted Roper's boot was "commensurate with" that boot having trodden first in the gentian violet, then in the soil around Mawsley, and finally in a patch of lime on the side of West Street. Traces of gentian violet had been found in a patch of lime and a footprint that bore similarities to Ted Roper's boot sole. But Mr. Partridge had been giving evidence in court on another case while the chemist was making his examination, and had been ridiculed by a barrister from London. The wounds were still smarting and Mr. Partridge didn't propose to be caught again. "Give me something absolutely conclusive," he said, "and I will sign the report." He was painfully aware that his reports were introduced into evidence in Court since the last one had become a battleground over which the prosecution and defence had fought battles, his own character and reputation the only real issues at stake.

Without the report, Aveyard refused to move against Ted Roper. "If I have to see him again," he said, "I want to be able to nail him to the ground."

★

Superintendent Aveyard rang the bell on the front door of Mawsley Hall; after a minute, the door was opened by Peabody.

"His Lordship is in his study," he said, faithful to the command that he admit the Superintendent or any of his men at any time.

"I don't think I need to bother him," Aveyard said, "if you can spare me a couple of minutes of your time."

"Certainly, sir," Peabody said. "Won't you please come in?" Aveyard followed him into the hall, then through to the agent's room where they had previously talked. Peabody stood in the centre of the carpet, his left hand clasped in his right, and waited.

"What I need to know," Aveyard said, "is quite a simple matter. The collection of guns in Mr. Cedric's room. What can you tell me about it?"

Peabody's lips had clamped tight at the mention of guns, his disapproval quite apparent. "Mr. Cedric acquired that collection during his fourteenth year," he said. "It was in the summer holiday when he was home from school. They were mounted on the wall a year later."

"By which time, Mr. Cedric had lost interest in them?"

"Yes, sir. You could call it a passing fancy."

"But while it lasted, you didn't approve . . . ?"

"Goodness gracious, sir, it wasn't my place to approve or disapprove."

"But you must have had some feelings about them?"

"Not about the guns, sir."

"But the choice of targets, perhaps?"

"I did feel that the 'choice of targets,' as you so aptly put it, left something to be desired. On several occasions, I myself was placed in that unfortunate position."

"I hope you were able to express your disapproval with sufficient force . . . ?"

"I must confess to having taken that liberty, sir."

For a moment, Aveyard detected the twinkle in Peabody's eyes, the memory of the no-doubt intense satisfaction he had drawn.

"And since those days, the guns have not been used?"

"No, sir. They are taken down each year, of course, for the spring cleaning."

"And cleaned by someone knowledgeable of guns."

"I'm afraid not, sir."

"Oiled and greased?"

"Yes, sir, I am able to perform that small service."

"Our forensic department said the guns had been well looked after. . . ."

"Thank you, sir."

"And now, is the collection complete?"

"Yes, sir, it is quite complete. Though I have no wish to usurp the function of the police services, I took the liberty of checking that fact the night of the unfortunate occurrence."

"Why? Did you have any reason to think Mr. Cedric might be involved? That the murder might have been committed with one of his guns?"

"That thought did pass through my mind, sir. As did the certainty that I would have to answer questions about the guns. I even took the liberty of rechecking the guns against the inventory kept here, in the Agent's desk. I'm happy to say all the guns are still present, sir, all hanging on the wall. That is a matter of some relief, sir, if you don't mind my saying so. . . ."

★

The forensic squad had finished its examination of the clubroom; a comparison of the prints of the people who normally used the room with the prints found there revealed only two extra sets, those of Constable Baron and Cedric Mawsley. No trace had been found of Ted Roper's fingerprints.

★

Westmacott had been found; he was innocently attending a technical sales conference in the Europa Hotel in London, and from the sound of his voice, enjoying his off-duty time. Aveyard spoke briefly with him on the telephone. "I'm not in the habit," Westmacott said, articulating carefully, "of accounting for my movements to anyone. Not even that fine lady I married." Aveyard said a written report could wait until Westmacott arrived, presumably sober, back in the village.

★

Cedric Mawsley's movements had been traced. He'd come out of the front gate of the Hall, looking "bemused" as one observer had said. He'd walked out of the village southwards, "as if not knowing where he was going." He'd sat on a stile a mile south of the village, "and appeared to be talking to himself." He'd walked back to the village, "gesticulating," and had gone into the back gate of the Hall.

★

Aveyard and Bruton were sitting in the Incidents Room. Inspector Roberts and his staff had gone out to lunch. "We'll hold the fort," Bruton had said, "until you all get back." He could see that the Superintendent was troubled by the commonplace chatter of the working party, by the normal conversational comradeship with which the men filled the hours of partial activity. Aveyard had been examining a dossier Bruton had compiled for him of the known activities of Police Constable Baron, prior to his murder.

"There's nothing in this," Aveyard gloomily said. "Just a series of routines in the life of a police constable." He flipped over the other papers Bruton had put on his desk. "Nothing here," he said, "absolutely nothing!"

"We might get some action today from the forensic lab," Bruton reminded him. That morning Aveyard had composed a strongly worded note of protest to Partridge, sending a copy to the Chief Superintendent, asking for action. "Or we could pull Ted Roper in. . . ."

"I'm still against that," Aveyard said. "Although Ted Roper is a known layabout, he still has the privileges of an ordinary human being. We have no right to harass him without something definite in the way of evidence against him. We've gone as far as we ought to go. We've asked him about going into the Hall, and he's given us an answer. It's up to us to produce *evidence* before we begin to doubt him, before we begin to give him the third degree."

"We could at least search his house. . . ."

"For what, Jim? All right, so we find a few pornographic pictures, perhaps a few things he's knocked off. But there are a thousand houses we could search and find the same thing. There isn't a man who works in an office who doesn't take home a few pencils, a stapling machine, a few headed envelopes. We've no right to impose on innocent people that way."

"That's not the main reason, is it, Bill?" Jim said. He knew Bill Aveyard was a stickler for strict honesty. Bill didn't admit to any bending in that inflexible code.

"No, it isn't. All my copper instincts are against Ted Roper for this one. It doesn't smell like Ted Roper. Look, even if we tie him in with those footprints, I can't see it. He goes into that room, walks around it in obvious sight of the chair where Baron was sitting. He comes round to the back of the chair, the position from which we think Baron was shot, and he only makes one set of footprints? I can't see it from that point of view. Nor can I see a lad like Ted Roper using an air pistol. All right. If he got in with a gang, if he was driving for a heavy mob and somebody stuck a pistol in his hand and said, 'Use it,' that might be different. But not on this sort of caper. It's all wrong. And, what's more, it's all wrong for Cedric Mawsley. Don't forget, he was bombed out of his mind. We know that from a score of witnesses. He was in no condition to hold a gun steady enough to use it, no condition, certainly, to use an air pistol for a shot that needed some degree of accuracy. Again, I can't see it."

"But you have no alternatives?"

"That's what's really bothering me. I don't have a single solitary idea. We don't have a single lead. There's nothing in any of this. Absolutely nothing."

"Except the fact, quoted by Lord Mawsley, that Baron had, most unusually, requested a late-evening interview."

"I think that's easy to account for," Aveyard said. "I think Baron was on to Cedric Mawsley's use of drugs. We've heard that he was conscientious, stubborn, loyal. He intended to stop closing a blind eye to Cedric Mawsley's peccadilloes and give him a warning. 'Come off drugs, Mr. Cedric, or I'll turn you in.' He wanted to have the old man standing by in case Cedric became abusive or obstreperous. Or perhaps he intended to tell the old man that he'd given an unofficial warning to his son."

"And Roper? Why do you think Roper went up to the clubroom? Assuming the footprints match and he did go?"

"I don't know. It could have been anything. Perhaps he had a date with a girl up there. Perhaps he went to steal something. We shan't know until we question him, and I don't feel I have any right to go for him until I have conclusive evidence that he was there. That's why I'm pushing Partridge as hard as I dare."

The telephone rang. Bruton answered it, then put his hand over the mouthpiece. "It's the Chief, Super," he said. "Maybe we're going to talk to Roper sooner than you thought."

He waited a second, then announced his name.

When the Chief had finished speaking, Bruton put down the telephone. "It *was* the Chief," he said, looking mystified, "but he didn't want to talk to you. He asked me to give you a message. 'Tell Superintendent Aveyard,' he said, 'to come to my office immediately.' "

"Just that?"

"Just that. He sounded most odd."

"I expect he's busy," Aveyard said, but he too was puzzled. The hierarchy of the police force is a delicate structure; Chief Superintendents don't usually ask sergeants to "tell" Superintendents to do things. "Yes, I expect he was busy," Bruton said.

★

The Chief Superintendent was sitting in his office, with the Assistant Chief Constable sitting beside him, both behind the desk, looking like some sort of tribunal.

Superintendent Aveyard was "admitted" to the office by the duty constable. He walked to where the senior officers sat in silence. Neither asked him to sit down.

"Superintendent Aveyard," the Chief Superintendent said formally, "a letter has been received the contents of which seem to indicate that, in the course of your duty as a police officer, you may have been paid, and may have received, sums of money in conditions which can only be described as bribery. I am hereby suspending you from all police duty until such time as an investigation into this matter has been carried out by an independent police officer, Chief Superintendent Beasley, of the Leicester Police Force, with such assistance as he may require. Subsequent upon the completion of those enquiries, charges may or may not be preferred against you. You may, of course, at any time you wish, engage any legal representation you feel you require, on your own behalf and at your own expense. You will hold yourself available to Chief Superintendent Beasley at all times until his enquiry has been completed. Is that understood?"

The Chief's voice was a cold whip that lashed out at Aveyard. His manner expressed all his disappointment, all his anguish, at his obligation to say these words to a man he had befriended and sponsored, actively securing his promotion in the Birton force against opposition.

"I understand, Chief Superintendent," Aveyard said. It was not the time for denial.

★

Detective Chief Superintendent Bill Aveyard was sitting at the desk in his office in the Headquarters of the Birton Constabulary, in a large country house in a park about a mile outside the town of Birton. Bill was making a chain of paper clips, fastening the doubled end of each one into the single end of the preceding one with enormous concentration. The chain he had so far constructed snaked across the green blotter at the centre of his desk in precise lines; it was at least four feet long and the cardboard box which had provided its raw materials was almost empty.

A knock sounded on the door and, without looking up from his task, Bill called, "Come in."

The door opened and a constable appeared, carrying a cup of coffee on a saucer into which several drops had spilled, wetting the two biscuits which lay beside the spoon. The cup and saucer were brown earthenware, in contrast to the white commercial crockery the canteen supplied. They'd been a gift from the Detective Chief Superintendent who, against all the protests at Bill Aveyard's youth and lack of seniority, had secured his promotion two years earlier. When the constable had gone, Bill looked at the cup and saucer. "I wonder if the Chief will want them back," he thought.

Bill Aveyard was making a chain of paper clips because, for the first time since that promotion two years ago, he had nothing else to do.

That's not strictly true. Bill Aveyard had many things he could be doing, several cases whose investigation was not yet completed.

Another knock came on the door. Bill Aveyard called "Come in," again. The door opened and Sergeant Jim Bruton walked across the office and, without being asked, sat in the chair which faced the desk. For a couple of minutes, neither spoke. Sergeant Bruton looked at the chain of paper clips, then sighed. "A right bugger, isn't it?" he said.

Bill Aveyard nodded but didn't trust himself to speak.

"I wondered if I could help?" Jim Bruton said.

Bill shook his head. Both knew the rules, the spoken and unspoken regulations that define that amorphous mass known as Police Force Tradition.

"I thought you'd say that," Jim Bruton said. He got up out of the chair, stood there heavily, looking at the blotter, avoiding Bill Aveyard's eye. They'd worked together for many years, back to the days when Bill Aveyard, too, was a sergeant. Jim Bruton had taken the younger man under his wing, watched with pride as his protégé rose above and beyond him, never once jealous or resentful that a junior had been promoted over his head. Jim Bruton knew he had found his own niche as a sergeant, never would want to rise to officer rank unless some benevolent Chief made him up to Inspector to increase his retirement pension. Jim had seen, from the beginning of the team relationship between the two men, that Aveyard would go a long way in police work. Bill Aveyard had the one thing Jim Bruton lacked, instinct. Jim was good with detail, with the slow, plodding method that constitutes 95 per cent of all police work. Bill Aveyard had instinct, flashes of insight in which he could quickly separate truth from fiction, right from wrong, genuine from false.

Bill Aveyard's instinct had let him down, very badly. Jim Bruton clucked his tongue against his teeth and left the room, shaking his head. At the doorway he paused briefly and looked back. "We're having steak and kidney pudding tonight," he said. "I expect there'll be enough for three."

Bill Aveyard watched him go, saw the door close before he returned to making his paper-clip chain.

The telephone rang. Bill Aveyard picked it up.

"Chief Superintendent Beasley here," the voice said.

"Superintendent Aveyard."

"Are you ready for us?"

"Any time."

"We'll come right away, if that's all right with you."

"Any time."

It took them less than a minute to arrive in his office. "They must have rung from the Chief's office," he thought. They were two, Chief Superintendent William Beasley from the Uniformed Division at Leicester, aged fifty-five, fat and florid but with the well-washed public schoolboy look, neatly knotted tie, and inconspicuous cufflinks. With him was Inspector Wallace-Smith, from Traffic, Leicester. Aveyard instinctively rose from behind his desk and walked to the other side. The Chief Superintendent sat in Aveyard's chair. "Sit down, please," he said. Inspector Wallace-Smith unzipped the black case he carried and held it open on his knee, his nose wrinkling as if it contained something distasteful to him. He looked across the carpet at Aveyard and on his face was the expression of every man who feels himself betrayed, who feels somehow that his stature and dignity have been diminished by the actions of another person. Aveyard saw that the black case contained only a few papers. When Wallace-Smith realized Aveyard was looking at the papers he turned his knees and lifted them so that the papers could not be read. A flicker of anger crossed his face. Aveyard had seen the same look on many a father, or many a brother, when a member of a family has been brought home from being charged with a crime, the look that said "How could you shame us like this?" Nothing is so easily bruised as a man's dignity, nothing so jealously guarded as his personal sense of integrity. The Chief Superintendent waited until Wallace-Smith had settled in his seat and had arranged his papers. He coughed politely, seemed ill at ease in Aveyard's chair, examining the desk top as if it might contain a clue. He picked up the chain of paper clips and, without speaking, allowed them to fold themselves one by one into the cardboard carton. Then, the desk clear in front of him, he placed his hands strategically on each side of the blotter. It could have been by accident that each pink and carefully manicured hand settled exactly five centimetres from the edge of the pad.

★

Inspector Roberts at fifty-two years of age had long ago resigned himself to the fact that he would never make Chief Inspector or Superintendent. With this resignation had come a great contentment which, coupled with his ability for taking pains and remembering facts, made him invaluable in the kind of investigation now taking place. The investigation itself had a sense of urgency and close family connotations, since it concerned the murder of a constable in D-Division of the Birton Police Force.

Inspector Roberts opened the Incidents Book and made a notation. Twelve forty-seven. House-to-house Surveys completed. He glanced at the constable who had just handed him the last of the questionnaires that had been carried round the village, completed in detail by the force of constables the division had assigned to the investigation.

"You can leave it here, lad, and I'll deal with it."

The constable went back to the far corner of the room, put a sheet of paper in the typewriter, drew one of the earlier completed questionnaires to his side, and began typing. In the old days he would have put seven carbons in the machine and the last copy would hardly be fit to read; now they had a copier on site manned by a girl from divisional headquarters, all the resources of a model office at their disposal.

Inspector Roberts glanced at the form to make sure all the sections had been completed, all the questions had been answered, the name and address of the person supplying the information had been carefully and correctly printed. He looked at the parish register which listed the names and addresses of all the voters in the village and place a tick against the name Westmacott, of No. 2, the Ride. "Right," he thought. "Let's see if Mr. Westmacott has anything different to tell us." Westmacott hadn't. On the night of the murder he had spent the time between eight o'clock and ten-thirty in the pub, The Pheasant. He was a member of the darts team and that evening was playing a home game against a team from The Cock in Birton. He left the pub at half-past ten and walked home down the High Street, turning left into the Ride. He met the following list of people on his way home and said good night to each one. The constable had carefully printed the names of the people and Inspector Roberts noted he had spelled one wrongly, Simmons and not Simonds. Inspector Roberts' memory clicked as he looked through the list, remembering the statements each had made. All had reported seeing Westmacott going home. Three had described Westmacott as being drunk, two had suggested Westmacott was "happy," one of them had said "Westmacott was carrying a number of bottles of beer," and Mrs. Jones of No. 4 the High Street had said that Westmacott "as usual was staggering disgustingly." Inspector Roberts was too old a hand to accept any one of these reports at its face value, knew how impossible it is to obtain a purely objective eye-witness report of any event without the subjective and often emotional opinions of the observer intruding.

Constable Baron had lived in the village, renting a cottage at No. 10, the Ride, where he lived with his bride of a year, Betty. He had made an offer for a site at the start of the Ride and that offer had been accepted. Once upon a time a glass-blowing factory had occupied that site but it had fallen into misuse thirty years ago; a few years ago the stone of the ruin had been sold for building, on condition the site was cleared and levelled and a hedge planted to surround it. Constable Baron had had an appointment with the builder, Jack Marsh, also of Mawsley, and together they had walked round the site, discussing what kind of a house Jack Marsh would build for the money Constable Baron would obtain on mortgage. When interviewed, Jack Marsh agreed it was a bit unusual to walk round a site at night, but he was a busy man and so was the constable and the previous four appointments they had made to look at the ground in the daytime could not be kept by one or other of them. He said that anyway there'd still been enough light to see what they wanted.

Jack Marsh left the site at nine o'clock. He was probably the last man but one to see Constable Baron alive. The other one, of course, was the man the police were trying to find, the murderer. Mawsley had a very active air rifle and pistol club which met frequently in a large barn placed at its disposal by Lord Mawsley. The police had impounded a whole arsenal of air pistols and rifles from the houses of the village and the forensic team at Birton were conducting ballistics examinations of them, with little hope of success. Lead pellets are not like exploded rounds; though some of the high-powered air pistols were rifled, the lead pellets did not hold the imprint of the rifling as accurately as a steel-jacketed bullet would have done. The piece of lead that had killed Baron and had been extracted from the base of his skull could not be matched to any of the specimens they had obtained from the village guns. Nor could they say definitely that it did *not* come from anyone of the guns.

Inspector Roberts pondered this and other matters as he read the Westmacott statement. He looked up when the door of the hall suddenly opened and Detective Superintendent Colby, the new Investigating Officer, came in. His face revealed no trace of his thoughts as he stood up. Everybody liked Detective Superintendent Bill Aveyard. Few people like Colby. The two Superintendents were similar in one respect. Both were young, both were efficient and came from the new school of Detective Officer, young men who brought an academic intellect to the business of crime detection. The older men on the force who'd risen through the ranks by dint of long service thought of this new breed of officer collectively as "the Whiz Kids." But whereas Bill Aveyard had borne his intellect lightly, Colby never lost an opportunity to flaunt his academic training and had little patience with or tolerance of his contemporaries.

Colby came quickly across the room, looked at the desk, took in the opened Incidents Book and the Westmacott statement at a glance.

"What's that, Inspector?" he asked.

Inspector Roberts looked at him for a moment before speaking. "Good afternoon, Superintendent," he said slowly, enunciating precisely.

Colby at least had the grace to look embarrassed. "Oh, good afternoon, Inspector," he said, then couldn't resist adding, "I didn't know we were doing the gracious bit!"

Inspector Roberts picked up the questionnaire. "We've talked with Westmacott," he said.

"What took so long?"

"You may have forgotten Westmacott left the village that night and hasn't been back since."

Superintendent Colby had not forgotten. Mentally he cursed himself. Why did he always have this instinct to make a glib flip remark, often causing himself to look a fool to his juniors. Of course he remembered Westmacott had left the village. That fact had been in Superintendent Aveyard's report when he handed over the case. Westmacott was a representative for a firm of boiler manufacturers and that night he'd caught the last train from Birton to London to attend a sales conference starting the following morning. Unfortunately he hadn't told his wife where he was going and they'd had a hell of a job trying to trace him, thinking naturally that he might have skipped the village because of Baron's murder. Aveyard himself had spoken to Westmacott on the telephone; sending the constable to compile the questionnaire had been no more than a formality.

Colby grunted and sat at his desk.

The door opened again, and Jim Bruton came in. Colby knew that Bruton and Superintendent Aveyard had worked together on many cases, but he couldn't risk changing sergeants in the middle of an investigation. Bruton came to the desk. "Good news, at last," he said. "I've just been having a word with Mr. Partridge of forensic. The cast of that footprint does match. And the gentian violet. He's prepared to sign the report."

"That sort of information ought to be entered into the book," Colby said.

"It will be, Superintendent, as soon as the report is received," Bruton said, resolving to offer no more advance information if that was the way it would be received.

Colby's eyes were gleaming with anticipation. "I think the time has come," he said, "to sort out Mr. Roper. I can't think why it wasn't done before."

"Shall I pull him in?" Sergeant Bruton asked.

"Yes. Take him into Birton. Meanwhile, forensic can search the house. When they've finished, you can bring Roper here and I'll question him."

"We'll need a Search Warrant," Inspector Roberts said.

"I know the procedures, Inspector," Superintendent Colby said. "Now let's get started; let's get some action into this case. . . ."

CHAPTER 6

Inspector Wallace-Smith handed a sheaf of papers to Chief Superintendent Beasley. Beasley straightened them on the blotter so that the distances between the edges of the paper and the edges of the blotter were exact.

"You understand this is an informal meeting," he said.

Bill Aveyard nodded. The procedure of a Departmental Enquiry is a more precise matter even than a court of law. A Departmental Enquiry has a primary unpleasant atmosphere, however, since the accused is a member of a trusted family. Many times Aveyard had sat on the other side of the desk and could remember clearly the distaste he had felt. For many years, the police force was regarded almost as a deity that can do no wrong; recent disclosures round the world and the number of books written about police corruption and venality have tarnished that image almost to a point at which to be a policeman is regarded as suspect, since all policemen are assumed to be "bent" in one way or another. It no longer mattered what rank an officer had achieved; the higher the man the greater the "take" was the way many people felt about police corruption. Of course the temptations were immense, especially since the police must often administer laws that make little or no sense to the lay mind. What did it matter if a few friends, gathered in a pub for an evening's conviviality and disturbing no one, should raise a glass of whisky to their lips five minutes after the arbitrary "closing time?" Did the possession of a piece of paper, a licence, suddenly elevate the drinking to some new, correct, status? What did it matter if a man pushed a wheelbarrow of oranges, parked them where he was causing no obstruction, and sold them to the passing housewives pennies cheaper than the shop prices? Administering these "laws" could make a policeman feel useless, superfluous.

Aveyard himself was a straight "letter of the Law" man. He didn't approve of some of the laws or of the professional men who shelter behind them, but he knew quite clearly that if he did not set an example, if every man employed by the Police Force did not behave with absolute probity, the country would decline even more quickly into the anarchy they could daily see growing about them.

"The purpose of this meeting," Chief Superintendent Beasley said, "is to inform you, of the evidence which has been placed before us which I, in my official capacity, will investigate. You understand that a statement of the receipt of this evidence is in no way used by me to infer or to imply that that evidence is wholly or in part correct. We merely wish to apprise you of what we have. Only when our investigation is complete will a decision be taken as to whether you will be charged or not with a crime. You understand that your suspension from duty at this moment is a matter of police procedure as defined by the relevance Police acts. You understand also that the suspension was made at the discretion of the Chief Constable advised by your immediate superior the Chief Superintendent and that that suspension can be lifted at any time."

"I would have preferred to stay at work," Aveyard said. "I have a lot to do."

"I know how you feel," the Chief Superintendent said. "This is a very unpleasant business for us all. You can take notes if you want to."

Aveyard shook his head. "I'd rather just listen," he said.

"Very well. This all began," Beasley said, "with an anonymous note received by the Chief Superintendent. Clipped to the note was a paying-in slip for the National Westminster Bank, Market Place Branch, Birton. The slip purported to show that a sum of one thousand pounds had been deposited in cash into an account which bears your name at that branch. The note attached to the payment slip was printed with a ballpoint pen and said 'Ask him why I am paying him off.' In accordance with procedures the Chief Superintendent immediately contacted me and I assigned an investigating team. That team discovered, by methods which you as a police officer will understand, that the payment was alleged to be made by a man known to you as Herbert Wilson who owns and operates a number of licensed betting shops in Birton. When asked if he had made this payment to your account, Mr. Herbert Wilson indicated that he had done so but declined to give a reason. His exact words were—" and here the Chief Superintendent referred to a paper on his desk, " 'You'd better ask *him*, hadn't you?' The 'him' to whom he referred he identified as Detective Superintendent Aveyard. He added the words 'and it's not the first time either.' When the Chief Constable was informed of this evidence—or rather should I say this statement—he gave me permission to interview you and if you will recall I did so immediately on an informal basis. You were good enough to give me permission to interview the bank manager, one James Riddle, a man you described as a friend of yours. James Riddle subsequently gave me access to the records of that account which contained a credit balance of two thousand pounds. The account had been opened by a letter written in familiar terms and signed Bill; it contained three specimen signatures on a piece of card of a type used in the box-filing system here at Police Headquarters, and fifty twenty-pound notes. The letter asked that this account be opened in your name and gave your home address. The second payment into that account was made the following day and was the subject of the paying-in slip which, after being stamped by the bank, appears to have been forwarded immediately to the Chief Superintendent. You supplied us with a specimen signature in presence of Inspector Wallace-Smith and this specimen signature appears to confirm the ones given to the bank. On receipt of this confirmation you were suspended from duty. The Departmental Enquiry has been initiated but as yet you have not been accused of accepting a bribe with an attempt to pervert the normal course of justice."

"Has Herbert Wilson been charged with offering a bribe?" Aveyard asked.

"Not yet, though he has been warned that he may be so charged."

Chief Superintendent Beasley shuffled his papers and when he had straightened them again he looked up at Inspector Wallace-Smith. "Inspector," he said, "I know it's irregular but I wonder if you'd care to pop down to the canteen for a few minutes. I'll join you there." Aveyard sat still as Wallace-Smith accepted the papers Beasley held out to him, zipped them into his briefcase, and left the room.

Beasley got up and walked across to the window looking out over the park. The sun was shining on trees which stretched as far as the eye could see. The park had been left open to the public. Several mothers were wheeling prams along the walks. In the distance he could see a flock of crows whirling over the tops of one of the trees and the blackness of the nests they had built. He turned around and looked back into the room, his facc carrying a look of puzzlement. Aveyard had moved in his chair and turned to face him.

"Look, Bill," the Chief Superintendent said. "You don't mind if I call you Bill?"

Aveyard shook his head. He knew the interviewing technique, had used it himself on company executives. "Tell us what we want to know; save your wife and family embarrassment. . . ."

"I've been talking with your Chief," Beasley said. "I don't know you personally, of course, but your Chief says this business with Herbert Wilson goes against your nature. Apparently, he staked his reputation to recommend you for promotion. That's one of the responsibilities of senior rank. We have to make certain there's a regular flow of talented younger men coming up. Sometimes we're right, sometimes wrong. We all make mistakes. All we ask is that, when a mistake has been made, the effects of it on the morale of the Force are kept to a minimum. All right, you could accuse us of being protectionist, but only when it concerns the general good of the force. Only you can know, at this moment, if your Chief has made a mistake. We can find out, of course, and you know enough about police work to be certain that we will find out exactly why that payment was made and what, if any, services were rendered to earn it; if there's any whiff of bribery, we'll prosecute with full vigor. You know that."

He paused. This was the moment Aveyard was supposed to say, "I've been a naughty boy, I've brought dishonour on my Chief and the Force." He said nothing.

"I sent Inspector Wallace-Smith out of the room in case there was anything you wanted to say to me," the Chief Superintendent said. "At this moment, the Chief Constable would accept a resignation and that could be the end of it."

Aveyard still said nothing.

"If you've done it, Bill, don't think about yourself. The Force comes first, you know; it has to. If we have to chase you and prove the accusation, it'll mean a hell of a stink for the *Force*; it'll mean imprisonment for you. As it is now, you could acknowledge you've made a mistake, give us a quiet resignation, and I promise you, that would be the end of it. No newspaper publicity, no departmental publicity, nothing. Just a bald announcement of your resignation."

"You'd give me a reference if I applied for a job outside?"

The Chief Superintendent smiled, thinly. "Now, that's asking a bit much. I imagine something could be worked out, some statement that said you'd served for so many years, had been promoted, just a statement of the known facts about you."

Aveyard shook his head again. "Look, Chief, let's put our minds into more profitable thoughts. I didn't do it. I didn't accept a bribe from Herbert Wilson. You can use that as your starting point. And forget this business about resignation. I'm not going to resign and, if I'm dismissed, I shall seek legal advice about the best procedure to fight wrongful dismissal."

The relief on Beasley's face was comical to see. He broke into a huge smile, clasped his hands together and shook them, hardly able to contain himself. "Your Chief will be so happy, so happy," he said, "and, of course, so am I. It's been such a nightmare, thinking a man of your rank could have accepted a bribe, especially one so highly thought of as you were. I can't tell you what's it's done to your Chief. It has been almost as if his own flesh and blood had been accused. . . ."

Aveyard had only seen the Chief once since the accusation had been made; the Chief's conduct had been icily proper, glacier cold.

"This is such a strange business," the Chief Superintendent went on, "such an odd affair. . . ."

"It doesn't make sense," Aveyard said. "In the first place *why* would Herbert Wilson need to pay me two thousand pounds? He's running a perfectly legal betting-shop business. He even has one of the best-known lawyers in this town on the board. I can't stand the man but he's a respected member of the community, on every committee you can think of. Herbert Wilson lives in six acres on the edge of the town and every Saturday night has twenty or thirty people for supper. His yearly drinks bill can't be far short of the two thousand pounds he's supposed to have paid me. Secondly, assuming I'd been daft enough to take two thousand pounds from him, would I have put it into an account in a bank in my own name with my own address? And finally, anybody can start a bank account using any name they like just so long as they don't use that false name with intent to defraud. You know the Law."

Beasley came back across the room. "I know the Law," he said, "but one thing police work has taught me—you can't examine any case on grounds of reason. How many cases have you had to deal with, how many cases have you solved because the criminal did an unreasonable thing? And particularly where money is concerned; how many men have knocked off a few thousand pounds and then have flashed it about unreasonably? We had a case only last week; a fellow working as a Company Secretary, robbing his employer blind. How did we get on to him? Because the silly devil bought himself a 4.2 Jaguar, started having his suits made in Savile Row, was seen eating in the best restaurants in the county, and went for his holiday to Bermuda! All on a nominal salary of thirty-five hundred pounds a year. When the fraud squad looked at his books he was a hundred and twenty thousand in the red and he didn't have a penny in the bank to show for it. Where is the reason in that?"

"I didn't do it, you know," Aveyard said. "I've never taken a penny."

"But the money *was* in your account; you could have drawn it out at any time. You can understand that we have to investigate it."

"Yes, I can understand that," Aveyard said. "It doesn't make it any more palatable. Word gets round. People are starting to look at me in a way I know I've looked at other people. I don't like it."

"You've not been charged. You've not been accused!"

"No, but I have been suspended from duty. When Colby took over the Baron case he could hardly bring himself to be civil. You understand I'm not complaining. I've always been one of the first to say that the Law is the Law and we must fight to maintain it. But it's bloody painful when you're the one caught in the long, slow grind. You can do me two favours," he said. "You can ask Herbert Wilson *why* he needed to bribe me and secondly you can get it over quickly. I want to get back to work."

★

Ted Roper had lived in the village of Mawsley all his thirty years. He was tall and heavy, a thickset, well-built man of small intelligence, well known to the police. His long history of petty crime had started in juvenile court when he was accused of assaulting a forty-five-year-old man. For years Ted Roper had been the village bully, and the man was the village schoolteacher with the unfortunate task of trying to cram some knowledge into Ted Roper's shambling hulk. When he had tried to chastise Ted Roper for horseplay in the schoolyard, Ted Roper turned around and hit him, breaking his nose and cracking three of his teeth. In the following years Ted Roper drifted from job to job, always starting out with good intentions but never realizing that his great strength could cause injury. Over the years his lack of intelligence resolved itself into a complete indifference to Law and Order and the rights of possession. Whatever Ted Roper saw that he could use, he took without thinking about its owner. Rather than walk home, he'd take the first bicycle he could see. Once he took a horse and left it to graze in the field behind his home. When he grew old enough to begin to understand engines, he started to take cars. He never intended to "steal" them, never tried to sell them. If he needed transport he'd smash a car door open, jump a wire across the starter switch, and use the car for as long as the petrol lasted. On the occasions he'd been caught driving such a vehicle he'd allow the officers to arrest him, then if they were foolish enough to give him the chance he'd crack their heads together and make his way back home. He'd been to Borstal three times and to prison twice and on each occasion had behaved immaculately while inside. The probation officers all despaired of him; the local police, all of whom knew him, would run a mile rather than arrest him. He lived in a cottage with his mother, a drudge who cleaned the floors in a factory in Birton. The house she kept was neat and tidy and she accepted Ted's absences with almost total indifference. Profoundly religious, she believed that everything that happened to her and her son was the Will of God and as such could not be influenced by the action of mortals. Whenever her son was in prison she went to see him once a week, baked the jam tarts she knew he liked, and sat opposite him for thirty minutes with hardly a word to say. She never reprimanded or admonished him. "Just make sure you wrap up warm" was the nearest she ever came to trying to influence the course of his life. Ted Roper himself didn't think the police were putting on him when they arrested him. It wasn't from motives of malice that he would crack their heads together, merely that he no longer wished to go where they were taking him and saw that as the only means of escape.

It had been an easy arrest. "The Super wants to talk to you," Bruton had said.

"Right."

"Wrap up warm," Mrs. Roper had said.

Ted Roper hadn't thought to ask why the Superintendent wanted to talk to him. He'd merely accepted the fact at its face value.

He'd been driven into the police headquarters in Birton, and placed in an interview room. No one had spoken to him, except the constable sitting mute in the corner of the room, cleaning his fingernails. After a while, the oppressive silence had got on Ted Roper's nerves. "Why don't you charge me?" he'd asked. The constable had looked at him with complete disinterest.

"Don't ask me, mate," he'd said. "I'm only here to act as nursemaid." After half an hour a sergeant had appeared and Ted Roper had been taken downstairs and put into a cell. "It's just for a little while," the sergeant had said. "We need the Interview Room for a meeting."

Meanwhile, though Ted Roper couldn't know this, the team from forensic had gone to his house, been admitted by his mother on production of a search warrant, and had started to go through the house from top to bottom. "The place is clean," his mother said as she followed them from room to room. "I won't allow any stuff to be brought here." The men of the forensic team have a thankless task, searching a premises often without knowing what they are looking for, scrabbling in drawers and cupboards for oddities, things that ought not to be there, seem out of place. Expensive radios in mean rooms, jewellery in a working-class woman's dressing table, floorboards that have obviously been recently taken up and put back again, plastic-wrapped packets in the cisterns of lavatories, heavily weighted lamp bases, notes in the tin boxes in underwear drawers.

They found nothing in Ted Roper's house to arouse suspicion.

"You keep a very clean house, missis," one of them said as they left. "It's been a pleasure to turn it over. Not like some, I can tell you." It was the first compliment anyone had paid Mrs. Roper in thirty years.

The leader of the forensic team went to report to Superintendent Colby in the Interview Room in Mawsley Hall. Colby was astonished, found it hard to accept there had been nothing in Roper's house. "No stolen goods," he asked, "no watches, no cameras, no radios?"

"Nothing."

"No cartons of cigarettes, bottles of whisky?"

The sergeant from forensic was a slow-speaking man. "In my department, Superintendent, when we say nothing, we mean, nothing!" He didn't even wait for the Superintendent to reply.

"Get Roper here," Colby shouted across the room. Inspector Roberts looked up at him. "Yes, Superintendent?" he said. "Did you say something?"

★

Superintendent Colby, prepared for Roper's arrival from police headquarters, had cleared the space before his desk and had placed five of his largest constables around the wall.

Roper was brought in and given a chair before the desk. The Superintendent looked at him for several moments in what was intended to be a quelling way, but Roper smiled cheekily back at him. "Right, Sergeant," Colby said, "you know what we need."

Sergeant Bruton perched himself on the edge of the desk. "Ted," he said, "you've got form, so you know there's a lot of rigmarole to be got through before we ask you questions."

Ted Roper's face broke into a huge smile. "Oh yes," he said, "anything I say will be taken down and used in evidence against me."

"You've got the idea," Bruton said, "only you've got it wrong. Anything you say will be taken down. We may use it; we may not. It all depends." He turned to look at the Superintendent who nodded. It wasn't the correct form of official caution according to the Judges' Rules, but they all knew that Ted Roper wasn't capable of understanding the full reasoning behind that set of regulations. If anything useful came of this questioning, Roper would be taken to Headquarters and there he'd be treated to the full dignity of the Law. For the time being it was enough that a caution, any kind of caution, had been administered.

"You know a police constable was killed?" Bruton asked.

Ted Roper nodded. "I should know," he said. "I saw him, didn't I?"

Bruton looked over to where the shorthand writer was inconspicuously taking notes. "Would you care to tell us how and where you saw him?"

Roper looked about him as if pleased at the attention he was receiving. "Well, he was in the clubroom, wasn't he?"

"Don't ask us questions," Bruton said kindly. "Just tell us what you saw."

"He was in a chair in the clubroom. Dead."

"How did you know he was dead?" Bruton asked.

"Well, he was, wasn't he? I mean there was blood on the back of his head. He looked a right mess."

"What were you doing in the clubroom?" Superintendent Colby asked quickly.

"What was I doing there? Well, I was cutting through the grounds of the Hall, wasn't I?"

"Don't ask me questions," Colby said. "You're here to answer questions, not ask them."

"You needn't get shirty," Roper said. "I'm telling you, aren't I?

Nothing to do with me, but I just happened to notice he was sitting there and saw he had blood on the back of his head."

"And what did you do then?" Bruton asked, his voice still kindly.

"Well, I had a look in his pockets. See if they had anything in them. But they didn't."

"You searched a corpse and tried to steal from it," Colby said, expressing his disgust.

"Steal? Who said anything about stealing. He was dead, wasn't he? Dead men can't smoke cigarettes, can they? Dead men can't use money, can they?"

Sergeant Bruton leaned forward. "After you'd been through his pockets, tell me what you did then."

"Well, I went where I was going, didn't I?"

"Where was that Ted?"

"Up to Fairville Cottages."

"What for, Ted?"

"To see if Slanky was working."

"And was he?"

"Yes."

"And then what?"

For the first time Ted Roper looked discomfited. "Well, you know . . ." he said.

"Know what, Ted?"

"You know!"

"No, I don't know, Ted. Tell me."

"Well, like, I went in, didn't I? You know!"

The light of understanding dawned on Bruton's face, but he refrained from smiling. "You spent some time with Mrs. Slanky," he said gently.

Ted Roper laughed. "That's a good one," he said. "Spent some time with Mrs. Slanky. Yes, that's right."

Bruton turned to the Superintendent. "Mrs. Slanky is a well-known local character, Superintendent," Bruton said. "SOA of 1956."

"You mean she's a tart!"

"A tart?" Ted Roper said indignantly. "She's a very nice lady."

"That's as may be," Colby said coldly, "but let's get a few facts, shall we? How much time did you spend with this 'very nice lady'? What time did you get there and what time did you leave?"

"What *time?*" Ted Roper asked. "How would I know? I don't carry a watch."

Colby leaned forward as if taking over the interrogation himself. "You must have had some idea of the time since, according to what you've just said, you wanted to make sure if her husband was working. Presumably her husband goes to work at a certain time each night, and you wouldn't go round before that time would you?"

"You're dead right!" Ted Roper said. "He leaves the house at ten o'clock. I was watching the telly. I left at a quarter to ten and took a short cut through the Hall."

Superintendent Colby had the satisfied look of a man who thinks he has detected a flaw in an otherwise impeccable argument. "If you hadn't spent time with Constable Baron," he said triumphantly, "you'd have arrived early at Fairville Cottages, wouldn't you?"

"Yes, like, but I didn't want anybody nipping in before me, did I? I mean, you've got to be quick round there. You'd hardly believe the queues I've seen sometimes."

Superintendent Colby rose quickly from his seat, walked across to Inspector Roberts' desk, bent down and whispered in his ear. "Send someone round to see this Slanky woman. Better still, go yourself. I want to know what time her husband left that night, what time Roper arrived, what time he left. And was there anything unusual about Roper. You know, all the usual stuff."

Inspector Roberts got up and left the room, and the Superintendent sat behind his desk again. It was a trestle table more used to carrying cups of tea and cakes than the bulk of a police investigation. When Aveyard had left the case, Bruton had taken away his favourite chair, and left a Church Hall bentwood one in its place, which creaked as Superintendent Colby leaned back. Colby became aware of the ominous sound, and quickly sat upright. "Right, Mr. Roper," he said. "I want you to start at the beginning, where you were sitting at home watching television, and tell me everything that happened before you got back home again that night. And, *en passant,* as you might say, you could tell us why you left a police constable dead in a chair and did nothing to help him."

CHAPTER 7

When Chief Superintendent Beasley had left, Bill Aveyard, tiring suddenly of making paper-clip chains while the walls of his office closed tighter about him, left Police Headquarters and drove his own car into the town of Briton. The market place was empty of stalls since this was not market day; he drove his car through the complex of steel poles on which the stalls would be constructed the following day, and found a vacant slot at the top near the Market Cafe-Restaurant. He sat in the car for a moment after he'd switched off the engine, not yet certain of the motive that had brought him into the town to park where he had.

He got out of the car, stood still, looking around him. Familiar sights, all of them. The church behind him, and near it the library. Bus station on the other side of the road. Baker's shop, Fish-and Chip shop. The Queen's Head. A policeman doesn't think of places in the abstract, identifies them by event or occasion. They'd staked out the Church after repeated acts of vandalism two years ago, caught the woman doing it, a religious maniac who believed God had deserted her. The library had been broken into. Who the hell breaks into a library? Turned out to be a boy taking his A levels, wanting text books they wouldn't let him borrow since they were classified for Reference only. The boy was suffering a brainstorm from overwork. Baker's shop, another break-in, but this time, a straight burglary aiming at the cash till. The Fish-and-Chip shop, with its corner where you could stand and eat your cod with salt and vinegar. Aveyard always met Fred there, Fred the Nark, a useful source of information in this town. Cod and chips, please, and don't wrap 'em; I'll eat 'em here. Back into the corner and find Fred the Nark. Who did that job in Fisher's factory, Fred? Who's flashing his money around the Working Men's Clubs? Fred would grumble. "I don't know why you're always asking me. If anybody knew I even talked to you, I'd wind up in the lime pit outside Artleknock."

You could stand at the bar of the Queen's Head, quietly, on a Friday night, keep your ears open, and learn more about what's going on beneath the surface of Birton than in any other single spot. The bar of the Queen's Head was the focal centre for the successful and the hopeful, the hard boys and the hangers-on hoping one day to join them, partners in crime. They knew Aveyard, of course, but somehow that didn't stop them talking. Almost as if the bar at the Queen's Head was the Confessional or a doctor's office and any information gathered there was sacred and confidential. It was often enough merely to observe who met who, who recognized who, who talked to who. Jim Lowndes, talking to two Wellingborough lads. Faces unknown, but look at their hands to know they're engineers. What's Jim Lowndes talking to engineers about? That's how it starts. The basis of police work is careful and correct observation; that's what the manual says. It's also using your nose and your instinct. Aveyard had smelled them, literally smelled the welding on them, and wondered what Jim Lowndes was doing with a couple of welders. Two weeks later, he'd had the satisfaction of knocking off Jim Lowndes on a charge of receiving. The welders worked at Corby Steel Works, and Jim Lowndes had fenced the half ton of copper they'd brought out, concealed in iron pipes they were supposed to be taking to a quarry to weld into the water system.

And now, as he looked around the city, he could imagine the hostile eyes that would look at him if he was charged. The local newspaper would pick it up, of course, and a photograph of him would star on the front page. Local Superintendent charged with accepting a bribe. Departmental Enquiry. That would be the end of his effectiveness in this area. Every petty crook, every lag, every layabout would sneer at him, 'Weren't you the one they charged with being bent?' Even if the charge proved false, the slime would stick, the taunts would continue. The most deadly of all the Britishisms is summed up in the one phrase, no smoke without fire. No one would ever believe that he was entirely innocent.

He turned to the right and walked quickly along Market Place, past the Cafe-Restaurant which emitted its usual odour of corn oil and cooking grease. Next door the glass shop, and then the betting shop, one of the chain owned by Herbert Wilson. His policeman's mind instinctively ran through the relevant sections of the Betting, Gaming, and Lotteries Act, 1963. He couldn't help himself, even though in no way could he consider himself on duty. Dammit, that was what made a copper, wasn't it? Section Three of the Fourth Schedule, the licensee must display his betting office licence on the premises . . . etc., etc., etc. Notice on the window showing times of opening, notice showing the name and the words "licensed betting office" *and nothing else*. Stuck on the notice was a piece of paper which said, "Vote for Blackwell, the candidate to WIN." The manager of the office ought to have seen that, ought to have razored it off the notice. Displaying the sticker on the notice constituted an offence at law. Aveyard could walk into the Betting Shop and close it down on a legal technicality. What was more important, as a police officer sworn to enforce the law, Aveyard *should* walk in there, *should* make certain the manager cleaned the notice.

Aveyard walked past. Turned right into the bank. "Is he in?" he asked the girl cashier.

She looked strangely at him. "Do you mean, Mr. Riddle?"

So it had started, Aveyard thought. When he'd come into the bank a month before, the girl, knowing him to be a personal friend of the manager, had shared a joke with him, had greeted him as a favoured customer, even though he did not keep his personal account at that branch. Now there was an edge to her voice. Did she know he had been suspended from duty, was about to be charged with accepting a bribe? She went on speaking. "Mr. Riddle is no longer here," she said. "Would you like to talk to Mr. Mumby."

"Mr. Riddle. Not here?"

"Didn't you know? Mr. Riddle retired last Friday. We had a party for him, here in the bank. Well, we had two parties, really, one in the bank and one in the Queen's Head. We gave him a canteen of cutlery. Very nice."

Aveyard cursed himself. Of course he'd known Riddle was near retirement, had talked about what he was going to do afterwards. Dammit, hadn't Aveyard recommended Riddle to Smithson's when they wanted someone to supervise their wages procedures after a couple of holdup scares. One day a week. Aveyard had suggested Riddle might like to do it after he retired.

"Oh, I'm sorry; I quite forgot," he said.

The girl looked at him. "You've got a lot on your mind right now," she said, ice lacing the edge of her voice.

James Riddle was dozing in an armchair by the fire when his wife showed Aveyard into the sitting room of their cottage near Wilby.

He struggled upright. "Forgive me, Bill," he said. "It's a little habit I've got into since my retirement."

"You've earned it," Mrs. Riddle said. "Stay where you are and I'll bring you both a cup of tea."

James Riddle rubbed his eyes, put on his glasses, looked into the fire, avoiding Aveyard's eye. Aveyard saw the *Financial Times* which had fallen to the floor beside the chair, the *Investors' Chronicle*, the *Economist* on the table beside him.

"Still keeping your hand in," he said.

James Riddle nodded. "It becomes a way of life," he said. "Funny thing, when you start working in a bank, money becomes unreal. It's just a column of figures. When I was a clerk I used to count the piles of it, thinking, 'Fancy me, James Riddle, holding one thousand pounds in my hand!' But very quickly it ceased to be a pile of money. It was merely a column of figures for which I held the responsibility, a certain number of slips of paper that had to be accounted for, a certain weight of coins. I remember how shocked I was the day I first weighed a bundle of notes instead of counting them. But gradually, the whole thing of 'money,' actual money, became unreal. Especially when I moved off the counter. It became such and such a person has credit, such and such a person hasn't. *A* can cash a cheque any time he wants to; *B* must have his account verified. It was almost as if money became a character reference. Which is all wrong, of course. A person isn't made any better by possessing money; a person isn't made any more valuable as a human being because his account shows a credit balance. One of the most saintly men I know runs a tiny village post office, does wonderful things for the old folk and the children. He's in every sense of the word, a good man. But there's never a spare penny in his shop account or in his personal account. The bank, officially, classifies him as undesirable because he often dips into the red without security. One of the nice things about retirement is that I'm no longer bound by the bank's attitude. Now I can form my own opinions about people, regardless of the state of their account."

Aveyard realized that James Riddle was talking to bridge what would have been an uncomfortable gap before his wife brought the tea and left them alone together. The door opened and she came in, bustling through the twilight with a trolley carrying two poured cups of tea, a teapot, a jug of hot water, milk, sugar, and a tin of shortbread. "You need a light on in here," she said, but didn't touch the switch. It was up to James to decide if he wanted to light the room. It appeared that he didn't. He leaned forward, took the long poker, and stirred the coals of the fire with it. The flames began to rise, casting a set of shadows onto the walls. This was an old-furnished room, in which the two of them had lived all their married lives, in which they'd reared two children in peace and tranquility. Now the two children had left home, started out on their own, and the couple could settle back for the last chapter of their lives together. Aveyard felt reluctant to disturb that peace, however briefly, to impose himself and his problems on that well-earned rest.

"I'm sorry to bother you," he said, when Mrs. Riddle had left the room.

"It's no bother," James Riddle said.

Aveyard could see, however, that his presence troubled the older man. Riddle was going to be asked to make a decision, to take sides, to occupy an attitude. Aveyard knew that Riddle would prefer to avoid that responsibility. His days of decisions ended when the staff gave him that canteen of cutlery. "We've been friends a long time," Aveyard said, "ever since we first met at the County Show when you were having trouble with your bank's stand. You remember. Somebody broke into it the night before the show opened, and I found it was that lad, Henry Lake, mad at you because you'd turned him down for an overdraft."

"I remember it well," James Riddle said. "A lot of water's flowed under the bridge since those days. A lot of people have changed. Many attitudes have changed. In those days you impressed me with your absolute probity. I wanted to let that lad off with a warning. You insisted on prosecuting him. You were right, of course. But perhaps you too have changed. . . ."

Aveyard had known James Riddle wasn't the man to mince words. There it was, a plain statement, an invitation to speak his mind.

"I haven't changed," he said. "I'd still prosecute that lad, because I think that anyone who breaks the law should be called to account."

"I didn't want to get involved in this matter," James said, "but you understand I had no choice. Now, you're the one being called to account. Now the boot's on the other foot."

"I didn't do it," Bill said. "I want to say that to you, face to face. I didn't do it."

James relaxed visibly. He reached out his hand and touched Bill's arm. "Thank you for coming here to say that to me," he said. "I couldn't understand how you could possibly have had anything to do with a man like Herbert Wilson. Not your sort at all. And bribery, that's not Bill's way, I said to myself." A frown creased his face. "But the evidence is there, Bill, make no mistake about it. You're going to have to prove you didn't do it. And that's going to be difficult."

"I haven't taken bribes from anyone," Bill said, as if anxious to leave no doubt in James' mind. "I didn't write to ask you to open that account. I've had no private dealings of any kind with Herbert Wilson. I've chased him a couple of times, officially, but I've never accepted any money from him, nor any of his famous hospitality. I've never placed a bet with him or in any of his shops; I'm not a betting man, anyway."

"You know they've checked the signatures on that card and they match yours? They even showed me the signatures, yours and the one on the card, to see what I thought. I examined them very carefully—you know we have techniques at the bank for comparing signatures—and, frankly, I would have paid out on either one of them."

"I know."

"Of course, there are many ways of forging a signature. We both know that. But you have to be something of an expert to do it in such a way it can't be detected. It's not something Herbert Wilson would know how to do, for example. You know it, of course, being a policeman, and so do I. . . ."

"I can tell you two Briton men who also know it. . . ."

"If you're thinking of Tom Maloney and Arthur Wentworth, you can forget them. They were the first two who came into my head. I know the quality of their work. In the old days we were caught by both of them. But this is out of their line. Tom Maloney's a draughtsman. He used to do the plates for the old fivers. None better. Wentworth has always specialised in documents, share certificates, Green Shield Trading Stamps. They're both specialists and I for one can't see them varying. Postal Orders, Money Orders, that sort of thing. Neither one of them would touch Herbert Wilson. He's a hoodlum, that one, and Maloney and Wentworth, whatever you may think of them, are gentlemen. Wilson is a thug, a well-polished, well-veneered, well-lacquered thug."

Both looked into the fire, thinking about what had been said. Accepting that the signatures on that card had not been put there by

Bill Aveyard, whoever had done it had been something of a specialist. There are several techniques for forging a signature. The first one is to trace the signature onto thin paper, then copy the tracing. Tracing, however, is never used by specialists since it contains the flaw, visible under magnification, of a wavy hesitant line. Even when made by a sick person, a signature runs smoothly from point to point with a flow impossible to achieve by tracing. A signature can be projected onto a plain piece of paper or card, and then copied, but again that reveals a lack of smoothness under magnification. The favoured method of the specialists is to practise a copy of a signature over and over until writing it becomes instinctive. Thus a result can be achieved with all the smoothness of an original. A signature, however, reflects the personality of the person making it and often small discrepancies can be found which expose differences in authorship. Some people exert an extra pressure on each downwards stroke, others on the upwards. To copy the outline of the individual letters of the name is not sufficient to deceive an expert; the style of pressure on each stroke must also be copied faithfully.

"Why didn't you write to me, acknowledging receipt of the one thousand pounds, and of my letter?" Aveyard suddenly asked. "Wouldn't it be normal business procedure to do that? And what about a cheque book, and a paying-in book. Surely, when a new account is opened, you'd send a cheque book through the post?"

"*I* wouldn't," James said. "Other branches might, but I wouldn't."

"Never?"

"Never. Look, I know you. You open an account. I'm bound to see you, sometime. I'd wait until I saw you and ask you what you wanted doing with the cheque book. Only if your letter specifically asked me to send a cheque book in the post to you would I do it. A man might have any one of a hundred reasons for opening an account with my branch. Most importantly, he might not want to let his wife know he had such an account. Bank accounts are supposed to be confidential, and the customer could be embarrassed if I send a cheque book in the post, which his wife might open, and ask for an explanation."

"But it's not the same in all branches?"

"Manager's discretion. It's up to the individual manager how he runs his branch. Most branches would send a receipt, post a cheque book and a paying-in slip and a paying-in book. But not me."

"You see what I'm getting at, don't you?"

"I can't say I do."

"Look, James, if I'd received a letter from you saying you'd received a thousand pounds and were enclosing a cheque book, I'd have been on the telephone immediately, wouldn't I, asking if it was some kind of a joke? When the second payment was made, we'd have been waiting, wouldn't we? We could have nobbled Herbert Wilson, then and there. A quick phone call from you; would you mind hanging on, sir, to Herbert Wilson . . ."

"Assuming, and here's another thought for you, that it was him. . . ."

"He says so, and he had the paying-in slip and he's not likely to incriminate himself, is he?"

"He's not incriminated, Bill. Look, what counts is not what he's said to the Departmental Enquiry. It's what he says in Court, if it ever comes to that. He can say the one thousand pounds was a winning bet, can't he? He can deny it was a bribe. If he's paying off a bet, the Court can't get him for bribery."

"And it can't get me for accepting a bribe. . . ."

"Not legally. But the stink would have been made, wouldn't it? It would finish you in the police force, wouldn't it?"

"The point I was trying to make earlier was that whoever decided to open that account chose your branch because they knew you wouldn't be writing to me. . . ."

"You have a point there. . . ."

"So, it was someone familiar with your technique of opening new accounts. . . ."

"If we check all the recent new accounts. . . ."

"Or, each member of your staff . . ."

James Riddle didn't like that suggestion. It had been *his* staff, hadn't it? Men and women he'd worked with, trusted in the way a bank manager must trust his staff. "They gave me a canteen of cutlery, Bill," he said. "Mumby's taken over now that I've retired. I recommended him for the branch and they gave it to him. . . ."

"I wasn't meaning Mumby. . . ."

"I know them all, Bill, *personally*. We were a *team*. We worked closely together. I never had a resignation, not for the last six years. They only left when they were promoted, or became pregnant. . . ."

"Whoever opened that account, James, knew for certain you wouldn't write to me. . . ."

Mrs. Riddle came bustling into the room. "How's your water," she said briskly. "Is it still hot? Look, you've not touched your tea, either one of you. That's no way to go about retirement, James, leaving your tea grow cold. . . ."

★

When Inspector Roberts came back into the Incidents' Room, Superintendent Colby glanced from the book he was reading, a copy of Neruda's poems he had ostentatiously taken from his pocket when Ted Roper finished his account of the events of the evening of the murder. For a few minutes Bruton had sat looking at the Superintendent whose manner expressed complete indifference to everybody else in the room, then he'd touched Roper on the shoulder.

"Go sit over there," he'd said, "against the wall."

He had seated himself behind Inspector Roberts' desk, reading the Incidents Book which by now contained twenty pages of entries, glancing through the box file in which Inspector Roberts had meticulously cross-referenced every single fact. Sergeant Bruton had a vague stirring of memory. If Superintendent Aveyard had still been on the case he knew they could have discussed his thoughts; from that discussion would have come something of value. Niggling at his memory was a tiny little oddness, one of those strange out-of-key facts a policeman is trained to spot. Something, somewhere, but what?

When Inspector Roberts walked into the room Superintendent Colby looked up from the Neruda. "Ah," he said brightly, "now perhaps we can get back to crime. What did Cleopatra have to say about Mark Antony here?" Anybody less like Mark Antony than Ted Roper would have been hard to imagine.

Bruton had risen to his feet. "Let's have you back over here, Ted."

Inspector Roberts had written the relevant facts and put a piece of paper on Superintendent Colby's desk.

Colby closed his book with a snap, tucked it carefully back into his inside pocket. "Come along," he said, "let's have the facts. I can't read your handwriting, anyway." That was a slander and they all knew it since Inspector Roberts had a meticulous, almost copperplate, hand. Inspector Roberts picked up the piece of paper and began to read from it. "Report of interview between Inspector Roberts and Mrs. Emmaline Slanky, known as Big Emma . . ."

"You don't need to go into all that," Superintendent Colby interrupted. "What time did he get there? What time did he leave? Let's draw a veil over the obscene events which took place between times, shall we?"

When Inspector Roberts spoke his voice was hard, brittle as broken glass. "He arrived at ten-five, *sir*, he departed at ten-thirty, *sir*."

Superintendent Colby could not leave it alone. "You mean he *left* at ten-thirty," he said. "Only trains *depart*."

"He left at ten-thirty," Inspector Roberts conceded and then irresistibly added, "That was the time of his departure."

"And what was the time of Constable Baron's *departure* from this life?" Superintendent Colby asked.

"According to Dr. Samson," Inspector Roberts said, "it was sometime before ten o'clock."

"I hope you're listening to this, Mr. Roper," the Superintendent said. "I hope the Inspector and I are not wasting our breath. Constable Baron was murdered shortly before ten o'clock. Shortly before ten o'clock, according to your own confession, you were in the clubroom in which Constable Baron's body was discovered. A footprint was found next to the body and a cast of that footprint has been compared with a pair of boots you confess belong to you and found to be exact. There is another similarity, but we'll go into that in Court. So far as I'm concerned all that is now missing is your further confession that you murdered Constable Baron." He leaned forward and an almost stifling wave of bonhomie oozed from him. "Come on, lad," he said, "let's get it over with. You knocked him off, didn't you? You went in to the clubroom carrying a pistol on your way to bag a brace of Lord Mawsley's pheasants. Constable Baron saw you. You know it's an offence to carry a pistol. He challenged you. You grabbed him, brought the pistol up behind his ear, and let him have one. Go on, tell us you did it. You can always plead self-defence in the court. Get yourself a smart lawyer, lad, and we'll never make a charge of murder stick."

Sergeant Bruton was sickened by the tone of this interrogation, which went against all his dignity as a policeman. "Superintendent Colby," he said, "could I have a word with you in private?"

Colby glared at him, annoyed with Sergeant Bruton for interrupting at the moment he considered he was winning over the suspect.

Ted Roper laughed coarsely. "You must be stark raving bonkers!" he said. "You must be round the bloody twist. Superintendent you call yourself. I've shit better coppers!"

Superintendent Colby glared at Sergeant Bruton again as if the insult was his fault. He half stood up in his chair. "Listen to me, you illiterate bastard . . ." he said, but Roper laughed at him again.

"My mother and father was married two weeks before I was born," he said, "so try that on for size."

Colby got up fully, walked around the desk until he was standing over Ted Roper. With a quick wave of his hand he beckoned Sergeant Bruton and Inspector Roberts forward. It was a moment they all knew, the get-tough technique. Neither the inspector nor the sergeant had the stomach for it but this was the Superintendent's enquiry and they were obliged to play it by his methods, whatever they may think of them.

"You were in that clubroom at the right time . . ." Colby said.

"That means you had the opportunity," Bruton added.

"Come on, lad, you may as well tell us!" Inspector Roberts adopted the role of friend.

It's a whipsaw technique. One man hammers home the fact, another explains them and the third one placates.

"We have your footprint . . ." Colby said.

". . . and it matches, lad!" Sergeant Bruton added.

"We have a casting of your footprint," Colby said, "taken from the floor behind the body!"

"The cast matches the sole of your boot perfectly," Bruton added.

"Come on, lad, you can't beat the scientists! Nobody can beat the scientists," Inspector Roberts said. "Tell us if you did it. It'll go a lot easier for you."

Ted Roper's head was swivelling from one to the other as if watching a three handed ping-pong game. "You're mad," he said; "all of you. I was going for a bit of nooky. Big Emma. You know Big Emma! Why would I stop and kill a copper when I was going for a bit of nooky? I knew Baron. He never did me no harm. I've even bought him a pint. He was lying in the chair. Of course you found my footprint there. I told you, didn't I, I'd taken a look to see if he had any cigs in his pocket, but he didn't have, so you can't even charge me with nicking 'em, can you?"

"We'll find that pistol," Bruton said, "and it'll have your fingerprints on it."

"I don't even own a bloody pistol. What would I be doing with an air pistol? Kids stuff that is. 'Can I have an air rifle, Mam?'" He looked at each of them in turn. "You've had me on the book a score times, but when ever have you got me with a weapon? I don't carry one; you know that! That's a mug's game."

For the first time Superintendent Colby allowed himself to look baffled. "I want his house searched again," he said. "Top to bottom. And I want to be there this time to make sure it's done properly."

"What shall we do with him?" Bruton asked. "Shall we charge him?"

"Don't be silly, Sergeant," the Superintendent said. All knew, including Roper, that there was nothing with which they could charge him. "He's assisting us in our enquiries."

Inspector Roberts had gone to the filing cabinet beside his desk and from it he produced a piece of paper. He held up the paper so that the Superintendent could see it. The Superintendent knew what it was, the Search Warrant executed by Mr. Mallory, Justice of the Peace. He knew also that such warrants are issued only for a single search. And this one had been used. He shook his head. The Inspector shrugged his shoulders, satisfied that Sergeant Bruton had witnessed him showing the warrant to the Superintendent. "It's my duty to point out to you, Superintendent . . ." he said.

"It's your duty to help me find that pistol."

A policeman has rights and also responsibilities. A special memorandum had been sent from the Home Office about searching premises without a warrant. Every officer of the rank of Inspector and above had had to sign to say he had read and understood it. Inspector Roberts knew that he and Sergeant Bruton were well within their rights to refuse to take part in another search of the Roper premises until a new warrant had been obtained. But they also knew that Mallory, the JP, was a liberal, and the chances of him granting two warrants to search the same premises were nil. They also knew the type of officer Superintendent Colby was. Like all brilliant men he had a flaw. His was personal arrogance. They knew that if they refused to do his bidding, if they made a case of it, he could and would make life hell for them. Roberts looked at Bruton. Was it worth it? Ted Roper was a thug; they owed him nothing. Baron had been a policeman and they owed him everything. Was it worth risking his career for a thug like Roper. The answer of course in abstract terms was 'yes.' The police had to conduct themselves with the utmost probity, they all knew that. But who can understand the motives that at any moment can make a coward of any of us.

"All right," Colby said, "let's get it over with. Let's go and take his house apart."

CHAPTER 8

Aveyard drove his Austin 1300 into a car park behind the house on the Birton road in which he rented a flat. The house had been solidly built by a leather merchant in the first years of the century, with high rooms that reflected a style of living of bygone years. As he got out of his car he glanced across the road at the new block of flats four stories high just nearing completion. The flats were small and mean with eight-feet ceilings and asbestos-board partitions through which every sound would be heard. He looked up at the house in which he lived, grateful for its more solid comfort. A curtain twitched on the ground floor and he knew Mrs. Nicholson had seen him arrive. He went to the door and opened it. Mrs. Nicholson was waiting in the downstairs hall with its two other doors, one leading to his flat upstairs and one to hers.

"My, you're home early. Don't often see you at this time of day. Have you run out of crimes?"

He knew that what prompted her questions was not nosiness but genuine interest and concern for his welfare.

"I shall be working at home for a little while," he said, "so you'll have to get used to me being around during the day. I shall be able to see all your boy friends coming and going!"

"Boy friends," she said with a cheerful laugh. "There's only one boy friend in my life and that's my husband. Not like you, who changes his girl friend more often than he changes his shirt." She inspected his collar critically. "That one could do with a bit of a stitch," she said. "Bring it down, and I'll see what I can do."

"That's what girl friends are for," Aveyard said. "Are you making me an offer?"

"Get on with you, I'm old enough to be your grandma!"

When he got upstairs he made himself a cup of coffee, black with sugar, the way he liked it. He put the Mozart Piano Concerto No. 21 on the Akai Stereo Cassette tape player, balancing the volume of the two speakers so that the sound belted out at him, a refreshing douche of clear crisp music he hoped would deluge his thoughts. It didn't work. He wandered round the flat, picked up a book then put it down again. He went into the bedroom, took off his coat, his shirt, and tie and put on a roll-neck sweater. He looked at the shirt. Dammit, he hadn't noticed when he put it on this morning that the stitching had gone on the collar. In a fit of anger he took the shirt between his two hands and ripped it from top to bottom. He went back into the sitting room, punched the button of the tape to eject the cassette, put on instead Beethoven's Ninth Symphony. He sat in his wing armchair and picked up the telephone.

Jane Prescott was not in her office and they didn't know when she'd return. Susan's mother said she'd gone shopping. Betty Maclean had gone to London for a couple of days. He had dialled Angie's number and the ringing tone had started when he slammed the receiver down, realizing that the last thing he wanted at this moment was the sound of Angie's county voice, the sight of Angie's county figure romping round his flat, Angie pulling him with that zestful bubbling laugh of hers into the bedroom for what she would doubtlessly call, "a bit of a lark." When he put the phone down he hit the stop button on the tape, and silence and gloom descended upon him.

"Sod it,"' he said; "sod it!" For the first time in years he gave way to a mood of black despair and self-pity.

It wasn't the first time he'd been accused. Once it had appeared as if he had killed a girl after raping her. (See *Cock-pit of Roses.*) Every policeman becomes used to false allegations. But that doesn't help to allay the feeling of frustration and hopelessness. How many times over the years had he asked himself if he was doing the right thing to cut himself off from the normal life other people seem to enjoy. Take Mrs. Nicholson as an example, living below him in the flat with her husband who worked as company secretary for a shoe manufacturer, a steady safe job that had given him a placid way of life, a wife who obviously adored him, and two kids now launched on their own, both married and likely to produce grandchildren at any time. Nicholson was a member of the Birton Amateur Operatic Society, the Birton Conservative Club, and had even bought a flat on the Costa Brava ready for his retirement. Every year he and his wife went there for a three-week holiday, came back happy and suntanned, content to work for another year.

Aveyard picked up his book of addresses. Dammit, why did the cover have to be black, making it like every other "little black book" with its addresses of readily available women? Women like Angie, County Set, wrote books for children and thought Aveyard and everything to do with him was "a bit of a lark," who gave her body and her time freely but would laugh herself silly if Aveyard proposed marriage and an annual holiday on the Costa Brava. Take Jane Prescott who worked as a designer, full of Womens Lib, believing the finest thing that had happened to the human race was the invention of the Pill and the acceptance by men that women liked sex. Jane Prescott would talk him out of marriage, take him to bed and persuade him nothing could be improved by any old-fashioned outmoded Church or Civil ceremony.

Where did it all go to? All the pride you took in doing your job. It wasn't easy to be a copper at a time when almost everybody called you a pig or the fuzz. Aveyard didn't expect it to be easy. He hadn't expected it to be easy those years ago when he turned his back on his economics degree and joined the Police Force as a trainee. In those days he'd been full of fire, full of his concept of the Police Force as a body of men who needed the leadership of trained minds. He'd used his trained mind, hadn't he? He'd tried to bring a new approach to the police work he'd been involved in. He'd tried to sort out in his own mind what made a criminal, why people do outrageous and often foolish things in the pursuit of gain. He'd succeeded too, got his promotions, always at an early age, passed the examinations, always well. His superiors had recognized that here was a younger man capable of bringing the discipline of intellect to the often crushing routine of police investigation. Aveyard knew there was a vacancy for a Chief Superintendent in Worcester and suspected his name had been put forward along with that of Superintendent Colby. By any standards he'd made a success of his career. But where had that left him personally? He was buying this two-bedroomed flat on a mortgage from the Prudential. He could sell it tomorrow and make himself a profit, an honest legal three thousand pounds. He had a wardrobe of good clothes, trendy but at the same time well made. He had six pairs of shoes, a stainless-steel Omega watch, a Parker fountain pen, and an N-registration Austin 1300 motorcar. He had a hundred and seventeen bottles of wine in the racks of the larder off the kitchen and twenty girls in the little black book willing to help him drink them one at a time. He was a good cook but he'd kept his figure despite the fact that he played no sports. He could ski on snow or water, skate on ice, sail a dinghy. But where did all that leave him? Why had he done nothing to protect himself? He was vulnerable, that was the word for it, vulnerable. A thug like Herbert Wilson could walk into a bank with twenty-pound notes in his hand, money he'd obtained by preying on the gambling weakness of mankind, and, by paying those notes into account someone had opened in Aveyard's name, he could jeopardise everything Aveyard stood for, everything he believed in, everything he'd worked for.

Bill Aveyard picked up the telephone and dialled a number.

Mrs. Bruton answered. "I'm expecting him," she said, "but he phoned to say they were doing a search and he might be late home."

"He offered me some of that steak and kidney. . . ."

"Then come over and have it. I'm giving him a special treat. He'll kill me when he finds out how extravagant I've been. I bought a half-a-dozen oysters to cook in it. You know the way Jim loves oysters in a steak and kidney. . . ."

"I'll bring a bottle," Aveyard said. "I've got just the thing."

"You and your bottles. I'd be happier if you were bringing some nice young girl to tell us you were getting married!"

★

James Riddle picked up the telephone and in his meticulous and precise tones announced the number and his name. When the caller identified himself James said, "Oh, Peter, thank you for ringing me back so promptly. I know how busy you must be balancing your ledgers."

"That's one job you no longer have to do, lucky devil. Are you enjoying your retirement? And what can I do for you."

James Riddle coughed nervously. All his life as a bank manager he'd done things by the book. What he was about to do now was a departure from the strict etiquette he had always observed. "I want to ask a personal favour, Peter," he said. He'd chosen his man carefully; it was largely due to his own efforts that Peter had managed to sort himself out after his wife had left him and had risen to be Chief Cashier at another branch of the bank. Peter would remember all the account codes from the Market Place branch, at least the ones in which James Riddle was interested. Peter had access to the computer link into the bank's headquarters in London. Establishing the computer had caused objections on moral grounds since it gave anyone with the right knowledge total access to the details of any account.

James Riddle had thought very carefully before he made the telephone call. It went against everything he had stood for during his years as a bank manager.

"I want you to ask the computer some questions for me," he said. "You'll be surprised when you find out what they are and you'll ask me to justify myself. All I can say is that the career of an honest man is at stake, and ask you to trust me. Will you do that?"

"You trusted me once," Peter said, "when my career was at stake, when I was going out and getting sozzled every night and turning up for work next day still drunk. You trusted me even when I started making mistakes. I don't see why I shouldn't trust you now. What questions do you want me to ask the computer? I guess you want the details of somebody's account."

When James Riddle gave him the list of names, Peter whistled. "My God," he said, "this chap of yours, whoever he is, must really be in trouble."

"He is," James Riddle said. "He is!"

★

Chief Superintendent Batty and Chief Superintendent Beasley were sitting together in a corner of the lounge of the Pilgrim's Club, which was empty apart from Rupert Dowdy, a Birton solicitor, who was pouring over papers at a table by the window. "Don't tell me you've got the road drills outside *your* office?" Dowdy had said when they came in. "They're taking up the road outside our place and I can't even hear myself think."

Membership of the Pilgrim's Club was by recommendation and unanimous vote; all were professional men from Birton and its environs. Each represented the privacy of the other members and anything heard in the Pilgrim's was considered sacred.

The steward brought a tray of tea and then withdrew leaving the two policemen in a pool of silence both were reluctant to disturb. Beasley had been carrying the black briefcase Inspector Wallace-Smith had given him. He opened it and from it produced several sheets of paper, handing them without speaking to Batty. Batty looked at them, put them back on the table, Beasley picked them up as if reluctant to let them continue to see the light of day.

"It's his word against the evidence?" Batty said.

Beasley nodded. "You can look at this from two points of view. Let's assume that your fellow Aveyard is guilty. Let's assume for the moment, however unpleasant it might be to you personally, that he's been on the take, probably for years."

"Hang on a minute right there. Why should he be on the take? No matter how little we may like Herbert Wilson and his betting shops, he's running a perfectly legal business. There's no reason why he should need to pay off anybody."

"Oh, come off it!" Beasley said. "You can't be as naive as that. So the man is running a legal business. There are so many ways a copper could make life difficult for him if he put his mind to it. How do you think a betting shop would survive, for example, if coppers were seen going in and out all the time? Dammit, two thirds of the clients who use betting shops are old lags anyway. They're not going to go in and make a bet, probably with bent money, if they have to rub shoulders with the fuzz everytime they get near the counter."

Batty thought for a moment. "All right," he said, "point taken. The man's running a legal operation but a ruthless policeman could still harass him. Go on with what you were saying."

"Well, we're still in the realms of conjecture. Let's say your man Aveyard has been on the take. It starts off with a twenty-pound note once a week, but we both know how it is—any man venal enough to go on the take is likely to get greedy; soon the twenty quid a week becomes forty or sixty. Perhaps Herbert Wilson got fed up of paying out. Perhaps Aveyard made a demand for a capital sum; shall we say a thousand pounds? Herbert Wilson saw the light, paid him his thousand, but then shopped him by sending that paying-in slip to you. Let's face it, there must have been some sort of transaction between Herbert Wilson and Aveyard. No man spends a thousand pounds to shop a police officer unless he has a reason for doing so! Aveyard may be telling the truth and didn't know anything about that bank account. In an odd sort of way, I'm inclined to believe that. Either Aveyard is a damn good liar or was telling me the truth when he said he knew nothing about the bank account; don't forget I'm not without experience in knowing when people are lying to me or not. But even if Aveyard *were* telling the truth about the account, that doesn't let him off the hook, does it? It could just be that Herbert Wilson used that method to shop him."

"I'd love to have a look at that chap's books," Chief Batty growled. "I bet they would tell a story."

"I bet the boys from the income tax and VAT would like to get a look at them too," Beasley said. "But that doesn't alter the fact that there must have been some relationship between the two of them."

"Wilson is putting his head on the block, isn't he?" Batty said. "After what he's told us we're bound to charge him with attempted bribery. If we can make that stick we can close down every one of his shops."

"That's where he has been very clever," Beasley said. "He hasn't told us anything about a bribery. He's told us that he's paid money to Aveyard. But he's entitled to pay money to anybody who places a winning bet with him. There's no law against Aveyard placing a bet and, if it wins, Wilson has to pay him out, hasn't he? When we asked him about the money he said, 'You'll have to ask *him* what it's for!' If we take him to court and accuse him of an attempted bribe, he can either say that Aveyard made a winning bet, or that somebody else did, and asked that the money be paid to Aveyard's account. He's committed no crime! It isn't a crime to open an account for the benefit of another person, is it?"

"But meanwhile, he's managed very successfully to smear one of my best officers. Aveyard's been suspended and the stain on his character will stick, no matter what we find out in the end! There'll always be people who'll say there must have been a grain of truth in it, or Aveyard's just beaten the rap because he's a Superintendent. This sort of thing tarnishes the whole police force, not just the individual officer. If Aveyard gets off, no matter how innocent he may be, there'll always be somebody to say he only got off because he was my blue-eyed boy. Believe me, I've never favoured him. Not in any way. I've put both him and Colby up for that job in Worcester, and personally, I can't stand the sight of Colby."

"But even if Wilson's intention was merely to smear Aveyard, there must be some reason. So again we come back to the suggestion that there must have been some contact, some sort of 'arrangement,' or 'deal,' or 'relationship' between them."

"Well," Batty said gloomily, "that's what your lads are trying to find out, isn't it?"

"I know Aveyard would like to get back on duty," Beasley said, but Batty shook his head vehemently.

"No," he said, "there's no question of that. The suspension stays. Until Aveyard is cleared, he never works as a policeman again."

"You realize that even after he's cleared you may lose him," Beasley said. "It's my guess that even if he walks out of a police court a free man, he may tell us to take the force and stick it as far as it will go right up your arses."

"Don't think I don't know that," Batty said. "That's exactly what I'd do in the circumstances. Now thump that bloody bell and let's get ourselves a couple of whiskies; you can make mine a double!"

CHAPTER 9

The bedroom measured twelve by ten and stank of unwashed feet and dirty underwear. The three-quarter-size bed in the middle of one wall had been made, the bleached calico sheet turned down over the thick army blanket, two pillows plumped in the middle of the headboard which bore a greasy smear of hair cream. On the table at the side of the bed was a tin alarm clock and an ashtray which had been emptied and washed. The edges of the table had been burned by an army of smouldering cigarette ends and looked as if a design had been made in poker work. A wardrobe made of plywood with plastic inserts, a dressing table with a mirror that had lost half its silvering at the bottom and distorted any reflections. One of the pieces of wood supporting the mirror had cracked near the bottom and the mirror canted crazily to one side. A lightbulb covered by a parchment shade hung in the centre of the ceiling; from above the shade a wire stretched across the ceiling and halfway down the wall to where it became an extension fitting. From the fitting one wire lead to a radio on the table at the other side of the bed, another led to a standard lamp which had no shade, and a third ran unprotected across the carpet to a record player with a plastic cover which stood on the top of a chest of drawers. From the record player two more wires issued, terminating in loudspeakers hung from nails driven into the wall to create that melodic stereophonic effect, said to enhance the quality of any music. Records in and out of their sleeves were shuffled on the top of the chest of drawers and the dressing table, the Lead Zeppelin, the Rare Earth, the Beatles, the Rolling Stones predominating. Bruton looked at the pick-up head; from it hung a quarter of an inch of wool and dust. "Music hath charm," he said, "to soothe the savage breast."

"We're supposed to be looking for a pistol," Superintendent Colby said, "not the Top of the Pops. You take the chest of drawers; I'll take the bed."

They'd turned over the living room downstairs, the cellar, the workshed outside the house. They'd examined everything in the pantry and now only the two bedrooms were left. Ted Roper's mother had been completely indifferent to the search. "Mine's a clean house," she said, "you won't find nothing here. Them other fellows didn't, did they? Everything here was bought and paid for, clean and tidy."

Bruton had to admire her. She'd obviously not had much money but with what she'd been able to put together, she'd made a home for this lout of a lad of hers. Granted the sheets on the bed were the cheapest bleached calico but they were clean and somehow she'd managed to find the time to make the bed and sweep the floor. The kitchen and the larder downstairs had been clean, though the stock of food wouldn't have fed a mouse.

He pulled open the chest of drawers. Inside was a different story. Ted Roper had obviously never folded a garment in his life, nor put one out for washing. Vests and shirts, underpants and socks were jumbled together, and from the drawer came the odour which permeated the room. Burton wrinkled his nose in disgust.

"You wouldn't like to change jobs, Superintendent, would you? You do the chest of drawers and I'll do the bed?"

There was no reply.

Wearily he pulled open the second drawer. He was about to plunge his hands into the morass of clothing it contained when Superintendent Colby said, "You can pack it in."

Burton turned around quickly. Superintendent Colby had pulled away the first pillow and was pointing to the second one.

Bruton walked to the other side of the bed.

"I think Ted Roper likes a hard pillow," the Superintendent said. He put his hands on each side of the pillow and pulled the cloth tight, straining it against the filling. The outline of a gun appeared on the cloth.

"Right," he said, "we've got him. We take the pillow down to forensic and let *them* get the gun out. And you can book that bugger!"

"I don't understand it," Bruton said. "Forensic searched this house from top to bottom. They couldn't have missed a gun."

"It's obvious, isn't it? Roper had hidden it somewhere else and brought it here after they'd done the search. Superintendent Aveyard was too busy thinking about where he was going to get his next thousand pounds to conduct the search himself, as any responsible officer would!"

With a masterly effort of self-control Jim Bruton resisted the impulse to react angrily to the sneering mouth of the Superintendent. "With respect, Superintendent, I take considerable exception to that remark," he said, "which I consider unwarranted and in extremely bad taste."

"Well, of course, you would, wouldn't you?" Colby said. "You were very close to Superintendent Aveyard. It probably comes a bit near the knuckle for you too, doesn't it?"

★

"I'll kill him; I'll bloody well kill him," Jim Bruton said. Aveyard reached out his hand and put it on Jim Bruton's forearm. "Eat your oysters," he said, "and don't guzzle down that Clos de Vougeot as if it was Watney's Pale. That's worth six pounds a bottle at today's prices. I don't care what Colby and people like him are saying. I know, and I think you know, that it's all a put-up job. If men like Colby have nothing else to talk about, what does it affect us?"

Aveyard was doing his best to calm Jim Bruton. Jim had arrived home in a blazing anger, threatening to resign, to complain to the Chief Constable, to kill Superintendent Colby. Mrs. Bruton, seeing the danger signals, served the steak and kidney pie without delay. When Bruton found the first oyster, he grunted about the expense and Mrs. Bruton brushed back a tear. So far Bruton had drunk three quarters of the bottle of the priceless wine without tasting a single drop. Aveyard had already decided that, in the circumstances, the Gevrey Chambertin with which he had intended to eat the cheese would be a waste! He was puzzled, too.

"I can't understand it," he said. "I just can't understand how forensic could have missed that gun. Dammit, I know Sergeant Dawson is one of the best; he wouldn't miss *a gun*."

Mrs. Bruton came round the table and took away his empty plate. "Cheese or fruit?" she asked.

Aveyard shook his head. "I ought not to have had that second helping," he said. "Perhaps a little cheese, a bit later on . . . ?" He looked at his watch. "Do you mind if I use the telephone?"

"Help yourself. . . ."

Aveyard dialled a number and Partridge answered.

"That pillow that was just brought in, did it have a gun in it?" Aveyard asked.

There was a pause. "I thought you were off the case," Partridge said. "In fact I thought you were off the force."

"Come off it," Aveyard said, "not you, too."

"Word gets around you know. I found it hard to believe."

"Tom, you've known me too long to think I would have my hand in Herbert Wilson's pocket. Let's forget about that crap. That pillow—was it a gun?"

When Tom Partridge spoke he sounded relieved. "Yes, it was a gun," he said, "and a really interesting one too. Almost a museum piece. B.S.A. dating from 1935. I remember when I was a kid I always wanted one. Double-helical spring and a piston-action chamber. Rifled barrel—one of the nicest air guns that was ever made. But then, as you know, Webley brought out their cheaper model and swept the market. I haven't seen one of these B.S.A.s in years."

"Have you looked down the barrel?"

"Yes, and I can tell you this. I think you're in luck. The barrel's rifled and there's a nick just under the foresight. I think we should be able to tie that up with the lead pellet, but I'll be able to tell you more when we've made the microphotograph."

"Would you care to hazard a guess?"

"Suspension hasn't changed that side of you, has it, you bugger? Always pushing, aren't you? Why can't you wait for the microphotographs and the written report?"

Aveyard laughed. "All I'm asking is yes or no. Come on, an educated guess."

"All right," Partridge said reluctantly, "but it's a guess and no more. This is the gun. And what's more, it's been looked after. Not a spot of rust on it. But what's more important, there isn't a single fingerprint!"

"I don't believe it," Aveyard said. "I just don't believe it."

"Well, you better," Tom Partridge said. "That gun was cleaner than a baby's bottom."

Mrs. Bruton had removed the remains of the meal, and now brought out a plate of cheese.

"Do you mind if I make another call?" Aveyard called from the hallway.

"Help yourself. You authorize my bills for payment," Sergeant Bruton said. At the sound of his slurring voice, Aveyard glanced round the door. Bruton's face was lobster red and he was staring in front of himself with disciplined intensity.

It took several minutes to get through the hospital switchboard, but eventually, Aveyard heard Dr. Samson. "Cedric Mawsley is in a bad way," he said. "It'll be touch and go. There are complications. It's good of you to bother, now that you're no longer concerned with the case. I haven't even heard from Superintendent Colby."

"He must be very busy. Tell me, if Cedric Mawsley was in such a coma, would it be possible for him to have held and used a gun? I mean, if he couldn't stand up, couldn't see?"

"It's extremely doubtful," Dr. Samson said. "The effect of the combined drugs and alcohol would be to impair the functioning of his central nervous system. I think that now, for example, we have evidence of real damage to that system. Those are the complications I was speaking of. The effect would be to paralyse all his motor responses. He would literally collapse. The chair happened to be there, and I suspect he collapsed into it. He sat there, immobile. Possibly couldn't see anything even though his eyes were, so to speak, jammed open. I can't see him being able to hold a gun, let alone do anything with it."

"But he walked two miles, I believe you said. . . ."

"Yes, and during that time the chemical substances were pumping round his system, gradually building up an effect. If you like to think of it this way, the walking could be compared to blowing up a balloon. When the balloon burst, he fell into the chair. Possibly he sat down before the balloon burst. But once the balloon had gone, he'd be incapable of any other movement."

"But, if the balloon didn't burst before he sat down, if it was still, to use your analogy, being blown up when he arrived at the clubroom, he could have used a gun before the balloon burst, and killed Baron?"

"That is certainly a possibility," Dr. Samson said.

Aveyard thanked him and put down the telephone. When he went into the room, Mrs. Bruton looked up at him. "Come and finish your supper," she said. He sat down, took a piece of cheese from the board, but didn't start to eat it. He was thinking. Mrs. Bruton was used to thinking men; it was part of the life of a policeman's wife to sit quietly and let her husband think.

"We know that gun didn't belong to Cedric Mawsley," Aveyard said, "and yet, I find it very hard to believe that Ted Roper would have anything to do with it. He's just not the type. Everything about him is wrong. He'd think of a gun like that as a kid's peashooter. Even if he did have it tucked away somewhere, he wouldn't bother to look after it. It would be dirty. He wouldn't, he couldn't, keep it oiled and greased. What do you think, Jim?"

Jim was having difficulty doing any thinking at all. When he spoke, his voice was slow, each word measured and thrust carefully from him.

"I don't believe it," Bruton said. "It's just not feasible that Roper could have anything like that and keep it clean. Take a simple thing like the needle on the pick-up of his record player—it had a beard on it half an inch long. Except where his mother cleaned, his room was filthy. He's dirty and untidy. How could he keep a gun so clean?"

Aveyard had decided after all to open the Gevrey Chambertin, savouring the full taste of it with the Cheddar cheese Mrs. Bruton had provided. "I agree it doesn't make sense," he said, "but then nothing these days makes sense to me."

Mrs. Bruton looked across the table at him, heard his voice slightly slurred. "Jim Bruton," she said, "you'd better leave that wine alone. Both of you better leave it alone or I shall be putting both of you to bed."

Aveyard took another sip. "We're living in a world," he said, "in which nothing makes sense. Lags like Roper who keep a clean weapon . . ."

". . . if you'd seen his underwear, you wouldn't say his weapon was clean," Sergeant Bruton giggled.

"*Jim!*" his wife said, scandalized. "I think it's time I went to bed and left you two to talk alone if that's the sort of thing you're going to say!" She got up and cleared the table, looking amused at both of them. Really, men are such boys. She didn't blame them. Each had had a bad day. She left out the cheese and the bread and the half-full bottle of wine. "The bed's made in the spare room," she said to Bill Aveyard, "and your toothbrush is in the top drawer from last time. Don't start singing again, that's all I ask!"

★

"Nothing is what it seems to be," Aveyard said, lost in a private world of alcohol-inspired speculation. Old lags who wipe their fingerprints off pistols, a whole village full of pistols, bookies who open bank accounts for people, Superintendents who get themselves suspended, policemen who get themselves shot. What the hell was Baron doing to let a lag like Ted Roper get near enough to fire a shot into his skull in the one place where the shot would kill him? Ted Roper's not a brain surgeon, is he? How could he know where to hold that gun? Half an inch to the left or the right and the pellet would have bounced off the bone. He turned and waggled his finger at Jim Bruton. "Bounced off the bone!" he said.

There was a buzzing in Jim Bruton's ear, pushing it's way through the fog of his mind. "Somebody's ringing a bell," he complained. "Is it you?"

"No, it's *not* me," Aveyard said.

The door opened. "You're wanted on the *telephone,*" Mrs. Bruton said. "Superintendent Colby. I told him you'd gone to bed but he said to waken you."

Jim Bruton made a visible effort and sat upright. "Tell him to come in and I'll speak to him."

Mrs. Bruton glanced at the wine bottle which was now empty, at the empty brandy bottle, and the empty glasses. "I can't tell him to come in," she said. "You'll have to pull yourself together. He's on the telephone." She went outside and they could hear her voice. "He won't keep you a minute, Superintendent," she said. "He's in the bathroom." Sergeant Bruton rose to his feet and with immense dignity slow-marched across the room, carefully avoiding the corners of the furniture. He stood to attention in the hallway and Mrs. Bruton held the telephone receiver to his ear. "Sergeant Bruton here," he said enunciating carefully. "To whom am I speaking?"

"Superintendent Colby. I've just been talking to forensic. That gun is the one that did it. I'm going to let Roper stew all night but then we'll jump him half past six in the morning. I want you there. Okay?"

"Your wish is my command, Superintendent," Sergeant Bruton said. "I shall be there, bright-eyed and bushy-tailed. And may I take this opportunity of wishing you a good night."

There was a pause. "Thank you very much, and good night to you," Superintendent Colby said, mystified, as he hung up.

Mrs. Bruton put the telephone back on its cradle, watched her husband head back into the sitting room, a barque under full sail. He looked at the bottle of whisky on the bureau, at Superintendent Aveyard sitting with his head in his hand like a Rodin sculpture. "Interrogation at half past six. It hardly seems worth going to bed." He reached out his hand to grasp the whisky bottle but Mrs. Bruton got there before him.

"No you don't," she said. "It's Alka-Seltzer for you and off to bed and if, when you waken in the morning, you tell me you've got a headache I'll flay the living daylights out of you! Now both of you, into the bathroom and brush your teeth. I'll have the Alka-Seltzer waiting. Men!" she said. "And policemen at that. You're like a couple of overgrown schoolboys."

Aveyard went into the hall, and started to struggle into his lightweight overcoat.

"Where do you think you're going?" she asked. "You're in no condition to go out." He shivered with concentration.

"There's something I have to do," he said, "somewhere I have to go."

"Bill, you're in no condition. Can't it wait until morning?"

"No," he said, "it can't. It's something I ought to have done days ago."

"You're not going to drive your car? You're in no condition to drive. If they catch you, that'll be the end of you with what you've drunk tonight."

"I'm not going to drive my car," he said. "I'm going to walk. Where I'm going I'll need a clear head."

★

It took Aveyard an hour alternately walking and jog-trotting down the back road that lead to Mawsley. The night air was cold and a bright but fitful moon projected deep shadows from the hedgerow. Two cars passed him but neither showed signs of slowing down. Within half an hour of leaving Jim Bruton's house, Bill Aveyard was ice-cold sober. When he arrived in Mawsley the village was deserted, only one light showing from the downstairs of a house in the Ride, gleaming across the front garden with it's neatly tended lawn, its flowerbeds in which the annuals grew in precise rows, orderly as a policeman's mind. Aveyard stood at the gate and looked up the path. The curtains had not been drawn in the front room and he could see her sitting and stitching a large sheet of linen, working a pattern of coloured thread into an enormous tablecloth that one day should have covered her own table in her own dining room in her own house. The memory of what might have been comes strongly to us in moments of tragedy, the plans we've made, the schemes two people concoct together, dreams that hover on the edge of future reality. "When I get my promotion, we'll buy a house and move out of this rented place!" "When we buy a house, we'll buy our own furniture and stop living with other people's about us!" "When we buy furniture, we'll get a nice dining room table!" "When we've got a nice dining room table, I'll embroider a cloth for it, a big square cloth with a pattern of flowers in the middle and leaves all round the edges. And it'll all be ours!" It's not a dream, is it? It's a future reality, the apex of the cone that begins with love. It's what makes two people cling together and hold together through the difficult times, two people moving reality daily a step forward, building a pyramid of tasks, willingly undertaken, lovingly achieved by two people. Aveyard had felt the need of this all his life but he'd thrust it from himself in the name of dedication, or so he thought. You can't be a copper, he'd always say, and live a normal life. Jim Bruton and his wife had disproved that point, hadn't they? Jim Bruton and his wife were a normal couple, weren't they? They had built their pyramid, hadn't they? Because they had love; being a copper made no difference to that. But what about Betty Baron with her tablecloth, and somewhere in the house she'd rented with her man, a lovingly constructed drawing of a paradise they would build and own together down the lane, and no doubt price lists from furniture and soft-furnishing shops, cuttings from the Sunday magazines of the wonderful things they'd send away for, solid foundations of a life together. That life could change. It had changed, hadn't it, when passion had come to it? Not the passion of the love of two people together, but from somewhere the devotion that had made Bobby Baron opt out of the comfortable secure life he could have known as a groom to Lord Mawsley, and join the police force, the passion that had made him chase Herbert Wilson for his gambling operation. And the girl, who found herself in love with a young man with a slow, lazy future caring for horses, had suddenly found herself bound to a dedicated policeman, a stubborn man, who wouldn't let go of his ideals. What had happened then to her dreams, to his dreams? Death respects no bonds of love; death slices between people, cuts apart the dreams, chops them through, and leaves only the ever-bleeding wound of memory.

Betty Baron led him into the sitting room. "It's late," she said, "but I can't sleep these nights."

"That's why I came. In the night the hours are twice as long."

"And there's only half of me to fill them. I miss him terribly. He was such a nice man. Oh, he had his faults. He was pigheaded stubborn. He was obstinate!" She indicated the tablecloth she was working on. "I wanted it blue," she said. "I've seen some crockery in that shop in the Market Place, blue pattern. I thought it would be nice to do the dining room all in blue. He said, 'Whoever heard of blue leaves and blue stalks!' We had such an argument about it. I couldn't change him. It had to be green because he said, 'Whoever heard of leaves and stalks that weren't green!' " There was a catch in her voice. "He was like that," she said, "always black and white."

Aveyard was sitting in the chair opposite her. She lifted her eyes from the tablecloth and looked across at him. "That was the only way we were different," she said, "the only bone of contention, if you like, between us. For example, I don't hate you."

"Hate *me?*" he said. "How do you mean that?"

"Well, you being suspended and all."

He looked at her mystified. "I just don't understand you," he said. "Why should you hate me because I've been suspended?"

She coloured. "Oh, I didn't mean to offend you. It's just that I thought, well after what he said, and then when I heard you were suspended, I thought it must have been you he was referring to. It was, wasn't it?"

"I haven't the faintest idea what you're talking about, Betty."

"Well, my Bobby—funny name for a policeman isn't it?" She wiped a tear away from her eye. "I often said the only reason he'd thought about joining the police force was because of his name. This last few months he's been very bothered. You know he always wanted to get into the plainclothes branch. Well, about three months ago, it seemed as if he'd changed. I could see something was bothering him, but he wouldn't talk about it. I tried to get it out of him, but couldn't. It seemed as if he sort of lost heart, lost his pride in being a policeman. I remember him saying once or twice 'What's the point, what's the point of being a policeman if that sort of thing goes on?' He used to talk a lot about corruption. Every time there was anything in the papers about detectives being corrupted, you know what I mean."

"No, I don't know what you mean," Aveyard said.

"You remember the big case three months ago. A police force up north. The Chief Constable had to resign. My Bobby said, 'It's happening a lot nearer home.' I asked him. But he wouldn't tell me."

"Let me see if I've got this right," Aveyard said. "Your husband was very happy being a policeman until about three months ago when he suddenly seemed to lose heart and began talking about corruption, 'nearer home,' I think you said, as if there might be somebody local, somebody high up who might be corrupt?"

"Yes, that's right," Betty said. "He's really suffered about that for the last three months. But then, it seemed to come all right."

"In what way?"

"The day he was . . . that last day . . ." She fell silent, bending over the tablecloth, fighting the need to cry tears that could no longer come, remembering dreams. "He was so full of himself that last evening, almost hugging himself, if you know what I mean. Like a man who's been ill for a long time and suddenly feels better. And making plans. 'Perhaps we can even have both,' he said, 'the green and the blue. You can make two tablecloths, one with green, another with blue. They can be his and hers, our little secret joke. The green will be mine, the blue yours.' But then he hugged me. 'I didn't mean that,' he said. 'Of course, they'll both be ours.' "

"It sounds like he'd had some good news . . . ?"

"That's what I thought at first. But he was so tantalising. I asked him about it, and he said, 'Let me go about it in my own stubborn way, and when it's over, I'll tell you about it. Just let me get this meeting over and done with. . . .' I asked him, 'What meeting?' But he wouldn't tell me; he was always a bit secretive."

"This is one time one could have wished he'd talked a bit more about things. It might help us catch whoever did it?"

She put down the tablecloth. "I'm not a very good hostess," she said. "Can I get you a cup of coffee or something?"

"No, nothing. Thank you." Bill Aveyard badly wanted a brandy, 'the hair of the dog that bit him,' but knew that brandy is beyond the resources of a constable's wife. As are two sets of crockery for the table. Bobby Baron had been expecting promotion, that much was clear to Aveyard. The most usual method of promotion for a younger man is by a particular achievement that brings him to the attention of his superiors. Was Bobby Baron hoping for such an achievement the night he was killed? Unfortunately, young constables tend to be secretive, to hug their discoveries to themselves, play them close to the chest so they can build up credits for arrests, a "sheet" that looks impressive when promotion time comes along. Aveyard had no doubt this secretiveness had killed Bobby Baron. "Would I be right in saying your husband implied he had a meeting that night? Other than his meeting with the builder?"

"Yes. He said he might be late. I wasn't to worry, even if it took him all night. He said it might make a 'stink that will last all night.'"

"And he seemed happy about making this 'stink'?"

"Yes. It seemed the end of a long miserable road."

"And you think it had to do with this business of corruption on the police force?"

"Yes, I suppose, in a way, thinking about it now, I *did* think that. I was glad, relieved to think that what had been worrying him was going to stop. And I was pleased, for his sake, that he was doing something positive to stop it, instead of moping about, as he had been doing for three months, letting things happen, not putting his heart into anything."

"And this 'corruption' concerned someone 'high up'?"

"Yes, that's right," Betty said. "That's why I assumed, when I heard about your suspension, that he'd been talking about *you.* Don't misunderstand me; I've got nothing against you personally, but I'm not like Bobby. I don't see everything black and white like he did." She bent her head over the tablecloth again and Aveyard knew that now she was crying silently. She lifted her head again, swept the hair back from her forehead in a defiant gesture. "He was right, you know," she said. "He was right all the time. Leaves and stalks should be green, not blue. If only I'd gone on looking, I would have found the identical plates in that shop in the Market Place with a green pattern. You've got to go on looking, that's all." Her eyes burned with an intensity of self-accusation.

"Will they find out who killed him?" she asked.

"I don't know about *them,*" Aveyard said, "but *I* will. You can rest assured about that."

CHAPTER 10

"We don't *need* a cough out of you," Superintendent Colby said. "We've got enough against you as it is. We've placed you at the scene of a crime by means of a footprint; we've traced part of your movements via Big Emma, which shows you were there at the vital time. We've found the weapon, hidden in *your* house, in *your* pillow, in *your* bedroom. What more do we need? I'll tell you. Nothing."

For the first time, Ted Roper lost his composure. Even he could see the tough spot he was in. He licked his lips nervously, looked from the Superintendent to Sergeant Bruton, to the constable in the corner taking notes of anything he might say, the constable standing near the doorway of this semi-basement room to which he'd been brought the previous evening. He'd been put in a cell and the door locked. "We're not arresting you," the station sergeant said. "You're merely assisting us with our enquiries. Anytime you want to leave the cell to take a walk to the lavatory, just holler."

He'd slept well; the bed was comfortable and the sheets clean. And then, suddenly, a light had flashed in his eyes jerking him from sleep, a rough hand had been laid on his shoulder, and a voice had barked, "Come on you, get dressed!" That had been half an hour ago and so far, they hadn't let him have either a cup of tea or a cigarette. He needed both, badly.

"I want a lawyer," he said.

"You've been seeing too many television serials. We haven't charged you yet."

"Yes, you have!"

"That wasn't a charge. That was the official caution."

"Why don't you get on with it, and charge me?"

Superintendent Colby stood in front of Ted Roper's chair, towering over him. "Don't take that tone of voice with me, lad," he said.

"You're in a lot of trouble, and the sooner you get that into your thick skull, the better for you."

Sergeant Bruton came forward. His voice was low enough to be a whisper and he winced as he spoke as if moving his jaw was an effort. "The Superintendent's right, Ted. You *are* in a lot of trouble. We're going to charge you with a murder. The papers are being prepared right now. We've got a case against you. With your record, you won't stand a chance in court. Finding that pistol in your pillow is the clincher. . . ."

"I don't know nothing about that pistol. I've never seen it before."

"That's what they all say, lad. It was there, in your pillow. I was there when it was found."

"It was planted. . . ."

Superintendent Colby stood forward, his fist doubled. "You suggesting the sergeant planted it, lad?"

Ted Roper shook his head rapidly, fear showing in his eyes. "No, I'm not making accusations," he said. "Only that whoever killed the policeman, whoever shot Bobby Baron, he planted it."

"Only one thing I don't know, Ted," Sergeant Bruton said, again quietly. "I don't mind admitting it. I don't know *why* you did it. Of course, in the Court, they won't be worried about why you did it, merely that you did do it. But, just for my own interest, I'd like to know *why*. Was it, like the Superintendent said, because you were after a couple of the estate pheasants? Constable Baron caught you at night with a gun?" Bruton missed not having Aveyard to back him up. This was the sort of moment the two of them worked best together, each complementing the other perfectly. Sergeant Bruton would supply the facts, Aveyard the intuition, but between them, they'd get a cough out of a lad like Roper. Colby was a bully and no help at moments like this. Colby would plough away at what he already knew, steamrollering Ted Roper into some sort of statement by sheer weight of words and length of argument. Colby was good at deduction, used his intellect very well on problems. The force ought to keep him chained up in a back room, like a tame computer, into which they could feed information. It was a great mistake ever to let Colby out on a case, Bruton thought. He ought to be in forensics, or Crime Prevention, or Planning, anywhere except on a case where he had to deal with human beings. Either he was too heavy with suspects, or too "intellectual"; somehow, he never seemed to get it right. There was no point in being "heavy" with a lad like Roper.

Roper had seen it all, been the whole route. You can be heavy with a bank clerk caught with his hand in the till. With a man like Roper, you need the human touch to try to get through the fog of his limited intelligence, the fog that deepened every time you threatened him. It was no good threatening Roper, he'd been hit hard by experts in his time and had developed the instinctive reaction to hit back, or to close up. Now he had closed up. He could be opened again, but only delicately by skilful probing.

"You won't be able to walk away from this one, I'm afraid," Sergeant Bruton said softly, careful not to shake his head in case it fell off. Blast Bill Aveyard and his French wines. Blast the cognac. Blast Colby for calling for a six-thirty interrogation. And blast the canteen for being slow with the coffee. "We've already got enough evidence to charge you," he said, "and I personally think they'll make it stick. But it seems a shame to me if you're charged with the wrong thing . . ."

"The wrong thing?" Roper asked. "How do you mean?"

Oh hell, Bruton thought, if only I had Aveyard now, backing me up. He prayed Colby would keep his mouth shut.

"Well, Ted, there's a lot of reasons why you could have done it. Let's say Constable Baron jumped you, suddenly; I mean there you are, in the clubroom with the lights out, and suddenly this figure jumps at you out of the darkness. It'd be natural, wouldn't it, to be scared for a moment, to lift the gun and pull the trigger? Then you switched on the lights and found it was a policeman. That's what I mean when I say, charged with the wrong thing. If that was the way it happened, you could plead justifiable self-defence, couldn't you? And I doubt if you'd be convicted of anything."

"And him a copper," Ted Roper said. "You'd throw the book at me. . . ."

"That's what I'm saying," Bruton said. "We wouldn't. We couldn't. Believe me, the fact that Bobby Baron was a policeman won't make a scrap of difference in Court. He was off duty, wasn't he? Off duty! The minute a policeman takes off his uniform, he's just like anybody else, isn't he? Especially if he jumps out of the dark at you. Is that how it was, Ted? Is it?"

"I could plead self-defence, did you say?" Ted Roper asked.

"Now I've got him," Bruton thought. "Now it comes."

"Come on, you damned fool, hurry it up," Superintendent Colby said. "You heard what the sergeant said. Tell us you did it in self-defence, then we can all go and have breakfast. We've got you, anyway; I don't know why we're bothering to ask for your motive. . . ."

Ted's face closed like a trap. "I didn't do it," he said. "I don't know how that gun got in my pillowcase. And you can sod off, the lot of you. I want a lawyer." No child ever said "I want my mam" with such plaintive pleading as Bruton heard in Roper's voice.

★

The ward door opened and Lord Mawsley came in, with Dr. Samson, and Mr. Paisley, the specialist, behind him. Cedric Mawsley was lying flat on his back in the centre of the bed with his eyes closed. Arranged at the far side of the bed was the apparatus that, so far, had kept him alive, the plasma bottle on its stand, the bottle containing the saline drip, the wires and tubes of the electrical and mechanical devices with which the hospital staff had fought to save his life. The nurse sitting beside the bed rose to her feet when she saw them. Mr. Paisley greeted her, then went to the wall and took down the chart with its columns of figures. He looked at the electrical machine which registered pulse and heartbeat information on a strip of paper, tracing the variations continuously. He showed the readings to Dr. Samson, who grunted with satisfaction. "Now it seems to be holding steady," he said. The specialist nodded, took a pen from the top pocket of his white laboratory coat, and wrote his initials on the slip of paper next to the last reading.

Lord Mawsley had crossed the room and stood still, looking down at his son. It would have been impossible to read the thoughts behind the calm mask of his face, but both doctors had enough experience of this sort of scene to gauge the emotional turmoil passing through his mind. So often they'd repeated this scene, with someone less capable than Lord Mawsley of controlling his or her emotions and expressions.

"May I touch him?" Lord Mawsley asked.

"Of course," Mr. Paisley said.

Lord Mawsley stretched out his hand and placed a finger against his son's temple. He didn't speak. His son didn't move, didn't open his eyes, though Lord Mawsley felt he seemed conscious of the touch.

"He's going to survive," Dr. Samson said, after a hurried glance to verify the specialist didn't want to speak. "There was considerable danger for a long time, but now he's going to pull through."

"Is there anything you can tell me about it?" Lord Mawsley asked.

Dr. Samson looked at Mr. Paisley. This, surely, was his department.

"Do you know, Lord Mawsley, that the physical actions of the body, lifting arms, moving legs, even flickering an eyelid, are controlled by a set of nerves activated from one part of the brain?"

"I didn't know that," Lord Mawsley said, "but I can imagine it would have to work like that, wouldn't it?"

"It's a very logical system. It works very well until we start to tamper with it, as your son did."

"The drugs and alcohol? I've suffered that myself, though in a different context."

"The drugs alone wouldn't have done it, nor would the alcohol, but in combination, the effect can be quite devastating. There has been a certain amount of damage to the brain but, so far as we can judge, the motor responses, the system of nerves I was talking about, are still all right. Your son will be able to walk again, lift his arms, etc."

"But what about the rest of him? What about his mind, his brain?" Lord Mawsley saw the specialist hesitate. "I shall want the truth," he said, "so you may as well tell me now."

Paisley looked at Dr. Samson. After all, he knew the patient, knew Lord Mawsley. "So far, Lord Mawsley," Dr. Samson said, "we have been concerned to save Mr. Cedric's life, to take care of the physical part of his existence. That's been a tremendous job, and has been successful. Now other people, other specialists, will have to take over. . . ."

"But you assured me that Mr. Paisley was the best brain man we could get, the best in the country. . . ."

"I make no such claims, Lord Mawsley," Mr. Paisley quickly said, "and I'm certain Dr. Samson would not wish to represent me as such. I've had a considerable experience of brainwork. This is why I was called in. But my experience has been in brain surgery, in the treatment of the 'brain' as a physical organism. Dr. Samson has told you that everything that can be done has been done for the physical brain of your son; now we must turn to men who have obtained experience of the brain as a housing for the mind, if I might so put it, the application of the physical state of the brain to the workings of the mind."

"Are you saying the mind has been damaged?"

"No one can say that yet, Lord Mawsley. So far, your son has not recovered consciousness. So far, no one has been able to judge the state of your son's mind. I've carried out certain tests, and so far as the brain is concerned, there is no longer any danger of damage. But I do not know, no one can know, until your son recovers consciousness and reacts to other tests, what use the mind can make of that physical brain."

Lord Mawsley was silent, thinking deeply. He stroked the side of his son's forehead again. Poor devil, was he doomed to wake up an idiot? A mindless idiot? If so, far better they had let him die. On the other hand, if he woke up with his "mind" unimpaired, what would he find in there? The death, the killing, of another man? Again, far better he had not awoken. If Lord Mawsley were to persist in calling for specialists, could he, perhaps, be responsible for reawakening his son to such a dreadful future? In Lord Mawsley's younger day the issues were much clearer, weren't they? A man himself judged if he was fit to live. Codes of conduct were strict, honor meant something. The death penalty for murder, eye for an eye, tooth for a tooth.

"One thing we can tell you, Lord Mawsley," Dr. Samson said, as if reading Lord Mawsley's thoughts, "your son didn't kill Police Constable Baron. He couldn't have. By the time he reached the clubroom, it was all he could do to walk across the floor and collapse into the chair. . . ."

"It's a miracle he ever got there and didn't pass out somewhere along the route of his walk," Paisley added.

"He wouldn't do that." Lord Mawsley said. "Despite the drug business and everything, he wouldn't want to put people about by collapsing on a public thoroughfare. . . ."

★

The old conception of a bank with ledgers, meticulously entered up in that activity time between the bank closing at three o'clock, and the employees going home at five-thirty, is completely out of date. Few banks, if any, keep any ledgers in the branches. Each transaction is typed onto a tape. Money paid in, money taken out, money transferred from one person to another, from one company to another. The electrical impulses on those tapes are fed at lightning speed down the line to the bank's computer, squatting in Lombard Street where once men in tall hats flourished quill pens with consummate copperplate grace and dignity.

As Chief Cashier, Peter Sinclair had access to the computer terminal, a machine similar to a large typewriter housed in one corner of the High Street Branch. Though he and the manager needed to be together to open the safe, Peter's key alone would unlock the terminal, since he often came early to work, to begin the day's billing. He glanced at the sheet of paper on which he'd printed the numbers remembered from his days in the Market Place Branch. He turned the key on the terminal, waited for a brief second, though the terminal with its transistors needed no warm-up period. He pressed the key marked "line," waited three seconds until the red "line" light glowed. Quickly he tapped a set of numbers on the keys. The numbers appeared on a sheet of paper on the platten. Then he spelled out the numbers which called for an accounting of transactions over the previous three months. There was a pause while the terminal made a clicking noise. The green light appeared, telling him the correct data base had been located. He pressed the activate key, and, almost immediately, paper began to spew from the platten, printed in neat lines at the rate of ten words per second.

When the paper stood still, another green light appeared as the computer, ever patient, awaited new instructions. He tapped the "wait" key, ripped the paper from the platten, and began to read. Only one set of figures caught his eye. He reactivated the computer and asked it a further question. The computer, dutiful servant, replied immediately, despite the millions of characters it needed to sort to get the answer he required. He ripped that piece of paper from the platten, and closed the computer down.

When Priscilla, the girl who normally worked the computer terminal, arrived, she looked at the torn paper. "Somebody's been at my machine!" she said. One look at Peter Sinclair's face convinced her not to pursue the matter further, though she ostentatiously dusted the terminal and the desk into which it had been built, before sitting down to begin her day's work.

When coffeetime came, Peter Sinclair left the bank and crossed to the lounge of the Royal Hotel. He sat in the corner, accepted the tray of coffee and biscuits old Annie wheezingly brought to him, and waited.

James Riddle appeared at exactly ten-fifteen and Peter Sinclair handed him both rolls of computer printout.

James Riddle instantly saw what Peter had spotted on the first roll, turned to the second. "Looks bad, doesn't it? Cash sums withdrawn every week. Large cash sums paid in every so often. Apart from that, the regular salary cheque going in each month, the regular household expenses coming out, the regular standing orders being made."

"He was near the mark a couple of times. Notice the cheque drawn for cash, entry number seventeen, and the large cash deposit the day after. If the account had been verified when the cash cheque was presented, it would have been found to be overdrawn. Lucky there was cash available the following day to meet it."

The pattern was quite clear and readable by either one of them. Who but a gambler withdraws cash sums of up to fifty pounds a week, makes infrequent cash payments in of up to a thousand pounds? Mostly the payments in were of the order of several hundred pounds. The balance of the account had suffered at the beginning of the year. It had started with a credit of two thousand five hundred pounds, approximately. Ignoring the salary payments in and the normal household expenses out, the account had dipped to as low as ten pounds in the first three months. Then four payments in had taken the account back up again. Again it had dipped; again it had gone up. At the present moment, it stood at three thousand eight hundred pounds.

"Does that tell you what you want to know?" Peter asked.

"All but one thing. I can't read the identification number."

Peter had known James Riddle all his working life. A year ago, he couldn't imagine James Riddle asking him to check the accounts of fellow employees secretly. Had retirement changed him already?

"You said something about a good man being in trouble . . . ? Do you want to tell me any more about that?"

"I can't Peter. The knowledge isn't mine to tell."

"So, I'm obliged to trust you . . . ?"

"I'm afraid so!"

Old Annie came back. "Want anything else, or can I make out your bill?" She handed James Riddle a piece of paper, but Peter took it from him. "I think I ought to pay that," he said. "I wouldn't want Mumby to be able to accuse me of having sold him down the river for no more than a cup of coffee and a digestive biscuit."

★

"You don't stand a chance," Sergeant Halford said. "Those guns were manufactured by the hundred and not even numbered. All stamped BSA, of course, and the A is a tiny fraction out of line. That's how we identify a genuine one from the Japanese copies. It was actually designed in 1933 by the Pieper Company of Liège; they were the ones who invented the Steyr-Selbstladepistole Modell 1908 that, as you'll remember, was made at Steyr and issued to the Austrian Police. . . ."

"No, I can't say I do remember that," Bruton said, smiling.

His headache had vanished; he'd lost his bile under the gentle enthusiasm of Sergeant Halford, a legendary figure of the Birton Police Force. Employed by Traffic he passed his days riding about in a patrol car. Evenings he spent with his collection of guns, and books about guns. Halford was an expert on all types of weapons, but handguns were his particular favourites; the collection in his semi-detached house was the envy of every weapons collector and expert. "You understand, I'm not too well acquainted with air pistols," Halford said.

"You could have fooled me. . . ."

"It's just that the action of that particular model is very similar to one developed for the French Fusil MAS Model, was it—yes, it was 49. . . ."

"I don't think we need go into that too deeply," Bruton said, trying to staunch the flow of information. "I just wondered if this gun would have a traceable history. . . ."

"Not a chance," Halford said. "As I told you, many were made and not numbered. They were bought before the war as target pistols, for shooting birds, etc. Rather a better quality than the ordinary air rifle and costing a bit more. They still turn up from time to time."

"And there's nothing special about this one?"

"Nothing. Unless you count the fact that whoever had it has taken good care of it through the years. I could go so far as to say it's probably been stored in a collection, with the kind of attention a collector would give it . . . but I can't go further than that."

"Just one other question. Is this the sort of gun a layabout would have?"

Halford shook his head. "I don't think so," he said. "They like Colts when they can get them, Smith and Wessons, or Webleys. There're still a lot of Lugers about from the war. Actually it's the Borchardt Luger, the Parabellum Pistole . . . but you don't want to hear about that, do you? Layabouts like guns, not air pistols. That's why they're layabouts, isn't it, because they like guns . . . ?"

"You like guns, too, don't forget!"

"I suppose there's no answer to that."

★

The Market Place in Birton is three-sided; to the north a parade of shops includes the Cafe-Restaurant, Malcolm's Porcelain-and-Glass Shop, and a branch of the National Westminster Bank. Along the south side another parade of shops encloses the Royal Hotel, a fish-and-chip shop, and the entrance to the Bus Station. To the west of this triangle the high wall of the church extends for a couple of hundred yards before it shelters the archway of the entrance to the Birton Public Library-and-Reading Room. A road runs through the centre of the triangle along the south side; the triangle has been paved and sockets built in at regular intervals to carry the iron pipework on which the market stalls are constructed on Tuesdays, Fridays, and Saturdays. Apart from the widening of the road and the surfeit of motorcars that seek parking spaces in every out of the way corner of the triangle, apart from the establishment of a betting shop between the Cafe-Restaurant and Malcolm's, few changes have taken place during the last three or four hundred years. Every building around the Market Place has become the subject of a Preservation Order. The shops were all built of red Northamptonshire ironstone, each constructed individually with different roofs and facades. Above Malcolm's a clock designed by Thomas Campion is still in going order; promptly on each half hour a door opens in the face, and a figure slides out carrying a large bronze gong which the figure strikes once. On the hour a group of figures appears and twirls in a stilted mechanical dance while the carillon plays a snatch of a tune said to have been composed in 1827 by the Bishop of Northampton specially for use in the "Horological Instrument," as the device was then called. Oddly enough, all the mechanical parts of the movement were copied from a design made by Leonardo da Vinci for the Duke of Milan.

Detective Superintendent Aveyard was sitting in his motorcar, parked in the corner of the wall at the north end of the square. Looking through the windscreen he could see along the footpath past Malcolm's to the door of the National Westminster Bank. He had been in position since half-past eleven. He was wearing a black seaman's jacket he'd just bought from the Army Surplus Store, a pair of black woollen trousers, and a flat cap.

This was a market day and the stalls had been erected and were selling a variety of vegetables, clothing, fruit, potted plants, plastic buckets, pressed-tin cutlery. Musical Minny was there with her stacks of gramophone records and sheet music. Aveyard remembered having bought the Vivaldi Four Seasons, conducted by Thomas Beecham, from her about a year ago. He'd copied the old seventy-eight RPM records onto a tape cassette he still enjoyed playing. Few people knew that Musical Minny had once sung in Covent Garden. Tommy Pincheon was there, a small inoffensive-looking man who sold wrist-watch straps and "silver" locket chains, and cut keys on a grindstone. Few people knew how much time Tommy Pincheon had spent inside—sometimes the keys he cut were made without the owner knowing, and Tommy used them late at night.

Promptly on the half hour, the door of the clock opened, the figure appeared, the gong was struck.

"Mumby used to prefer an early lunch hour," James Riddle had said, "but now that he's manager he'll have a lot of entertaining to do." A constant dribble of people went into and came out of the bank. An armoured car drove up and the men appeared from it wearing paramilitary uniforms and steel helmets. Aveyard grunted when he saw them. He recognized that Security Express men were vulnerable to attack but thought the way they dressed invited aggression. For a long time he'd argued against the men in Birton being allowed to carry wooden clubs hanging from a strap around their waist. He knew the Security Express Forces would like to be armed, and so would many policemen, but Aveyard stubbornly resisted all such suggestions. The Security Express men took over five minutes to collect their cargo of money from the bank and then drove east from the Market Place.

Mumby appeared at the door of the bank at a quarter to twelve. Aveyard slid out of his car and stood by the side of it. Mumby threaded his way through the market stalls and went into the tobacconist's shop on the south side of the Square, next to the Royal Hotel. Aveyard had walked alongside the wall and took up a position where he could see the door of the tobacconist's no more than twenty-five yards away. When Mumby came out he was smoking a small cigar. He waited on the pavement for a car to pass and then crossed the road back into the busy Market Place itself. Aveyard followed him, closing the distance between them to ten yards. Mumby did not look around. He went through the market without even glancing at the stalls, then into the Cafe-Restaurant, to stand at the long counter at the far end. Aveyard had positioned himself near a pile of empty boxes; he could see inside the Cafe-Restaurant through the large front window. He read the notices on the window skilfully written in whitewash. "Cod and Chips," "Steak Pie and Chips." Suddenly he felt hungry. Mumby was still standing at the counter talking with the manager, drinking a cup of something the manager had put in front of him. A stallholder came to Aveyard and temporarily blocked his view.

"You from the rubbish department?" he asked. "When're you going to shift these boxes?"

"The van's late," Aveyard said.

"Too bloody right it's late! It's always late!"

"I'll have a word with the mayor," Aveyard said.

"No need to get cheeky!"

Mumby had come out of the Cafe-Restaurant. He stood in the doorway. A knot of people walked past, blocking him from Aveyard's view. When they had passed the Cafe-Restaurant, Mumby had disappeared.

Aveyard cursed, quickly searched along the street with his eyes. There was no sign of Mumby.

Aveyard crossed the road, looked inside the Cafe-Restaurant to see if Mumby had returned in there but could find no trace of him. Aveyard turned right, walked the fifteen yards along the pavement to the betting shop next door. It had formerly been a grocer's shop with large windows and a glass door. The windows had been painted over from the inside so that one could not see through them. The glass door had also been painted. Aveyard pressed the handle, opened the door, and went in. A small wood-and-glass screen hid the room from his view but he could hear a faint murmur of conversation. He went round the screen and saw Mumby standing at the cashier's cage in front of the small heavily barred window. The room was thirty feet by twenty; all round the walls were green boards with matt surfaces on which lists of runners had been chalked. One long board extended the width of the room behind the three cashier's cages and on that board the odds had been chalked. Four pillars extended from floor to ceiling and around them were hung flat surfaces on which were pads of betting slips. The ten men in the room were all reading the back pages of newspapers as avidly as if this were a public library. They traded secrets in hushed voices. Aveyard stood at one of the pillars feeling conspicuous without a newspaper. He reached into the wastepaper bin and pulled out a crumpled sheet of the *Daily Mirror* which he smoothed out on the table in front of him.

Mumby was still standing at the cashier's desk but now the cashier had gone. A man Aveyard took to be the manager came out of the back office and beckoned to Mumby to go to a door at the end of the counter. Aveyard couldn't hear what was said but he saw Mumby shake his head as if to say "I don't have time." He took a piece of paper from his pocket and showed it to the manager. The manager examined it and then went to a safe which stood against the back wall in full view. Hiding the knob with his body, he opened the door of the safe and from it took a bundle of notes. He came back to the counter and to Aveyard's surprise counted off ten of the twenty-pound notes and handed them to Mumby. Mumby counted them, wrapped them in the piece of paper he'd shown the manager, and placed them in his inside pocket. He half-turned and Aveyard ducked behind the pillar.

"Righto, see you later!" Mumby said, turned round and left the betting shop. Aveyard waited a moment and then followed him and was just in time to see Mumby going up the steps into the bank.

★

"It's the blatancy of it that gets me," Aveyard said. "Two hundred pounds handed over, just like that. Of course, perhaps they're being clever. If I hadn't been looking for it, I wouldn't have spotted it. The piece of paper he showed the manager, so far as anybody knows, could have been yesterday's betting slip with a winning bet on it."

Detective Chief Superintendent Batty looked at him. He'd granted this interview with considerable reluctance. Batty had a strict sense of protocol and so long as Aveyard was suspended Batty wished to have nothing to do with him. "Look," he said, "I don't approve of you engaging in police activity of any sort when you have been suspended from duty. You had no right to put that man under surveillance. I don't know by what means you obtained information to cause you to follow him. Betting is legal, even for a bank manager! We may not approve of it, but there is no reason why even a bank manager shouldn't have in his possession a slip relating to a winning bet and why he shouldn't go into the betting shop and collect the money, which is legally his." He got up from behind his desk. "Superintendent Aveyard," he said, "you must *know* how I feel! I don't want to see, hear, or talk to you until this matter has been cleared up. Superintendent Beasley is a competent officer working with a competent team. You say you have not taken bribes and I fervently hope Superintendent Beasley will be able to confirm that statement by means of his investigation. In the meanwhile I must insist you stop any activity such as the surveillance of Mr. Mumby. Don't ask to see me again until I send for you because I will not receive you."

★

After Aveyard had left the office, Batty picked up the telephone and spoke to Beasley.

"I just had Aveyard in here, but sent him away with a flea in his ear. I had to. But he may be on to something. Mumby, the manager of the branch at which that account was opened in Aveyard's name, appears to be a betting man and uses Herbert Wilson's shop. I know that's not illegal but it's surely unusual. Dammit all, managers of banks are not the sort of men you expect to play the horses! Whoever made that signature had to know about forgery—assuming it is a forgery and Aveyard's telling the truth. Who better to know about forgery than the manager of a bank? I think it will be worth investigating Mumby, don't you? I can't see a motive as yet but let's say somebody wanted to put a fix in on Aveyard. With Mumby's help the phony account would be an easy way to do it, wouldn't it . . . ?"

★

Police prosecutions are initiated by a special legal department, the Public Prosecutor's Office, men skilled in Criminal Law who also have an astute knowledge of the climate of the Court.

"This is a tricky one," Thomas Kavanaugh said. "These circumstantial cases always are."

"You can hardly call it circumstantial to find the murder weapon in a man's pillow in his own bedroom," Superintendent Colby said.

"That's what's so tricky," Kavanaugh said, a worried look on his face. "We're not going to be able to put up anyone who can say definitely that it actually is the murder weapon. The best we're going to be able to get in Court is our expert saying 'it could be.' Frankly, if the defence knows what it's doing, on re-examination they'll get our expert to say 'it doesn't have to be.' You know, Superintendent, I always shudder every time we have to take an expert in to Court."

"But what about the footprint at the scene of the crime?"

"You've done a good job there, don't misunderstand me! I'm very happy about that! You've done a very good job of connecting your suspect with the place and time of the crime. This builder fellow, Jack Marsh, will make a good witness, to say that Constable Baron was still alive at half past nine when he left. Everybody knows Dr. Samson. Dammit, he's been a pathologist so long and so often on the stand that we hardly bother to cross-examine him any more. He knows what both sides want and delivers it. It's only some of these smart alecs from London who tend to have a go at him! Mrs. Slanky will be good value, too." He chuckled. "I like her story that the suspect had gone to see her about helping with the Church Bazaar. We'll have a word with defence before the trial and they won't question her about that. Of course, everybody will know what the score is but, in deference to her husband, we'll keep quiet. She'll be a good witness as to the time of arrival. Frankly I would have been happier if we'd been able to find someone who'd seen him walking about in the village. His mother says he left the house at ten to ten but she's unreliable and the defence could shake her. We may not even introduce the mother. It's all a bit vague, you know, and his story is plausible. Just the sort of thing one or two members of the jury could believe; he's either being very honest or very clever about robbing the corpse. Nobody will believe a man would voluntarily confess to something like that unless it was absolutely true."

"He did it!" Colby said. "He killed Baron! When Baron was lying there dead he tried to rob him! *I want a conviction.*"

Kavanaugh's eyebrows shot up. "You want to watch that, Superintendent," he said. "I hope you're not going to say anything like that in Court?"

Superintendent Colby coloured, realizing his tactical error. "I don't like to see policemen being killed," he said quietly.

"My dear chap, none of us does. None of us likes to see anybody being killed. But it's our job and, I might add, our duty to see that justice is done. We are only interested in proving the probable. In this office we're not concerned whether a man is guilty or not; only with what we can prove. Above all we don't have time for moral judgments. That's not to say that if you give us a good case we won't do the best we can with it. If only you'd found some fingerprints on the gun. Or what about ammunition? I don't know anything about it but I would have thought that if you'd found the gun you'd also find a box of ammunition or something. As I understand it there were two searches. The first one was negative and the second search turned up the gun. Not up to me to tell you your business, but if you could have found a box of ammunition with the suspect's fingerprints on it, for example . . ."

Colby got up to go. "You'll prosecute," he asked, "even without that?"

"We'll prosecute," Kavanaugh said. "The Chief Constable has agreed and the papers have already been prepared. I just pray that between now and our going into Court, you'll be able to turn up with something a little less circumstantial than we have at the moment."

CHAPTER 11

The bouncer stepped out of the shadows. "It's a bit young for you in there, Dad," he said.

"Dad? Come off it," Bill Aveyard said. "I'm young enough to be your grandson." The bouncer may have been hired for his brawn not his brain, but even he could recognize the determined quality of Aveyard's voice, could tell instantly this wasn't a man to tangle with. Dammit, it was very difficult to be a bouncer these days, what with the kids learning karate and Kung Fu, and dodging about like fireflies so you couldn't hit them, kicking their legs up and shouting Japanese. "You might be all right," he said. "It's the night for the Golden Oldies. Bill Haley and the Comets. One o'clock, two o'clock . . . and I'll be glad when it's four o'clock so I can piss off home."

Aveyard paid fifty pence and went into what was advertised as The Hangar, a converted shed on the south side of the little private aerodrome outside Birton. Its walls were made of corrugated iron lined with cellotex board. Inside the doorway a curtain mercifully shielded the inside from view. Aveyard went past the curtain and all his senses were immediately assailed. The shed was full of young people and of noise. From each end a light projector emitted a pattern of slides which changed every minute, beaming them onto rotating mirrors which flung them haphazardly around the room. Aveyard saw the face of Myrna Loy before it slid off to be replaced by a sepia-tinted Laurel and Hardy, then a coiled cobra ready to strike. There must have been twelve speakers round the room, each two feet in diameter, all wisely hung out of reach eight feet from the floor, all pounding out the demanding rhythm of early Rock, those compulsive, mind-stunning, sledgehammer sounds. Two long light guns sprayed parallel beams of primary colour onto a six-foot triangular mirror prism hanging in the roof of the centre of the shed. Colour splashed on the heads of the dancers like falling rain, their faces alternately hellish red or blue, green or yellow, the cosmetics the girls used standing out black as if smeared on by charcoal.

Ben Topham was standing just inside the curtain; he had not yet had time to fight his way across the room. His eyes were searching the dancers and the girls standing around waiting. Many girls were dancing together, their bodies gyrating in an exhibition they hoped would attract a more worthwhile partner.

Aveyard reached behind Ben Topham, quickly grabbed his wrist, and pushed it up between his shoulder blades. Topham started to turn but Aveyard twisted the wrist.

"It's easy to break a hand," he said. "Hello, Ben, how are you?"

Ben stood stock-still. It wasn't the first time his arm had been pushed between his shoulder blades.

"Oh, it's you," he said. "Inspector Graveyard."

"I've been promoted. Didn't you know? They made me Superintendent."

"I'd heard they'd *un*made you too."

"Don't get cheeky. I can still tear your arm off."

The smile on Ben Topham's face was one Aveyard knew he would see many times, the price he'd have to pay for suspension. It would take a hell of a lot of work to wipe that smile away from lads like Ben Topham.

"I'm clean, you know," Ben said. "I haven't done a job since I got out. There's nothing on me. If you plant something on me, they'll never believe you, will they? You being suspended and all. I mean if it's your word against mine, what's the difference between me and a bent copper?"

"A little dicky bird told me you've made yourself a bob or two! The little dicky bird said you were flashing twenty-quid notes only today. Five of them."

A look of uncertainty crossed Ben Topham's face. The information was too accurate. He'd put a bet on that very afternoon in Wilson's. A hundred pounds to win. Blue boy. Five twenty-pound notes. The tip had been good, but the horse had lost. "What are you after, copper?" he said.

"I thought with all that money you might like to buy me a cup of coffee," Aveyard said.

"They don't sell coffee, only Cokes."

"I didn't mean here. We'll take a little walk down the road. But don't try and run away, will you?"

"Not on your nellie! I want to find out which dicky bird tipped you off about the money. And then I'll go and thump him!"

Bill Aveyard had parked his car at the edge of the aerodrome, and drove to the Chinese Take-away on the outskirts of Birton. In one corner of the shop was a table. Ben Topham wrinkled his nose as they sat down and Lee Hu Fook brought them two cups of Nescafé.

"You don't eat this crap?" Ben asked Aveyard. "Give me a good curry anytime!"

Lee Hu Fook flashed a smile at him. "We cook chicken," he said. "Cully house cook cat."

"I never thought of you as a gourmet," Aveyard said blandly.

He sat back in his chair, obviously in no hurry. Jim Bruton would have recognized the technique instantly. Ben Topham played the game for a few moments and sat drinking his coffee, but his eyes were wary watching the policeman, waiting for his first move. Finally he could stand it no longer.

"Who was it that told you?" he asked. "Of course you've got the inside track at Wilson's! I suppose one of the cashiers tips you off when he pays you the money."

Aveyard grinned. "You can suppose what the hell you like, lad," he said. "The fact is that I know all about you. I know you're twenty-three years of age and live at 2, Corby Rise, Birton. You've never done a day's work in your life. You left school at fifteen because they kicked you out; we collared you the first time within three weeks breaking into the Co-op in Finedon. I know your form sheet like I know the back of my hand. You've just come out after serving a year of a two-year sentence for robbery with violence. Since you came out you haven't worked! Where did you get five twenties from? If you tell me you won them at Wilson's, I'll laugh right in your face."

"Well, I did, you know. Well, I mean you can verify that through your contact."

"My police contact . . . ?"

"No, well like I mean, your other one, I mean . . ."

"You mean what, lad?" Aveyard asked, his voice hard, bleak, icy.

"The fix. Everybody knows a fix is in. It has to be, hasn't it? Or they wouldn't be able to keep going." A smile came across his face. "And I wouldn't have been able to win my hundred quid, would I? Fancy that bloody twenty-three coming up three times like that."

Aveyard's mind raced, trying to remember the last betting slip he'd ever seen, the last list of runners. Yes, the horses *were* numbered. But what could he mean, "coming up three times like that?" Let's say the horse paid three to one. Three to one winning a hundred means a bet of twenty-five quid. That's an odd sum for a lad like Ben to play. "You won more than a hundred. . . ." Aveyard said, guessing.

"Well, a hundred and five. But I left the quid lie and chucked the fiver back at them."

Daylight dawned, the penny dropped! One pound straight up on a number twenty-three on a *roulette* table pays thirty-five pounds. It's traditional to leave down a winning bet; the ball spins again, drops back into the twenty-three! It can happen. A roulette ball has no memory of where it's just been. In the South of France a ball went into the same slot seven times running when a punter had the maximum stake on number. He cleaned out the casino. Well, Ben Topham hadn't cleaned out the casino but he'd won three times thirty-five pounds and that's a hundred and five. He chucked a fiver back at the croupier and he left his one-pound stake at the table not daring to hope the ball would go in twenty-three a fourth time. He didn't care; he was a hundred pounds to the good! All for one pound. The playing of roulette in England is illegal except in certain circumstances in a private home and in a casino legally authorized and licensed by the Gaming Board. The return of any portion of the winnings, even of a legal game of roulette, to the croupier or to any employee of the casino, is also illegal!

No wonder the fix was in, if Herbert Wilson was greedy enough and fool enough to be running an illicit roulette wheel, probably behind one of his betting shops. "Where did you win this money?" Aveyard asked. It was a dangerous question and depended how naive Ben Tophan really was.

"You know!" Ben said. "Dammit, you're the one with the fix in."

"Let's get one thing straight, lad; there may be a fix and there may be not. If there is, it's not with me. I don't know anything about it."

"How the bloody hell did you know I'd won a hundred pounds at roulette?" Ben Topham asked. "It speaks for itself, doesn't it . . . ?"

★

It was ten o'clock in the morning and Ted Roper was sitting on the iron chair bolted to the floor in the centre of his cell, when Inspector Colby came in. His solicitor had just gone and what he had had to say was not very cheerful.

"They've got you, lad, I'm afraid. Of course, it's all circumstantial but you do have two things against you. Firstly, there's the fact that that gun was found in your pillow, and secondly your past history is one of violence. Of course, they won't be able to bring up the past history, but I'm afraid the court will realize there must be something. What we'll have to do is get you cleaned up. Get your hair cut, get you a nice navy blue suit and a white shirt and a tie. I want you going into that court looking like a choirboy. It would help if you could learn to stand up straight and not shamble about. Try standing to attention the way soldiers do; put your hands behind you and pull your shoulders back. We shall get you a good barrister, but he won't appear on the scene for some time yet. In fact, you may not see him until just before you appear at the Assizes in Nottingham. In the meanwhile, you'll go through Magistrate's and Crown Court, but that will be a formality to remand you in custody. There's no point in applying for bail; they won't give it to us especially since the man you murdered was a police constable, and in view of your record of violence." The solicitor was in no doubt about his client's guilt. A kindly man, he was more used to house conveyancing and Company Law than criminal offences. The only reason he accepted Legal Aid cases was to obtain publicity for the firm he had just started. A solicitor isn't permitted to advertise; it does no harm to be seen in court, especially winning a few cases! He felt no hope of winning this one. That air pistol in his client's pillow was too much of a clincher, even without his client's fingerprints.

Although Ted Roper was too unintelligent to understand the true meaning of the word "irony," it struck him as "funny" that in his lifetime he had got away with so many things and now, apparently, was about to be done for the really big one he had not actually committed.

"How are you feeling, lad?" Superintendent Colby asked. "Are they treating you all right?"

Ted Roper looked up, surprised. He hadn't seen this side of the policeman before. "As well as can be expected," he said.

Colby pulled a packet of cigarettes from his pocket along with his handkerchief. He held them out and Roper, surprised, took them while Colby used the handkerchief to blow his nose. Even that small act seemed to make him more of a human being in Ted Roper's eyes. Colby handed him a box of matches.

"I seem to have caught a bit of a cold," he said. "Go on, have a smoke."

Ted Roper took one of the cigarettes and lit it.

"Take some more and hide them under your mattress; you can keep the matches." Roper did as he was told. Colby, he felt, wasn't such a bad guy after all.

"You realize we have to prosecute," Colby said, "with the evidence we've found. We don't like having to prosecute people. I know you call us pigs and all that sort of thing, but we're not really sadists." He blew his nose again. "My, I have got a cold," he said. "I'd better get out of here. We don't want you catching it. I'd better take the pack of cigarettes with me. They'll only search the cell if they see it. And where would you be without a smoke . . . ?"

"I didn't kill that policeman, you know, Superintendent."

Colby patted Ted Roper's shoulder. "I know you didn't," he said, "but we have to prosecute. I mean you could save yourself and us a lot of bother if you gave us a cough. It's not up to me to tell you what to say, but the sergeant laid it out for you, didn't he? We're only trying to be helpful, you know. If only you'd say that he came at you out of the dark . . ."

"It's not true, Superintendent."

"Who cares what's true or not, lad? We've passed that kind of thinking. The way it stands now—believe I'm only saying this to be helpful—the way it stands now, we're going to prosecute you. Your solicitor must have told you the court will find you guilty. You'll get thirty years!"

"I didn't do it."

"That's no longer important, can't you understand that, Ted? It doesn't *matter* whether you did it or not. We have evidence enough to charge you. In a court of law you'll be found guilty. You'll get thirty years. If you do as the sergeant suggests and tell the court that Constable Baron came at you out of the dark and you put up your hands to defend yourself and the gun went off in your hand, we shall never get a conviction. The only thing they can charge you with is 'carrying a loaded weapon in a public place after dark,' and, frankly, a good solicitor like Mr. Peverill will be able to make a case out of the fact that the clubroom is private property, not a public place! If the worst comes to the worst, you'll get six months. Two months off for good conduct and you'll serve four. Four months inside is nothing to a lad like you. You can do four months standing on your head." Superintendent Colby blew his nose again, picked up the packet of cigarettes and stuffed it and the handkerchief into the side pocket of his jacket.

"I didn't do it," Ted Roper said.

"Then you're a stubborn pigheaded fool," Colby said and closed the cell door behind him.

★

Jim Bruton was pushing his lawn mower over the six-yards-by-five apron of grass that extended in front of his semidetached house when Bill Aveyard turned his car into the concrete driveway, parked, and got out. Jim's cheeks were red with morning exercise and Bill Aveyard could smell the sweet-sour odour of cut grass hanging heavy on the morning air. He stood and looked around the small garden, at the golden privet hedge which separated it from its neighbour and from the roadway. There was no trace of weed in any of the flower beds which surrounded the lawn. Aveyard wondered how Jim Bruton managed to find the time; the police force kept him busy sometimes twenty-four hours a day. Jim Bruton emptied the grass box of the lawn mower onto a plastic sheet by the front door which already contained a sizeable mound of cuttings. "Nothing like grass cuttings for making compost!" Jim said. They'd long ago given up the artificial habit of wishing each other "Good morning," "Good afternoon," "Good night."

"I like these," Aveyard said, bending to sniff at a large rose from a bush at the edge of the drive. It had a delicate apricot colour with a heavy white center and a pungent odour that reminded Aveyard of his youth, when flowers used to smell and shop food used to taste. And policemen were figures you looked up to and even called "sir" and not pig.

"Day off today," Bruton said. "They're charging Roper; I was just going to stop for coffee."

Aveyard cast aside the memories of his youth. "That'll be nice," he said.

"We'll have it in the back; it's sunnier there." They went through the side gate in the screen of trelliswork which carried the intertwined shoots of a clematis. Aveyard watched amused as Jim Bruton twitched the end of one of the shoots behind one of the ties. Bruton didn't like stray ends in anything. They sat on a wooden bench against the back hedge and let the sun shine fully on them. Aveyard felt more relaxed than he had for weeks, listening to the sound of a bee droning somewhere in the climbing rose that part-covered the back wall. From where they were sitting he couldn't see another house; they could have been deep in the country. "I have been doing a lot of thinking," Aveyard said.

"And you want to try your thoughts out on me? Well, fire away. This is a morning for thinking."

"I couldn't understand why Herbert Wilson would need protection. I thought he was running a legal betting-shop business. Now I discover he's running a roulette wheel. But let's face it, who on the Birton Police Force could cover Herbert Wilson without me knowing? We could have a dozen quite legitimate reasons for turning over any one of Herbert Wilson's shops. There are six JPs in Birton and any one of them could give us a search warrant. Let's say some copper stumbles on the fact that Wilson has a roulette wheel, takes twenty quid to keep quiet about it. Who can say that the next copper to stumble on that wheel will be the same man? Have you ever been approached by anyone about Herbert Wilson running a roulette wheel?"

"You know I haven't. Or I'd have come to you."

"It seems to me that the only logical reason Herbert Wilson could have for fixing that bribe the way he did has nothing to do with the roulette wheel. Would you agree with that?"

"I'd go even further," Bruton said. "I was thinking about this in bed last night. My missus goes to sleep faster than I do. You'd be surprised how long I lie there sometimes, just thinking. It seems to me that paying the money into an account like that was done for only one reason. . . ."

". . . to get me suspended!"

"That's right. Herbert Wilson, or the man behind him, wants you off the Police Force."

Aveyard was silent for a moment. "I've come to the same conclusion myself," he said, "but why? That's what I don't understand. I had nothing against Herbert Wilson. I wasn't involved in any investigation that had anything to do with Herbert Wilson."

"So far as you know. . . ."

"So far as I know."

Jim Bruton took a sheet of paper out of the back pocket of his trousers and unfolded it. "I went into Records yesterday," he said. "I don't know why, but on a sort of instinct I suppose—though the instinct department belongs to you—I looked through Herbert Wilson's record. I just wondered if there might be something you'd forgotten that gave him a grudge against you. But there didn't seem to be anything. He was done for drunken driving, arresting officer, Hargreaves. He was arrested for allegedly running an illegal betting shop back in the days before they were legalized. Arresting officer, Moale. He got away with that one. He must have got rid of the betting slips before Moale got him into custody. He was done in 1972 for illegal possession of a firearm. Arresting officer, Blake on a tipoff. He told the court that as a licensed bookmaker he kept large sums of money in his house and felt he needed protection. The court told him to keep his money in the bank. They gave him a suspended sentence. Apart from that he's managed to keep his nose clean. Of course, he's had to, otherwise his licence wouldn't have been renewed. But I couldn't find anything in his record that either directly or indirectly involves you."

"It's a mystery," Aveyard said, "and the further I look, the bigger the mystery becomes."

Jim Bruton got up from the bench walked over to a bush and took off a dead flower head. "That's a nasturtium," he said.

"No good telling me flower names, Bill," Aveyard said. "They all look alike to me."

"Time you got married," Jim Bruton said, "then you'd learn about flowers in self-defence. Nothing like pruning a tree when you've had a domestic quarrel. Look," he said, "since you're here and we can't seem to get any further with Herbert Wilson, could I ask you about something that's bothering me?"

Aveyard nodded, pleased of an opportunity to forget his own tangled thoughts for a moment. "As long is it's nothing to do with flowers or pruning," he said.

"It has to do with that lad, Ted Roper. Superintendent Colby is pushing him a bit, you know. Ted Roper never shot Bobby Baron. It goes against the grain of everything you and I have talked about in police business."

"I was flabbergasted when you told me he was being charged. I could only assume you'd turned up something new."

"You know about the gun, of course, and there being no fingerprints on it. I just can't see Ted Roper using a gun. I just can't see it! If he'd had a gun in his hand, he'd have hit Baron with it, not fired it at him."

"I talked with Betty Baron," Aveyard said. "It would be worth your while to ask around a bit. From what Betty said I think Bobby Baron was on to something. I don't know what, something to do with police corruption. It seems he was very upset by something he discovered about three months ago. You might like to find out what Bobby Baron was doing three months ago. If he was on temporary detective duty or anything like that. Strange, isn't it, but if one were paranoiac one could create a link here. Bobby Baron, bothered about corruption in the police force, is murdered, and I am suspended from the investigation of his murder because of alleged corruption."

Both heard the front-door bell ring at the same moment. Mrs. Bruton had gone shopping. Jim Bruton started for the back of the house but whoever rung the bell had not waited long for a reply. They heard footsteps coming down the side path and the door in the trelliswork which screened the garden from view was flung open and Inspector Colby came through. At first he didn't see Aveyard. "I thought I'd find you back here," he said, "on the cabbage patch." Then he saw Aveyard. He stopped dead as if in one of those childish games of Statues, the arm still outstretched with which he had summarily dismissed all Jim Bruton's gardening endeavours. "Oh," he said, "I'd forgotten the two of you were thick as thieves." He turned on his heel and started back through the trelliswork door. "If you can spare a moment for your *official* duties, Sergeant," he said. "I'd like to have a word with you."

"Whenever I was obliged to interrupt a sergeant's day off," Aveyard said, "I always had the courtesy to apologize."

Colby turned back. "It would seem, Superintendent, there were lots of little things you used to do that the rest of us would be advised to avoid."

Aveyard came to his feet but Sergeant Bruton flashed out an arm and grabbed him.

"This is my house," he said. "I can be the one to decide when apologies are needed." He led the way through the french doors into the sitting room and Colby followed him.

"You want to be careful who you're seen with, Sergeant," Colby said. "You don't want people to be able to say you have the wrong friends. That sort of thing can harm your promotion, you know!"

Sergeant Bruton looked at him coolly. "Yes," he said, "that's one of the drawbacks in the police force. You can't always choose the people you're obliged to work with."

If Colby noticed the implied insult he chose to ignore it. "I want another search made," he said, "and I want you to take charge of it. It suddenly occurred to me that Roper's gun would be no good without ammunition. I want you to take that house apart again and see if you can turn anything up."

"This will be the third time," Bruton said. "You have a warrant, of course?"

Superintendent Colby produced it triumphantly from his pocket. "There you are," he said. "Find me some lead pellets suitable for use in that gun. They could be anywhere, in a tobacco tin, a chocolate box, the tea caddy."

"Or a box of ammunition," Bruton said drily.

★

It took Sergeant Bruton an hour of diligent searching, during which he emptied every canister in Mrs. Roper's larder,—not that there were many—looked into every vase, every jug, every container he could find in the house. They were in a box of Rothman's cigarettes standing by Ted Roper's record player. The bottom inch of the cigarettes had been cut off and the pellets were in the space left in the bottom of the packet, twenty-seven, wrapped in a piece of cotton wool. They matched the gun but more importantly the cigarette packet, of course, had Roper's fingerprints on it.

★

Detective Chief Superintendent Batty was on the telephone. "Yes," he said, "I think I can release Superintendent Colby for further interview next Tuesday. He's just in the process of wrapping up a case. You may have heard of it, Chief Constable. The murder of Constable Baron. It may turn out to be manslaughter but, I must say, Colby has done a good, fast job on it. I'll be giving you a full report to add to Colby's dossier. It should stand him in good stead at the interview. Good competent police work. About the other chap, Superintendent Aveyard, well, I have a bit of a problem there and I don't quite know how to deal with it. If I can tell you something for your ears alone, sir, and not for the other members of the interviewing board . . .

". . . I'm afraid I had to put the Superintendent under suspension pending certain enquiries being made. Obviously if these enquiries clear the Superintendent, as I fully expect they will, no mention needs be made of them when he comes for his next interview in opposition to Colby. Of course, if we can't clear him in time, I'm afraid I shall have to withdraw him or rather withdraw my support of him. You understand it's a tricky situation for me, personally, but I'll keep in the closest touch with you."

CHAPTER 12

When he left Jim Bruton's house, Aveyard drove to the Market Square and found the same space available for his car. He waited in it until the gong had been struck for half-past eleven, then got out and walked along the pavement to stand outside the bank. When Mumby came out, Aveyard was waiting for him. "I'd like a word with you, Mr. Mumby," he said.

"Official?"

"You know I've been suspended; it can't be official." Mumby took one look at Aveyard's face and something he saw there told him this was not a Cafe-Restaurant conversation. He turned and led the way back into the bank and into his own office. He picked up the telephone. "I don't want to be disturbed, Irene," he said. He locked the two inside doors and sat in the armchair by the small table on which was a cigarette box, a cigarette lighter, and a copy of the *Financial Times*. Bill Aveyard sat in the chair at right angles to Mumby's. The springs on his chair were much less worn and he seemed to be perched in it. The leather on the arms of Mumby's chair was slightly discoloured. It didn't take much deduction to realize which of the two was Mumby's favourite.

"There are two ways of conducting an investigation," Aveyard said. "One is to assemble all the information you can from many different sources and use that as a background from which to verify the answers to the questions you put, leaving the other person in suspense, doubtful as to how much you know. The other way is to ask direct questions, to state directly what you know and let the interrogation develop as it will."

"Let me guess. You're going to use the second method?" Mumby was cautious, but it would be hard to say which influence his caution derived from, the type of job he did or the type of man he was. But what type of man was he? Bank managers don't gamble, except with the bank's money and then only on sure things.

"I'm going to say something, Mr. Mumby, that will upset you, most probably make you angry. I can't help that! My reputation is at stake and within limits I'm prepared to do anything to safeguard it. I've been suspended from the Police Force and I'm not here in any official capacity, but that doesn't make the answers to my questions any the less important to me."

"Or presumably any the less dangerous to me," Mumby said unsmilingly.

"I suppose that's right. I have reason to believe that you are a gambler and that you frequent the betting shops of Herbert Wilson."

"Ah, the police's famous 'reason to believe.' Why can't you chaps ask questions directly or better still, to save both our time, let me ask the questions and supply the answers. Do I gamble? Do I use Herbert Wilson's shops for gambling? Assuming those two questions to be connected the answer to both would have to be no. I've never placed a bet in my life and therefore have never been into Herbert Wilson's or any other betting shop to do so."

"You've been seen in Herbert Wilson's betting shop."

"I've been seen in the bar of the Royal but that doesn't make me a drunkard. Really, Superintendent, it's not up to me to teach *you* how to do *your* job. I can only suppose that being suspended from duty has made you forget anything you may have known about interrogation. Interrogation is something we bank managers have to have at our fingertips. If you knew the number of would-be borrowers who come to us with a flawless story until we start to pick it apart . . ."

"Okay," Aveyard said, "I take your point. Maybe I have been affected by my suspension."

"Look," Mumby said. "I'd like to help you. I really would. Obviously I know all about this charge. I've had to see Superintendent Beasley and that other man, what's his name?—Wallace-Smith. I don't believe, from what I know about you, and admittedly that isn't much, that you're the sort of foolish young fellow who'd risk a promising career for the sake of a few pounds. But unless you tell me clearly what's on your mind, I shan't be able to help you. And don't worry about making me angry. Anger for me is a very private emotion."

"Okay," Aveyard said, "let's do it that way. You take cash money out of your account every week and you spend it. You receive much larger sums of cash money at irregular intervals and deposit them. I saw you in Herbert Wilson's betting shop receiving two hundred pounds. Can you, will you, explain those facts to me?"

Mumby was angry but managed to retain the anger within himself. He thought for a moment and then laughed. In the silence that followed his laugh Aveyard could hear the sounds of the bank from behind the closed doors, the very faint murmur of voices, and the clatter of machinery. Somehow the utter impersonalness of the background emphasized the very personal nature of what was happening in that room, in which a man's secrets were being laid bare and he was being called to account for them. All this was being done in the name of intimate personal humanity, one man appealing to another man to help him out of his troubles. Aveyard felt acutely that he had no right to do this, unless Mumby himself chose to surrender a part of his own personal freedom, to grant Aveyard that right.

"Somehow you got that information from James Riddle," Mumby said, "and I shall call James Riddle to account. Let's take the second one first. Yes, you could have seen me in Herbert Wilson's betting shop, though I didn't see you. The explanation is quite simple and, though it has nothing to do with you or me, I'll tell you what it is. That shop banks with us. The manager had paid in a sum, in cash. He'd been careless about writing the figures in the paying-in slip, and what looked like a five was in fact a three. Only after he left the bank did the clerk notice the difficulty. Since I was going out for lunch and knew I would be passing the shop I thought it courteous to go in and show the manager the paying-in slip, and ask him to write the number more clearly. He explained that instead of three hundred he had deposited he wanted to deposit five. He therefore inked over the figure to make it more clearly a five, and gave me two hundred pounds in cash to make up the difference. I said I would make the deposit for him, wrapped the two hundred pounds into the paying-in slip, and brought it into the bank to give to the clerk. If you care for me to do so, I will call the clerk to verify what I have just said. Now about the other matter. Well, that's something different and my own personal private business. Obviously, I'd rather not tell you about that but I know you want me to and therefore I will do so. But you understand that you force me to surrender part of my freedom as an individual and that, I regret to say, is something I shall not forgive you for." He held up his hand to stop Aveyard speaking. "No," he said, "I'd rather you didn't say anything. I'm not altogether convinced," he said, "that I want to spend the rest of my days as a bank manager and therefore, as an individual, I am trying to start a business. I allow myself fifty pounds a week of investment capital. I hope that explains the regular sums of cash I take out of my account. From time to time I sell the results of my efforts for cash and that, I hope, explains the capital sums of money I pay into my account. You'll see now why I found it very difficult at first to answer your question about whether I am a gambler or not. Yes, I am a gambler. My stake is fifty pounds a week and over the course of the year I hope to show a gross profit, 'winnings,' if you like. This year it amounts to about a thousand pounds. Well, that's twenty-five per cent of capital employed, one of the yardsticks we use for assessing the success of a business. Next year I hope to go even higher."

Aveyard noted Mumby was saying nothing about the nature of the business. Could that be a professional secret? A businessman's caution?

"When I asked about Herbert Wilson," Aveyard said, "you were careful to point out immediately that if I needed it, I could get corroborating evidence by calling in your clerk. Does your business activity also have corroborating evidence?"

"I was afraid you were going to ask me that," Mumby said. He seemed to be having some sort of inner conflict which resolved itself. "All right," he said, "in for a penny in for a pound! I'm a keen amateur photographer. Each week I engage models and take photographs. Every so often I put together a selection of the prints and sell them for use in publications. I've always had a dream, if you like, of being a professional photographer. When I first began it was just a hobby. Now I think I could turn it, possibly, into a profession. There are greater opportunities now then when I started."

Bill Aveyard asked himself what kind of publisher pays for prints in cash these days. Yes, there were greater opportunities for "publishing" certain kinds of pictures which used models as their subject. The confusion existing between the Obscene Publications Act of 1959 and '64, the Vagrancy Act of 1824 and '38, The Town Police Clauses Act of 1847, the Customs Consolidation Act of 1876, The Post Office Act of 1953, combined with the tolerance of the modern permissive society, had exposed many loopholes through which a certain kind of publisher could derive a profit. Few professional photographers of any standing, however, would supply that sort of material. The transactions between "publisher" and "gifted amateur" were often conducted in cash, for tax evasion and security reasons, among others.

"You can see some of my work," Mumby said.

"I imagine I already have," Aveyard said, "in my official capacity."

★

The man with the manure arrived at Jim Bruton's house at half past four. Six bags well rotted. Jim Bruton paid him two pounds and the man dumped the bags in the entrance to Jim Bruton's drive. The lorry had just disappeared round the corner when Mrs. Bruton came home. She stopped on the edge of the pavement and eyed the bags of manure effectively blocking her entrance.

"If you think I'm going to jump over lot . . ."

"Hang on a minute!" Jim Bruton said. "Don't be in so much of a hurry!"

Mrs. Bruton noted his tone of voice. "No need to lose your temper," she said, surprised. "Come on, I'll give you a hand."

Jim Bruton grabbed one of the bags and started to drag it out of her way. The bottom of the bag was rotten and snagged on a splinter of wood on the gatepost, ripping all the way across and depositing the best part of a hundred weight and a half of manure in Mrs. Bruton's path. Jim let out a curse the whole of the street must have heard. "Why couldn't you wait?" he said. Mrs. Bruton looked at him. "My, you did get out of bed on the wrong side this morning, didn't you?"

Jim Bruton didn't reply, stomped off down the drive through the trelliswork to bring his wheelbarrow and a spade. Dammit, he thought, he ought to have asked the man who delivered the sacks to put them in the back. It would have been worth a tip if they were all going to split when he tried to move them.

As soon as she saw him go Mrs. Bruton hoisted her skirt and climbed over the sacks. Unusually, she had been away from the house all day travelling to Leicester to help her sister buy a new coat. She'd expected to find Jim relaxed after his day off but he seemed to be in a foul temper. She went immediately into the kitchen and felt the kettle. He hadn't even made himself a cup of tea. She put just enough water in the kettle for two cups and switched it on; it wouldn't take many minutes to boil. When the tea was made she called him in. He was wheeling the second load of manure along the drive and put the handles of the wheelbarrow down immediately. "I'm sorry I snapped at you," he said sheepishly.

"That's all right, love. That's what wives are for."

He kissed her on the lips. "I disagree," he said. "You're an angel and I'm a bastard sometimes."

"Yes, you are," she said, "but only sometimes. Some men are bastards all the time."

"I've been working," he said.

"On your day off?" She knew that "working" meant police activity, not pottering about in the garden. No wonder he was bad-tempered. "They ought to leave you alone," she said.

He sat at the table and drank his tea. When he put the cup down she recognized the distant look on his face. He was still working! "What's the matter, love?" she asked. "Something bothering you?"

"Yes, it is. We did another search. I found that ammunition in a packet of cigarettes. The packet has Roper's fingerprints on it. It doesn't smell right. I only just got home."

"You and your 'smell right.'" she said. "I thought it was Superintendent Aveyard who got the smells. You miss not having him on the case, don't you? You don't like working with that Superintendent Colby, do you?"

"No, I don't. I think half the smell comes from him."

"Then, why don't you talk with Superintendent Aveyard, only this time without a bottle of wine to fuddle your tongue."

He was silent for quite a long time. "Oddly enough," he said, "that's not what I am thinking about. What's bothering me is something else. Something I think we've all missed. I think I'll just run over to Mawsley, have a word with Inspector Roberts. . . ."

"You can't," she said. "You can't get your car out! Not until you've shifted that manure."

★

Inspector Roberts was packing up the Incidents Office in the Parish Hall in Mawsley. Already the machinery had gone back to Headquarters, the extra desks, the tables, some of the filing cabinets.

"You haven't sent the Incidents Book back yet?" Jim Bruton asked.

Inspector Roberts wrinkled his nose at him. "Where have you been, Jim? In a farmyard?" He produced the Incidents Book and the box file of questionnaires. Jim leafed through them, rapidly finding the one completed by Westmacott. He read the number of people Westmacott had reported as having seen and then ticked them off against the identities of the people he named. Then, searching his memory for names, he flicked through two others. He showed the questionnaires to Inspector Roberts. "I knew there was something wrong," he said. "Read through those again and see if anything strikes you."

Inspector Roberts read through them. "There's one person unaccounted for," he said. "In each one of them. Dammit. I was so busy cross-checking the listed names that I failed to add them up and come to the right conclusion."

"And that conclusion . . . ?" Sergeant Bruton asked.

"There was one extra person in the village that night. One person nobody knew or at least nobody put a name to."

Jim Bruton bent over the table, took a sheet of paper, and drew a little plan. On the plan he put three rings and one dotted line. "Mrs. Jones saw our mysterious friend and her point of view extended over the Ride and the crossing with the High Street. Westmacott saw him and his view is a moving one represented by this dotted line. Finally this man Fisher saw him and all he can see is the High Street down here below the pub. We know therefore that whoever this person was, on the night of the murder he made a journey down from the High Street in the vicinity of the pub and past the end of the Ride."

"But we have no description of him, no identification, and no evidence he went into the grounds of the Hall!"

"Not yet," Bruton said, "but I'm going to see those four people again."

★

It took an hour. By process of elimination he was able to establish that the "other person," now so dimly remembered, was a male about six feet high, wearing a gabardine topcoat and no hat. The person walked normally, was not known to any of the villagers, had no distinguishing features, had never been seen before or since. Mrs. Jones thought he looked like "that first police officer that was asking questions on the case"—Superintendent Aveyard.

"That's great," Inspector Roberts said, "but where does it get us?"

"I don't know," Jim Bruton said, but the smile had come back to his face. Jim Bruton didn't like untidy investigations and was less concerned with the results than the fact that the enquiry had been correctly carried out with no loose ends lying about. Above all he was more than ever convinced of Ted Roper's innocence. "Find the man in the gabardine topcoat," he said to Inspector Roberts, "and I'll bet we find the murderer."

Inspector Roberts didn't share his feelings about Roper. "We already have our murderer in custody, Sergeant," he said, "and you'd do well to remember that."

★

Colby went back to see Ted Roper that evening. This time he took Mr. Peverill and Thomas Cavanaugh of the Public Prosecutor's Office with him. Mr. Peverill had wanted Roper brought up into a "civilized" office but Inspector Colby had insisted on seeing Roper in the claustrophobic atmosphere downstairs. "Look, Mr. Peverill," he said, "you want to help your client, don't you? The best way you can do that is by persuading him to co-operate with us."

Peverill privately agreed. "They have a lot of evidence Mr. Roper," he said. "You would do well to listen to them. You understand that, as your solicitor, I can only make suggestions and watch out for your interests. Frankly, I've no wish to see you tried on a charge of murder if there's any possibility of our pleading self-defence to a case of manslaughter."

Colby beckoned Thomas Cavanaugh forward and the prosecutor shuffled the half step that brought him claustrophobically near to the bolted iron chair on which Ted Roper was sitting. The harsh light beating down from the fitting in the ceiling threw the shadows of their features down their faces. To Ted Roper, looking up, the three figures pressing close around him seemed like some devil incarnate, the scene in one of those horror films he had enjoyed watching in which the mad doctor bends over the body of his victim.

"We have all the evidence we need," Thomas Cavanaugh said.

"Listen to him, lad," Colby said.

"We have your footprint and the gun. . . ."

"Mark what he says, Mr. Roper."

". . . and now we have the ammunition. . . ."

". . . from the packet of cigarettes. . . ." Colby said.

". . . on your dressing table, Mr. Roper."

". . . with your fingerprints, lad."

"We have a certain case," Thomas Cavanaugh said.

Their heads slowly backed away and Ted Roper looked wildly about him; their voices stilled, their heads no longer shielded the hard bright light which now beat mercilessly down upon him. He looked from one to the other, saw compassion on the face of Mr. Peverill, certainty on that of Mr. Cavanaugh and the brittle glitter of conviction that shone from the Superintendent's merciless eyes.

"We know how it happened, lad," Colby said. "You went into the clubroom—I'm not even going to ask you why. The light was out. A dark figure leaped out at you, your hand came up to protect yourself."

"It's only natural, Mr. Roper. Any court would believe that!"

"There was a gun in your hand and it went off and the dark figure fell dead in the armchair."

"It's the most natural thing in the world, Mr. Roper, the most natural thing in the world. A man has the right to defend himself against attack. It's the most natural thing in the world."

They gave him time to think and then Cavanaugh said, "Or would you rather spend thirty years inside on a charge of murdering a policeman? Thirty years. You'll be an old man when you get out."

"I can have you out in six months, Mr. Roper," Mr. Peverill said, "if you behave yourself, as I know you will. You look like a sensible man to me, Mr. Roper."

They stood back, each waiting. Roper suddenly seemed to shrink, to slump on his chair. Now he was no longer the braggart, the bully, the self-confident lout who uses violence as his only means of self-expression. Now he was frightened and defenceless, a victim of a system he did not know how to fight.

"All right," he said. "He came out of the dark at me. It was self-defence."

"I'm sure you didn't mean to do it," Mr. Peverill said, looking at Cavanaugh, establishing quickly the matter of motive. "I'm sure it was an *accident!*" He stressed the last word and Roper seized on it. "Yes," he said, "it was an accident; it was all an accident!"

Colby sighed with relief, like a punctured tyre. He stood further back, slapped one fist into the palm of his other hand, and looked away from Ted Roper, as if he had lost all his interest in him. "I knew it had been like that," he said, "and I knew we'd get a cough!" He walked to the cell door and rattled on the bars, Ted Roper and Mr. Peverill completely forgotten. The constable, who'd been waiting down the corridor, let them out, his face impassive though he must have heard Roper's confession.

"We could have done him for murder," Cavanaugh said disgustedly as he walked out of the cell. "With that ammunition. I never had a better case."

Mr. Peverill had stayed behind with his client. "You've done a very wise thing, Mr. Roper," he said. "you've been a very prudent man."

"I'll rather serve six months than go through that again."

CHAPTER 13

Mrs. Jones was sitting in the window again. "I'm pleased you've come back," she said. "It's been real quiet the last few days. I notice that young Superintendent doesn't come any more. Has he been moved to another case . . . ?"

"Yes, he has," Jim Bruton said.

"I don't suppose you like that, do you? The two of you seemed to get on very well together."

Bruton was surprised; he hadn't thought Mrs. Jones possessed that much perception. "You don't miss much, do you?" he asked.

"Not much. A body gets lonely, you know. Looks for detail to fill out memories. It's not enough to remember what happened; you want to include the way people look and feel and think, as well as the way they behave."

"You missed one detail, that night. . . ."

She looked at him. "Go on with you, Sergeant. What did I miss?" It was an offence to the opinion she held of herself for him to suggest she had not been thorough.

"The man in the gabardine coat."

"I included him. Walking down the road."

"But he walked back up again. . . ."

"He never . . . !"

"And, what's more, I think he went into the Hall. . . ."

"He never . . . !"

"None of us is perfect, Mrs. Jones."

She was silent, thinking back over the evening of the murder. "Come to think of it, it was strange, wasn't it? I mean, him being a stranger, walking down the street like that. Going nowhere? Chances are, he'd come back, wouldn't he?"

"But you missed him?"

"Haven't got eyes in the back of my head, have I?"

"How do you mean?"

"Well, I have to go sometimes, don't I?"

"And you, er, went, that evening, just before ten?"

"I always go, in the evenings, settle myself down. Regular as clockwork I am."

★

Jim Bruton came out of Mrs. Jones's and walked along Church View to the junction with the High Street. To the left through the twilight he could see the coloured lights on the outside of the pub. One of them, he noticed, was missing or the bulb had blown. He looked along the High Street. Six people in sight. Six! The mind is better than we allow it to be, he thought. The eyes are better scanners than any mechanical device, if only we'd let them do their job. Aveyard had told him that, but then, despite being a younger man, Aveyard had told him many things, had put into words so many thoughts Bruton had never been able to express. As Jim Bruton looked down the High Street he noticed one of the figures limping and recognized Jimmy Althorp. He walked down the street and caught Jimmy Althorp just as he was about to turn into the gate of the small brown-stone cottage in which the Althorps lived.

"Could I have a word with you, Jimmy?" he said.

Jimmy looked up at him. "You're the sergeant from the police, aren't you?" he said. "Have you found the murderer yet?" He opened the gate. "Would you like to come in, Sergeant. I hear you've arrested Ted Roper. Is he the murderer?"

"No man's a murderer, Jimmy, until the court says so."

Jimmy looked up at him again. "You wouldn't think so to hear the village people talk," he said. He showed Sergeant Bruton into the front room of the house, behaving in a completely adult manner. "It's the police sergeant, Mam," he said. "It's all right! He's come to ask me some questions."

Mrs. Althorp came through from the kitchen, wiping her hands on her apron. "Oh dear," she said, "is anything wrong?"

"Nothing's wrong, Mam. He doesn't want to talk to you. It's me he's come to see."

Jim Bruton smiled. "Only a few routine questions, Mrs. Althorp," he said. "I don't think I need to bother you. I can see you're in the middle of baking." Mrs. Althorp looked down at her arms liberally dusted with flour. "If you're sure it's all right," she said. "Our Jimmy is a very grown-up lad for his age. You'll find him very sensible to talk to." She patted Jimmy's head, leaving a smear of flour on his hair. Jimmy squirmed. When she had gone through into the kitchen he closed the door. "Would you like a glass of Sherry?" he said, playing an adult role with obvious satisfaction.

"No, thank you."

"I know how to pour a drink, you know!"

"I'm sure you do. But you probably also know that a policeman never drinks on duty."

"Oh, of course not," Jimmy said. "Now what were your questions?"

"I don't have my notes with me," Sergeant Bruton said, "but I seem to remember that last time we talked you told me your bedroom is upstairs at the front of the house and you were sitting in the window doing your homework on the night of the murder. You gave me a very good account of all the people you saw. I seem to remember you even saw Mr. Westmacott come out of the pub?"

"That's right," Jimmy said. "I suppose a policeman has to have a good memory, especially if he's a sergeant."

"It helps, Jimmy. Now, I've been able to find out that there was another man in the High Street that night. A man you haven't mentioned. Can you go through your memory and see if you can remember anyone wearing a gabardine topcoat, you know, one of those sand-coloured coats? The man would be just a little bit taller than I am."

"Somebody from this village?"

"I don't think so. A stranger."

"I know everybody in this village."

"That's why I've come to you."

Jimmy swelled with pride. His face was grave as befitted someone being "consulted" by the police but, unfortunately, on the subject of the man in the gabardine coat his mind was a blank. "I can't remember seeing anybody that evening you'd call a stranger," he said, "I can't remember anyone with the kind of coat you described."

"Don't worry, lad," Jim Bruton said. "In police work you learn that a *no* can just be as important as a *yes*. I remember you telling me last time I was here that you were sitting at a table in the window doing your homework. I want you to cast your mind back to the time between half past nine and ten o'clock. That's the most important time so far as I'm concerned. Can you remember if you left the table during that half hour? For example, did you go downstairs to get yourself a glass of pop or something? Did you go to the bathroom?"

Jimmy's face looked serious and carried a very odd expression when he spoke. "Can I take it, Sergeant, that this conversation is confidential?"

"Of course," Sergeant Bruton said. "We're just talking man to man, aren't we?" Jimmy Althorp nodded. "Yes, of course we are. I did leave the table, Sergeant." He made it sound like a confession of guilt. "I was supposed to be doing arithmetic homework. Mum's very strict, you know. I can see that she has to be. Homework till ten o'clock and then bed."

"But you got up from the table and stopped doing homework, is that it?" Jim Bruton asked.

Jimmy Althorp nodded, too guilt-ridden to speak.

"You sat on the bed and read the comic you keep under your pillow?"

Jimmy Althorp nodded. "Wow, you're quite a detective, aren't you?" he said awed.

Jim Bruton didn't tell him that, looking over the boy's shoulder he had seen the corner of what was doubtless the same comic peeping out above the folded sheet. "We all need to relax a bit sometimes," he said, "but eventually we have to face our responsibilities again. When you came back to the table to finish off your maths, you looked out of the window, of course. Did you see anything different?"

"Yes. The car. Parked outside the pub."

Sergeant Bruton felt his interest quicken. The man in the gabardine topcoat would need transport to get to and from the village and where less conspicuous to park than outside the pub?

"Did you get the number?" he asked, but Jimmy Althorp was shaking his head.

"I knew you were going to ask that," he said, "but it was sidewards on."

"There must have been some distinguishing feature, something different, for it to stick in the memory. What kind of a car was it? What colour was it? Can you describe it to me?"

"It was a Ford Escort, Series 5, Mark II, 1800 cc, bottle green."

"Well done, lad, but there are a lot of Ford Escorts about."

"This had a sticker on the side window. I collect stickers. I hadn't got this one."

"What kind of a sticker?"

"Naisby Point-to-Point Car Park sticker."

"No other distinguishing features? No dents; no scratches?"

"None on the side that I could see. Nothing except this Point-to-Point sticker."

"And you didn't see anyone getting into or out of that car? What time did you go down for your supper?"

"Ten o'clock."

"Your Mam gives you a slice of jam and bread and a cup of cocoa, eh?"

"Wow, you're a real detective, aren't you? How can you possibly know that?"

"My Mam used to do exactly the same thing to me, exactly the same," Jim Bruton said. "Tell me, just between the two of us, do you do what I used to do . . . ?"

". . . pour the cocoa down the lavatory?" They both laughed.

★

The records of the Secretary of the Naisby Point-to-Point Meeting revealed that twenty-five car-park stickers had been issued in advance by post in addition to the five that had been sold at the gate.

"People are very bad, Sergeant," the Secretary explained on the telephone. "We charge two pounds for the car parking; it's for a good cause and all goes into the fund. But that wretched man, Javits, *that pig farmer* who owns the field next to our car park, lets the people into there for fifty pence a head. I know they get a better view of the Point-to-Point, but you'd think people would be a bit more *loyal,* wouldn't you?"

"You can't expect loyalty when money is at stake," the sergeant said.

The list of twenty-five names contained that of the Chief Constable, Detective Chief Superintendent Batty, Superintendent Colby, two Justices of the Peace, the MFHs of the Pytchley, and the Woodland Pytchley, and, doubtless for professional reasons, Herbert Wilson.

★

Bruton was coming out of the post-office box in the High Street of the village when he saw the familiar car approaching and held up his hand. The car stopped and he got in. "I thought it was your day off," Aveyard said.

"And I thought you were suspended from duty."

"Right, neither of us has an excuse for being in Mawsley."

"I have," Bruton said. He was so relieved to see Bill Aveyard, so pleased to learn that he was continuing to take an interest in the case. He explained what he had discovered about the extra man in the village, the man in the gabardine topcoat, about the unknown car with the sticker on it, about the list of people who'd been issued with Point-to-Point stickers.

"Seems to me the best place to start," Aveyard said, "would be in the pub. They'd remember a man in a gabardine topcoat if anybody would."

But they didn't. Fred Walton was quite certain that the only men who'd been there that night were the regulars and the visiting darts team, all of whom were known to him since the two teams played often against each other. No man in a gabardine topcoat had been in the pub that night.

When Aveyard and Bruton came out, Bruton said, "Where were you going when I stopped you?"

"To Baron's house."

"Consoling the widow?"

"You know me better than that." It was Aveyard's turn to do the explaining and he told Jim Bruton what he discovered about the state of Baron's mind prior to the meeting with Jack Marsh, the builder, and the other "meeting" on which it would seem Baron had pinned so many hopes.

"It's always been a problem," Bruton said, "and it always will be. So many young men want to get out of uniform, want to build up a file that will get them into the detective branch. If only they'd talk to a sergeant, if only they'd put their thoughts on to a piece of paper."

"I have a feeling," Aveyard said, "that Baron might have done that very thing."

Betty Baron was sitting in the front room again only now she was reading a book, the embroidery lying forgotten on the table beside her. "There didn't seem any point in going on with it," she said. "I've talked to Major Rothgill at the Estate Office and he told me Lord Mawsley said I could have the renting of this house for as long as I like. Everybody's been very kind. Look at you, with all the problems you must have over your suspension, bothering to take time to find out what really happened to Bobby. Everybody's saying Ted Roper did it."

"Do *you* think Ted Roper did it?" Aveyard asked. "You know Ted Roper; you lived in the same village."

"He was always a big loudmouthed bully."

Aveyard changed the subject quickly, not wishing to bring Betty's mind back to the details of her husband's death. "That night," he said, "you remember I came to the house and had a quick look through your husband's bureau. I have a feeling I may have missed something. I have a feeling your husband may have written a report that would be very helpful to us. Assuming he had done so, where do you think he would have put it? Did he have a private place where he kept his things?"

"I have a shoebox at home," Sergeant Bruton said, to help set Betty Baron's mind in the right direction. "It's a bit of a joke between my wife and me. We don't keep secrets from each other—I don't suppose you and Bobby did—but sometimes a man likes to have a few things he keeps to himself. I keep mine in a shoebox, tied up with string. My wife wouldn't touch that shoebox for all the money in the world. Did Bobby have such a thing? Did he have a shoebox?"

Betty Baron was thinking. "Well the top right-hand drawer in the bureau, we always called 'his drawer.' But you went through that, Superintendent."

Aveyard could remember. Two pages torn from a practical homeowner magazine—How to Make Your Own Work Bench. A tin with six foreign coins in it. A cutting from a newspaper offering a collection of roses. A paperback copy of a book on body building. A tube of cream that promised to make your hair thicker. No sign of a report. There had been some pages from a police jotter written in Bobby Baron's spidery handwriting, but they'd been the normal Ways and Means Calculation of any young man contemplating taking a mortgage, having a house built and furnishing it. Gradually a picture had emerged during that search of a careful, precise young man, possibly a little too careful, a little too precise. Aveyard remembered the way the man's ties had been hung from a set of bull-dog clips on nails on the back of the wardrobe door. Most men hang their ties over a string. Bobby Baron's few pairs of shoes had all been cleaned before he'd put them in line at the bottom of the wardrobe;

the three off-duty suits he'd possessed were on hangers. A clothesbrush was hanging inside the wardrobe door—Aveyard couldn't remember the last time he'd used a clothesbrush.

"If your husband had some writing to do," he said, "where did he usually do it? At the bureau? On the kitchen table?"

"No," Betty said. "He always said he had to concentrate! He used to work on that table in the spare bedroom."

"Do you mind if we have a look around?"

"I'll put on the kettle, and when you're finished we'll have a cup of coffee."

"It's a bit late for coffee for me," Jim Bruton said, "but I'd love a cup of tea."

They went together up to the spare room. A divan bed in the corner with a blue quilted eiderdown on it. Under the window a plain wooden-topped table three feet long and two wide. On the table a tray containing three heavy crystal inkwells with brass covers that had been polished and then painted with clear lacquer. A wooden kitchen chair stood in front of the table with a yellow plastic cover seat. In the corner opposite the bed behind the door a single-size wardrobe stretched from floor to ceiling. Aveyard opened the wardrobe and the drawer beneath it. Both were empty. A chest of drawers to the left of the door was empty too, lined with newspaper dating two months ago. Beside the divan one of those wooden cupboards in which a chamber pot used to be stored now contained three paperback detective books—all Perry Mason—and a glass ashtray. They took the eiderdown from the top of the divan bed, lifted the box-spring mattress. The divan itself was also box sprung and buttoned. They pulled the mattress away and stood it against the wardrobe. The divan bed was on squat legs only one inch high. They lifted it and examined the thin cotton cloth pinned across, completely hiding the interior of the divan. Bruton examined the round brass-headed pins. All had been there, he would have said, since the divan was made. The cotton cloth had no sign of a repair in it and it sealed the interior of the divan completely. They let the divan down again. Bruton brought the mattress from in front of the wardrobe and put it back in place, laying the eiderdown carefully along the top of it. Both stood up and looked round the room. The floor was covered by linoleum that had been tacked down along its edges near the skirting board. Bruton lifted the square of rug in the center of the room and saw only linoleum beneath it, without a break in it.

"I've got it!" Aveyard said. "Give me a hand." He went to the left of the wardrobe and beckoned Bruton to the right, both reached up and grasped the eight-inch trim on the wardrobe top. When they drew it forward the trim slid off, exposing a gap between the wardrobe and the ceiling.

"We had one like that at home," Aveyard said, "meant to hide the dust!"

Neither was thinking about dust. In the space was revealed a green metal cashbox, about ten inches by six by four. Jim Bruton used his handkerchief to lift it down and carried it over to the table. "I don't know where constables get their money," he said. "I have to make do with a shoe box!" The keys were still on the metal ring on which they had doubtless been supplied, hanging from the lock. Jim Bruton used his handkerchief on the edges of the key and lifted the box lid. The first thing they saw was a stack of twenty-pound notes bound round with a paper cover on which was printed the insignia of the National Westminster Bank. Beneath the insignia the figure 200 had been written with a ballpoint pen, and below that, £20. Aveyard lifted the notes from the box. Beneath them was a folded sheet of paper. He opened it by its edges and spread it out. Across the top of the page was printed the word *Notes*. The word had been underlined several times and round it an elaborate doodle of circles and half circles showed the pensive and indecisive state of Baron's mind when he had sat down to compose this dossier. The first entry was a date just over three months ago. After the date, the words were written—'*Received from HW the sum of two hundred* (200) *pounds. Notes numbers 106–126, initialled.*'

Aveyard looked at the twenty-pound notes again. The small initial BB could be seen in the bottom left-hand corner of each. Beneath that entry was another, the single word "*Who?*," underlined three times with no less than seven question marks after it. Beneath that was another item, headed by the word, "*possibilities.*" This time there was no underlining. Had the thinking that provoked this part of the dossier been more determined, more precise?

(*a*) *if bribery, who? Could be anyone. How to know who to go to?*

(*b*) *if take a chance and arrest, what result? Possibly anon tip-off? Plus newspapers?*

(*c*) *best demand confrontation or threaten exposure. Only way.*

The last two words were heavily underlined, and Aveyard counted seven asterisks.

"If only Baron had talked to his sergeant," Jim Bruton said.

"He couldn't, poor devil. Don't you see? He couldn't trust anybody."

CHAPTER 14

"It could come from our branch, or any other," Mumby said. "Those wrappers are in use throughout the bank."

Aveyard had taken the notes and wrapper to Mumby as soon as the bank opened the following morning. Now they were contained in a plastic bag, with no danger of extra fingerprints smearing any that might be on them.

"So you can't tell me anything about them?" Aveyard said disconsolately.

"I didn't say that . . . Take this number, *200*, written on the wrapper over the figure £20. That tells me something."

"I wish it told *me* something. . . ."

"It tells me, for example, that the bundle of notes has never been through a cashier's drawer. Otherwise, as notes were taken out of the bundle, that figure would have been changed. It tells me that the notes you have there, or rather the wrapper, were originally part of a drawing of four thousand pounds. That's a heavy cash drawing, Superintendent, in twenty-pound notes."

"A wages packet?"

"Could be a company drawing cash to make up wages packets, yes. Could be a private individual, though I doubt that. Can I try out the packet on my clerks? One of them may recognize the handwriting."

"You won't let it out of your possession?"

Mumby smiled. "Of course not, Superintendent. I realize I shouldn't be seeing this packet at all, that it should be in the possession of Superintendent Colby, along with any other evidence he might have. How it came into your possession is no concern of mine."

Aveyard and Bruton had argued what to do with the packet and the safe-deposit box after they had found it. "It's evidence," Jim Bruton had said, "and as such I'm obliged to give it to forensic and enter it into the case, along with the other evidence."

"It isn't evidence, yet," Aveyard had argued. "Give me twenty-four hours with it, Jim. Let me see what I can find. If I'm unlucky, we'll put it back on the top of the wardrobe, and you can bring Superintendent Colby here and let *him* find it!"

"It still belongs in the case . . . along with the pistol and the ammunition. . . ." Bruton was worried; he was desperate to help Bill Aveyard all he could, but all his instincts as a policeman rebelled against keeping the knowledge of this box and its contents from the properly appointed Investigating Officer. And that was Superintendent Colby, not Aveyard.

"There's one other aspect you ought to consider," Bill Aveyard said. "Think what this will do to Baron's reputation, if it gets out that he accepted two hundred pounds from HW and said nothing about it? HW—that's obviously Herbert Wilson. The two hundred pounds was obviously meant as a bribe. We know Baron didn't use it; he marked it and kept it here as his idea of 'evidence,' but the tongues will wag, Jim, and we'll have injured the reputation of a lad who can't defend himself, a lad I believe is as innocent as I am. You don't want *that* on your conscience, Jim. . . ."

That was the argument that convinced Jim Bruton. "All right, Bill," he said. "Twenty-four hours. No more, Then I'll work it out, somehow, to get Superintendent Colby to 'discover' the box where we found it."

Mumby took the plastic-wrapped packet and went out into the bank, leaving the door partly open. After a couple of minutes, he came back into his office. "You're in luck, Superintendent," he said. "The second clerk I showed it to recognized the writing. She'll come in as soon as she's locked her drawer."

The clerk was about twenty-five, tall and willowy, with long brown hair she kept brushing nervously back from her forehead. She came into the room diffidently, stood inside the door until Mumby beckoned her to come forward. "You know who this gentleman is, Jenny?" he asked.

"Yes, Mr. Mumby. Superintendent Aveyard. . . ."

"Don't be nervous, Jenny. You think this is your handwriting on the wrapper?"

Jenny looked at each of them in turn, unwilling to commit herself until she knew the consequences of her statement. "You've nothing to be afraid of," Bill Aveyard said kindly. "We're just trying to identify the packet of notes as coming from this bank."

She nodded. "I think I wrote that twenty pounds on it," she said, "in fact, I'm fairly certain."

"Why is that, Jenny?" Mumby asked.

Jenny was barrying a ballpoint pen in her hand, a badge of rank, an instrument, a prop to give her confidence.

"Could you give me a piece of paper, Mr. Mumby? I can show you better than I can tell you."

Mumby pushed a note pad across to her, and she wrote the figures £20. "If you look at the £-sign," she said, "you'll see I always put a double loop along the bottom of it. I don't know why, but I've always done it."

Aveyard looked at the packet. Now that it had been drawn to his attention he could clearly see that the bottom "stave" of the £-sign contained an extra loop. "May I use your pen?" he asked. Jenny handed it to him, and he made the £ sign. It only had one loop along the bottom stave, beneath the vertical. He handed the pen to Mumby, who made the £ sign. His had a flourish at the top of the upright stave, and the bottom stave was long, with a loop on the end. Jenny's £ sign was quite unmistakeably similar to the one on the wrapper.

"Everybody writes the £ sign in his own way," Mumby said, "almost as if there were a philosophical reason for it. A pound means so many different things to different people. That's one lesson you learn quickly, working in a bank."

Aveyard was not interested in philosophy. "That wrapper, Jenny, does it tell you anything?"

She looked at it, trying to cudgel her memory. "Nothing comes immediately to my mind, Superintendent," she said.

"Look at it," he urged. "Take your time. The figure, two hundred. It represents an unusually large sum, doesn't it, an unusually large transaction? How many twenty-pound notes are usually stacked together?"

"Fifty," Mumby said quickly, but Aveyard beckoned for him to be silent, to let Jenny speak.

"Mr. Mumby's right," Jenny said. "Twenty-pound notes are usually bundled in fifties to make up a thousand pounds."

"So you'd expect there to be four bundles to make up four thousand pounds?"

"Well, you might; sometimes, when we make up a wages packet, for example, we get four wrapped packets and put an extra wrapper round them. That's usually when we write on the wrapper, to show what's in the packet."

"So this was probably the wrapper round four packets of notes made up at the same time?"

"That's what I'd think."

"And the sum of money. Four thousand pounds is a lot of money to be handling in cash. Most transactions for four thousand pounds would be carried out by cheque, wouldn't they?"

"I would expect so. The only time we'd make up that much cash would be for wages. . . ."

"The *only* time, Jenny?"

She thought for a moment. "Sometimes we make up a lot of cash for the shops. . . ."

"But not four thousand pounds in twenties . . . ?"

"No, that's usually ones, fives, and fifty and ten pieces."

"There *is* one other account that uses a lot of cash, Jenny," Mumby said, prompting her.

"Ah, yes, I'd forgotten that one. They could have drawn four thousand in twenties. . . . I'd forgotten. Ever since their shop in Kettering was burglarised and the safe blown open, they've used our night safe. They draw cash. . . ."

"Four thousand pounds worth?"

"Sometimes!"

"In twenties, Jenny?"

"You're right. In twenties."

"And who's that, Jenny?" Aveyard asked softly.

"The betting shop. Herbert Wilson's betting shop."

★

Superintendent Bill Aveyard was just leaving the bank when one of the clerks came up to him. "Excuse me, it is Superintendent Aveyard, isn't it?"

"Yes."

"You're wanted on the telephone."

"Take it in my office," Mumby said, then to the clerk, "tell them to put it through on my line."

Mumby tactfully waited outside the office while Aveyard went in and picked up the telephone. There was a click on the line and he heard the voice of Jim Bruton.

"You just caught me, Jim. I was just leaving. It could have been who we thought and it came from this branch."

"I didn't doubt it," Jim Bruton said. "In fact I was so sure that when I came in this morning I looked up the records again. You remember me telling you that a certain person had been done for the illegal possession of firearms based on a tip-off. I had a sudden thought; do you know who that tip-off came from?"

"I haven't the faintest idea."

"Pity, he's an old friend of yours. Arthur Wentworth. He knows how to forge a signature all right. . . ."

★

Arthur Wentworth lived in a tumbled-down cottage on the outskirts of Birton. However skilful he might have been with pen and ink, he had no skill with building work. The gate had been repaired with string, nails, and the wood from an old packing case. The front path had been concreted at one time, but the surface had cracked and the path was a long pool of dirty water. One window had been broken and repaired with cardboard from a shoe carton. To the right of the front door a stack of wooden crates with wire fronts housed sad-looking chickens. On the right of the front path a discarded tin bath stood half-full of water, covered with slime and duckweed. As Aveyard walked towards the front door, three frogs who'd been sunning themselves on the edge of the bath and squawking, dived into the slime. Aveyard could see the wriggling tails of half a dozen tadpoles, their heads already showing the mean expression of a full-grown frog's face, their bellies pink and bloated. He knocked on the door and felt it move under his hand. A bedroom window opened and a coarse female voice shrieked down. "Don't push the door in; come round the back." Aveyard stepped gingerly through the heap of rubble which bordered the path, through the thicket of uncut grass and spreading brambles around the side of the house, passing a broken bicycle, an old pram half-full of water which also contained frogs, a motor bicycle from which the guts of the engine hung like tripe, a pile of coal, and three bags of cement.

The woman was waiting for him at the door.

"Is Arthur Wentworth in?" he asked.

She cackled. "In?" she said. "Of course he's in! In *bed*, the lazy bugger! You won't catch him getting up in the mornings." She turned round and shouted and the glass of the windows shivered under the impact of her strident voice. "Arthur," she yelled, "there's a *gentleman* to see you."

He heard Arthur's voice from somewhere within the cottage, a voice used to making itself heard above the raucous boom of this woman, a voice that had grown rusty with exposure to too many pints of beer and hand-rolled cigarettes, a voice that rasped at the lining of your ears. "Tell the 'gentleman' to piss off," the voice said.

"*You* tell him! He's a *copper*." She turned to Aveyard. "I don't suppose you'll want to come in?" she said and burst into a gale of laughter. "You with your fine suit and all."

When Arthur Wentworth appeared he was the very opposite of what one might expect a meticulous, precise, forger-craftsman to be. His hair stuck out on top of his head like grey wire. His face had not been washed or shaved for several days. He'd obviously been sleeping in his shirt and the zip of his trousers was stuck halfway up. His fingers were heavily stained with nicotine, a half circle of which grew above the cigarette dangling from his upper lip.

"What do you want?" he said. "We haven't done anything!" When he recognized Aveyard a momentary flash of fear crossed his face, quickly replaced by a smirk. "Oh, it's you, is it?" he said.

"Who is it?" his wife asked. "Who is it?" Her interest immediately aroused.

"Shut your gob, woman," he said without even looking at her.

He turned and led the way through the kitchen. Aveyard held his breath and followed him through the door into the passageway that led to the front of the house. Arthur Wentworth opened the door to the left of the hall and they went into the room beyond. The room was about twelve feet square; the walls had been whitewashed and the floor of bare wood was spotless. Along the wall beneath the window a board about three feet wide sloped downwards with a rim at the bottom, stained with black drawing ink; several pens nestled against the bottom rim. On a table at the far side of the room stood a photographic enlarger. A corner of the room was screened off with a black curtain. In the centre of the room, a purpose-built table three feet square had a flat metal top. A large plate camera, a Hasselblad camera, and a bank of spotlights, each with the electric wire curled neatly around the base, stood on a shelf to the left of the room.

Above the metal-topped table a frame of Dexion was suspended from the ceiling.

Arthur Wentworth saw Aveyard looking round and smiled. "Never seen a forger's den before, have you, copper?" He went to a drawer and produced a black folder from which he took several pieces of paper in turn and offered them to Aveyard. "That's a receipt for the enlarger," he said. "Two hundred and fifty pounds, paid in cash; there's one for the Hasselblad, there's one for the Eumig, and one for the lights. I'm as clean as a new pin!"

Aveyard looked him up and down. "Hardly," he said.

Wentworth went to an artist's portfolio leaning against the wall and from it he drew a half a dozen paper sheets each about fifteen by twelve. He spread them out along the top of the working surface beneath the window and Aveyard looked at them. Arthur Wentworth handed him a magnifying glass. "You'll never see work like that again," he said. Aveyard whistled in amazement. Each picture was a scene, he recognized one immediately as the corner of the Market Place in Birton where sometimes he parked his car. It was the most exquisite drawing and the magnifying glass revealed the full detail. Every single stone of the facade of the church had been drawn in India Ink with the great precision of the old masters, the faces of all the people in the crowded scene complete in every smallest detail. On one face that occupied no more than a tenth of an inch of the paper, he could even distinguish the hanging earring. "My God," he said, "that's wonderful work. You have an amazing talent!"

Arthur Wentworth laughed sardonically. "You try selling that kind of work nowadays," he said. "All they want is Coca-Cola bottle labels stuck on bits of old carpet and large splashes of colour chucked any way over a piece of hardboard! You can't make a penny with this kind of stuff."

"I don't care if you make a penny or not," Aveyard said, "you're an artist. That's the best work of it's kind I've ever seen." He was examining each of the drawings as he spoke, using the magnifying glass to reveal the details. Bicycles, a half an inch high in which every spoke was drawn with precision. Every detail of the metalwork faithfully reproduced. Seeing Aveyard's appreciation Wentworth's face softened and his lips lost the cruel cynical smile. He took the cigarette end away and Aveyard saw he was careful to press it out in the tin he used as an ashtray.

"You really like it, eh? Well, tell me what you think about this?" He produced another sheet of paper from the portfolio and Aveyard gasped when he saw it. It was a drawing of the face of the crone who had met him at the door, done in a technique Aveyard had never seen before of crisscrossed coloured lines. Looked at from a distance it could have been a coloured photograph but when he put it under the magnifying glass he saw that the tints and the shadows, the highlights and the lowlights had been created by varying the distance apart of the lines and the strength and intensity of the strokes. Somehow Arthur Wentworth had managed to catch an expression on the woman's face as if she knew that once she had been beautiful and now her beauty was no more, as if she was aware of what she had been and what she had become, some inner wellspring of strength and pride that could sustain her through the difficult days of the present. "That's the most marvellous thing I've ever seen!" Aveyard said.

"You really like it?" Wentworth asked. "You really like it?"

"Like it," Aveyard said. "If it's for sale, I'll buy it."

Wentworth smiled with a warmth and friendliness that contrasted completely with his previous antagonism. "No," he said. "I'll have to go a lot further down before I sell this."

"You have gone a long way down, haven't you?" Aveyard said, sympathy in his voice. "Associating with men like Herbert Wilson."

"I haven't gone so far down I'll start squealing, if that's what you're after. I've still got that much pride left."

"Who said anything about squealing? You're not an informer. . . ."

"Too bloody right I'm not."

"Though you did help us once. Herbert Wilson and a firearm! Look," Aveyard said, "all I ask is a fair crack of the whip."

"Now you know what it's like to be the underdog, don't you?" Arthur Wentworth said. "Doesn't feel so good, does it, to have everybody suspecting you, especially for something you didn't do? You want to know something? How I got started? When I was a young lad, drawing was always my hobby. I had an ambition to be a book illustrator. One day I showed some drawings to a fellow and he asked me if I could do lettering. He said he had a certificate that had sentimental value for him but it had got torn and could I draw it up again, only this time he'd frame it. I was young in those days and stupid. Do you know what his certificate was? A certified bank check! He said it was the first money he'd ever earned and he was keeping it for sentimental value. I drew it up for him. The bugger cashed it. Then he told me what he'd done and blackmailed me into doing others. Now you know what I felt like in those days."

"I also know something else," Aveyard said. "*I* know that I didn't take a bribe. *I* know that I've been wrongly accused, but it seems as if you do too. How do you know? So far as you know I could have been bent."

"But you're not, are you? We both know that!"

"One thing is baffling me," Aveyard said. "You turned Herbert Wilson in for the illegal possession of firearms. You gave us the tip that he was carrying a gun and yet not so very long afterwards here you are helping him by copying a letter with my name on it to the bank. It's not so hard to work out how you could get hold of a copy of my signature—I've signed enough pieces of paper in my time—but why would you help a man like that after turning him in? Looking round this room, seeing the drawings you've showed me, I can form a picture of what kind of a man you are. Oh, I know we coppers are thought to be inhuman; I know we're supposed to think about nothing but who we can do next for some minor traffic offense, who we can push next, whose collar we can grab. But we do have our human side. I can see you now for what you are—a man with an enormous talent who somehow has never had the chance to let that talent come into full flower, to be recognized for it. You got off on the wrong foot and instead of spending your life with people who could appreciate what you could do for its own sake you've got yourself involved with people who only look for the use they can make of you, only look for the ways in which they can turn your skill into money for themselves. I'm not going to give you that 'Hearts and flowers' routine, that 'it's not too late', 'Salvation Army', routine. But I'll make you a promise. I think you can help me get out of the jam I'm in. If you *do* help me, I won't go against you for what you've done. When it's all over and done with, I'll see what I can do to help you with these drawings. Christ, man, there must be a hundred people who can use a talent like you have. I know a lot of people who could help and advise you. You'd be surprised at the number of people a copper gets to know. For example, there's a young girl I know. Oh, she's dreadfully county and all that sort of thing and she thinks that everything's a bit of a lark, but she writes children's stories. In fact, the biggest lark she ever had was when the BBC asked her up to Birmingham to broadcast some of them. Her doing the stories and you doing the drawings. I bet you'll get on marvellously together."

"You'd do that? You'd do that for me?"

"Try me," Aveyard said. "All right, I won't ask you to be a squealer. Herbert Wilson came to you. I don't know why you agreed and at this moment I don't want to know. But he asked you to write a letter as if that letter came from me. He asked you to sign that letter with my name in such a way that the experts would be completely baffled. I won't even ask how you did it. All right, if I'm wrong, tell me so and I'll go. If I'm right, just hold your tongue and when I get rid of this suspension you and I will have a talk about the future."

"I've got some drawings of animals here," Arthur Wentworth said. "I've always thought that if I could meet somebody, somebody like that man who wrote *Watership Down* . . ."

★

Bill Aveyard had met Jim Bruton by arrangement in the Eagle's Nest, the fanciful name for the restaurant built into the long corridor that straddled the six lanes of the motorway and served cooked cardboard to its captive customers. Normally neither Bill Aveyard nor Jim Bruton would be seen dead there, but they'd settled on it as the one place where no one who knew them would be likely to go.

"Why? Why? Why?" Aveyard asked. "I just can't understand why Herbert Wilson would want to fix me!"

Jim Bruton had been gazing out of the window, watching the cars zip by beneath them, feeling an unreal sense of floating disembodied in the air above reality. But the bribe was reality, wasn't it, and the method of doing it a reality?

"Would Wentworth stand up in court?"

"Not a chance. I promised I wouldn't reveal him officially as the source of the information. Herbert Wilson would pay somebody to carve him, or do it himself!"

"You're too accommodating, that's your trouble," Bruton said. "If it had been me, I'd have grabbed his collar and marched him into the nearest station. If he won't stand up in public court, what about the private departmental enquiry? There's no danger of Herbert Wilson getting to know the results of a departmental enquiry, is there?"

"Let's think about that for a minute, Jim," Aveyard said.

The waiter, a long haired dropout, wearing a clean linen jacket, obviously supplied by the restaurant, over a dirty shirt, obviously supplied by himself, stood languidly at the side of the table holding the computerized bill in one hand and a pencil with a bitten end in the other.

"You didn't want anything else, did you?" he said. "It's my time to go off." Aveyard shook his head and the waiter started to move away from the table. Aveyard's arm flashed out and held the waiter's wrist in a bone-crushing grip. "Look, you creep," he said, "you're supposed to be a waiter. For the price we're paying for this warmed up horseshit, we have a right too expect some service. So get busy; take these dirty plates away and get out your little brush and sweep away the salad you dropped on the tablecloth when you slung the dishes down. Smarten yourself up, or I'll put my foot right up your arse!"

The waiter's Adam's apple bobbed up and down as if about to sink for the third time in a sea of his own spittle. Aveyard and Bruton watched silently as he took away the used plates and the cutlery.

When he had finished, Aveyard picked up the bill as he had supposed it contained a printed item, "Service charge 15%," the amount of which had been added to the total. He crossed out that item and retotalled the bill including the VAT. "Right," he said, "now you can piss off."

Bruton was looking at him in quiet amusement. "You don't often lose your temper, thank God," he said, "but when you do you can be a bastard. I wish you'd lost it with Wentworth. We might have had an answer to that question you were just asking. The question 'why?' Or had you forgotten why we came here? I must tell you, you're the only man in the world for whom I would suffer a motorway cafe meal."

Bill Aveyard had switched off the waiter and had switched on the matter of the bribe. Once again Jim Bruton had to admire the way he could do that. "We both agreed," Aveyard said, "it could have nothing to do with the roulette wheel."

"Both agreed. Let's face it, if Wilson was paying both you and me fifty pounds a week, there's nothing we could do in the Birton police force to help him run an illegal roulette game. Dammit, even if he were paying the Chief Super to give us a nod and a wink, one of us would be bound to knock on the door of the Chief Constable. Some men on the police force go on the take sometimes, men who accept a pound or a fiver not to arrest somebody. But any bribe is usually a one-off job. People read books about bribery and corruption in London, Chicago, New York, where an entire force can be on the take over the numbers racket or something like that, but it can't and doesn't happen here! I stake my reputation on that! What's more, Bill, if I thought anything like that was going on I'd resign tomorrow."

"We have to face the fact," Aveyard said, "that for reasons of his own Herbert Wilson wants me suspended from duty."

"The immediate thought occurs to me," Bruton said, "that Herbert Wilson wants to stop something you are doing. Something you *were* doing the few days prior to your suspension. I've looked into all your cases, as you know, and with one exception none of them had a connection with Herbert Wilson. We know now that there was a connection between Bobby Baron and Herbert Wilson. We suspect that Bobby Baron found out about the roulette, but from your conversation with Betty Baron and the two hundred pounds we found in Bobby Baron's box, it would seem as if he's known about that roulette for three months."

"But did nothing about it! Why would that be? Bobby Baron was young and ambitious. We know he was stubborn and tended to see things in black and white. Dammit, if he'd walked in with that roulette wheel sewed up, we'd have had him in the detective division right now."

"We also know now," Bruton said, "that it was general knowledge among the lags that a fix was in! Didn't Ben Topham say he thought you were the one with your hand out?"

"All right, let's speculate. Let's say Bobby Baron heard that rumour. Perhaps a name was attached to it. You remember I reported to you that Bobby Baron said to his wife, 'It's much nearer home than that.' Supposing Bobby Baron thought that I or another of the Superintendents was involved in a fix. We know from his notes that he didn't know which way to turn. So he sits on it for three months. You can imagine how he must have felt, a conscientious young copper thinking that one of his superiors was on the take from a lout like Herbert Wilson. Baron had the two hundred pounds which, so far as he was concerned, was evidence that some bribery was going on. Of course, an inexperienced lad like Baron didn't know that is not the way we get evidence in a bribery case.

But we can forget that side of it." Aveyard turned and looked out of the window deep in thought. Jim Bruton looked out too, waiting, knowing the wheels were turning in Aveyard's mind.

"I think I've got it," Aveyard finally said. "Look, Wilson has bribed Baron. Baron has been murdered. Word get's about that I'm on the case. Wilson is afraid that in turning over the Baron case I'm going to find out about the bribery and therefore he has me suspended from duty. . . ."

"There's a flaw in that argument," Jim Bruton said. "The next officer to be put on the case would be in the same position you were in. What is to say that he won't find out about the bribe?"

"That's the second part of what I was going to say. When I was suspended, there was no doubt who was going to get the case. Superintendent Carmichael is on a course, Superintendent Joseph is on that fraud case, so it had to be Superintendent Colby."

"Yes, but I still don't see it. If Superintendent Colby hadn't got this fixed idea about Roper, if he had kept an open mind and checked into Baron's effects the way we did, he would have found out about the bribery."

"You said Colby, in your opinion, was trying to get a quick conviction of Roper. Has it occurred to you that Colby, for reasons of his own, might want to get that case closed quickly? It was inevitable from the moment of my suspension that Colby was going to get the case and may in fact have said so to his friend, the one who'd been giving him money, the man who didn't want a full investigation of the Baron case and therefore had fixed me so that I would be suspended, knowing that his friend was going to take over. . . ."

"You mean . . . ?"

"You've got it. . . ."

"Superintendent Colby could have been the officer who was taking the bribe."

"It's a nasty thought," Aveyard said, "but it becomes even worse if you carry it to its logical conclusion. . . ."

"The gun?" Bruton said, "and the ammunition . . . ?"

"That's one side of it, but there's another side too. It would be interesting to know where Superintendent Colby was on the night of the murder."

CHAPTER 15

Inspector John Biddy had been the Incidents Officer on the previous case on which Superintendent Colby had been the Investigating Officer. John Biddy was young, unlike Sergeant Bruton and Inspector Roberts, and fiercely ambitious. He belonged to the no-nonsense computer school, read the works of Criminal Psychologists, studied the Criminal Mind. Although Superintendent Colby would not admit it, John Biddy had solved Superintendent Colby's last crime for him. That too had been a murder. In a factory. A murder without an apparent motive. John Biddy had performed a statistical survey as a result of which he'd concluded that the two men employed in that factory would be homosexual. The victim was one of those men; and his murderer had turned out to be the other. Or, as Biddy said with unconscious irony, "Vice Versa."

Bruton found Biddy in the Records Office at Police Headquarters with a note pad in his hands and one of those pocket-sized electronic calculators. John Biddy was looking at the charts hanging on the wall and when Bruton came in he took his arm. He was a man from whom thoughts and words spilled in a constant cataract. Few men could follow the rushing ideas, few float safely out of the rapids of John Biddy's turbulent mind.

"I've just discovered something very interesting," he said to Jim Bruton. "We're going to have a taxi-driver murder in this city within six days! It's long overdue! I've just done a survey of the profession of all the men murdered in ten cities of comparable size to Birton. Would you believe it, taking into account the number of Hackney carriage licenses issued in those cities and the hour of termination of the bus routes I get a consistent figure of 2.7 per cent? If you look at the Birton figure you find that at the present moment we are running at 1.9 per cent. That residual 0.8 per cent represents a time span of seventeen months. Would you believe it's eighteen months since a taxi driver was robbed and murdered in Birton?"

"So what do you suggest?" Bruton said.

"There are two things we can do. We can either put a policeman in every taxi that operates after the hours of ten o'clock at night because statistically . . ."

". . . those taxi drivers are robbed after the pubs turn out?"

"Oh, you knew that, did you?" John Biddy said. "Interesting figure. Eighty-three per cent speaking nationally of course, of taxi-driver murders are committed between the hours of 10:30 P.M. and 12 P.M."

"And a 100 per cent of the men who come out of the pub with a skinful of beer and no money to pay for the taxi are left-handed Siamese conjurers," Jim Bruton said.

John Biddy's face creased into a smile. "You're putting me on," he said. "There's absolutely no racial characteristic thrown up by the records. It's not an ethnological problem, you know!"

Bruton laughed. "Well, that's reassuring," he said. "Have you got a minute?"

"Sure," John Biddy said. "Sure. What's on your mind?"

Jim Bruton knew he was on sensitive ground. But without the benefit of an electronic calculator or a book of logarithmic tables, he knew the only way to tackle John Biddy was head on. John Biddy had no time for finesse, no room in his fact-crowded mind for social or emotional delicacy. "You were Incidents Officer," Bruton said, "on that Pouf murder. As I remember, you wrapped it up on the twenty-eighth, the day after we started the Bobby Baron case."

"That's right," John Biddy said. "Did you know that 37 per cent of all murders are solved within twenty-four hours? Ours came in the second category, the 8 per cent that takes from one to seven days."

"Can you tell me where Inspector Colby was at ten o'clock on the night of the twenty-seventh?"

"Oh, that's easy," John Biddy said. Jim Bruton had not noticed the small attaché case on the desk top until John Biddy opened it. The inside of the lid was painted white. John Biddy took out a black box about four inches long and two inches square and put it onto a metal slide which clipped to the attaché case above the handle. Next he produced a plywood box and took a roll of film from it. He inserted one end of the film into a slot and pressed a button. A light emitted from the end of the black box projected onto the screen on the inside of the attaché-case lid. He pressed a button and to Bruton's amazement a page of writing was projected onto the screen. John Biddy went on pressing the button until the page of writing carried the date, the twenty-seventh.

"My God," Bruton said, "what is that?"

"It's microfilm," John Biddy said. "I always microfilm the records of cases I work on. I've been trying to get the Chief Constable to issue the equipment to every Incidents Officer. Just think," he said, "we could put the whole thing onto a data base."

"Imagine the confusion," Bruton said.

"Confusion?" John Biddy asked. "What do you mean?"

"It may have escaped your attention," Bruton said, "that you've got the bloody thing upside down," He had, too, but such considerations did not bother John Biddy. Nor, or so he said, the computer.

"Superintendent Colby—here we are—checking out of the Incidents Office—nine o'clock. That's twenty-one hours, you know. We really ought to start using the International Time Base, but until everyone understands it . . ."

"Where was he going?"

"Reason for departure—Interview, Mrs. Chase, 4 Ormsby Villas. Wovenhoe. She was the landlady of the man who subsequently turned out to be the murderer. I told Superintendent Colby before he left. You know, statistically . . ."

"I know," Bruton said. "One hundred per cent of homosexuals turn out to be queer. . . ."

★

Chief Superintendent Beasley listened sympathetically to Superintendent Aveyard, then shook his head. "I'm afraid that, unless you give me carte blanche, I can't do anything with this man Wentworth. *I* believe you. I believe him when he says he was instructed to forge your signature on that letter by Herbert Wilson. But you must see that such evidence in inconclusive. We must prove it to clear you. And that means I must bring him before the Departmental Enquiry. I can't grant him immunity from prosecution when I do so. I just can't do it. Either you must let me bring him in, or I can't use his evidence at all."

"I've given him my word," Aveyard said.

"Then, I'm sorry, but there's nothing I can do."

★

"Yes, I remember that day," Mrs. Chase said. "It was my daughter's birthday. The Superintendent—what did you say his name was? —Colby. Funny dry stick he was! He interrupted my daughter's birthday tea."

"Birthday tea? At nine o'clock at night?"

"Nine o'clock? Whatever makes you think we have tea at nine? It was half past four when he came here, nearly five o'clock when he left. The kids were very angry. They had to wait for their jelly and trifle."

★

"Four-thirty?" John Biddy said. "You've seen the diary for that day. At four-thirty, Superintendent Colby was reported to be on his way to his office in Birton. He came back at six o'clock."

★

"The twenty-seventh?" the desk sergeant said. "That would be a Thursday, wouldn't it? Well, I was on duty, yes, but I can't specifically remember if I saw Superintendent Colby or not? Why do you want to know?"

"It's a bit of a joke," Sergeant Bruton hastily said. "A bit of a lark I'm having with Inspector Biddy."

"Lucky buggers, you detectives. Here on the desk, we don't have time for a 'bit of a lark.' No, I'm afraid I can't remember if I saw Superintendent Colby that afternoon or not. . . ."

★

"We have the following things," Bruton said. "Superintendent Colby does possess a garbardine coat, does have a Point-to-Point sticker on his car and the car's the right sort. He was missing at the crucial time, and lied to his Incidents Officer about his movements. Furthermore, he *could* have planted the gun—I wasn't watching him all the time we were in that bedroom together—and he could have planted the ammunition."

Sergeant Bruton had driven to Bill Aveyard's flat after he had spoken to the desk sergeant, when he had completed the enquiries that seemed, to him, to implicate Colby in the web of suspicion they had spun together. Aveyard was not yet convinced, Jim Bruton could see that from the way he walked restlessly about the sitting room, unable to settle down. Jim Bruton watched him, willing him almost to sit somewhere and listen to what he had to say.

"They're going to hound you off the force, Bill," he said, "just as they are trying to hound Roper into a prison sentence. . . ."

"Oh, come off it, Jim. That's a pretty tough word. Nobody's *hounding* me; they're all behaving very correctly. And really, nobody's *hounding* Roper. Look at it from their point of view. They have what looks like evidence against both of us, and they're just pushing that evidence to its logical and legal conclusion. It'd be very easy to become paranoid. I know I felt a bit sorry for myself, at first, and wondered how they could be doing this to me, a loyal police officer. But now I can see they're just following a chain of evidence that *I* believe has been laid for them. But we have no reason to believe that the same factors apply concerning Roper, the gun, the ammunition. Anyway, hasn't he confessed?"

"Yes, but to the charge of manslaughter. He'll plead self-defence in Court. Colby will get a quick conviction, and be on his way to that Chief Superintendent's job in Worcester."

Aveyard had settled down; he sat in the deep armchair by the window, looking out. "Like you, Jim, I'm a bit sceptical about that gun and ammunition. But, you know, it's easy to let our minds go always along the same paths. And when, occasionally, we see something a bit out of place, a bit out of the normal, we tend to say, that can't be. We know what kind of a lad Roper is, so we tend to say, a crime with a bit of finesse to it is out of Roper's capability. You and I both should know, by now, that the only predictable thing about police work is its unpredictability. Right now the Chief Superintendent is suffering this way. He's been wandering down a path of perfectly reasonable assumptions; suddenly someone throws a stone in his way, a letter that suggests I have been taking bribes. Both you and I know it's inconceivable that I would take a bribe from a layabout like Herbert Wilson; but the Chief, who *should* know that, doesn't. From one line of assumption, he goes off along another, the assumption that, because an account has been opened in my name in a bank, I must have some connection with it. Certainly I believe he ought to have made an enquiry, but not the way he has. And, what's more, I don't propose to fall into the same trap."

He picked up the telephone and dialled. When the operator came on the line, he said, "Extension 347."

A constable was kept on duty as a part-time secretary to the Chief Superintendent, a runabout, a screen protecting his privacy from unwonted invasions. "Would you go in to the Chief Superintendent," Aveyard quietly said, "and tell him that Superintendent Aveyard would like a word with him? I know what he'll say. He'll tell you to tell me to speak to Chief Superintendent Beasley. If he does that, tell the Chief Superintendent that I intend to resign from the police force, but would like to have a word with him first."

As Aveyard had predicted, the Chief Superintendent came on the line. "No man's guilty until he's convicted," the Chief said. "Don't be a bloody fool! Anyway, I won't accept your resignation while a Departmental Enquiry is hanging over you. I thought you were a conscientious fellow and could take the knocks. I admit this is a knock, but take it like a man!"

Aveyard laughed. "That's better, Chief," he said. "At least, we're communicating with each other again."

He then told the Chief Superintendent about his plan.

★

An invitation from the Lord Lieutenant of the County is not something lightly to be disobeyed. The Assistant Chief Constable received one, as did Sergeant Bruton. Chief Superintendents Batty and Beasley were there (but not Inspector Wallace-Smith); Superintendents Colby and Aveyard were both requested to attend. The invitation, delivered by a policeman in each case, was hand-written by Lord Mawsley himself on an impressive piece of white gilt-edged card, which bore the coat of arms of the Mawsley family. "Would you be so kind as to attend a Crime Conference at the Hall this evening at six?" It was a command.

CHAPTER 16

Peabody greeted each guest at the front door and led him to the morning room. The "staff" had been brought on duty for the occasion and Millie, pert in a black dress with white collar and cuffs, stood by the sideboard dispensing drinks. Rogers, the housekeeper, stood by another sideboard on which were canapés Amy the cook had prepared that afternoon in some haste; when all were assembled, Millie and Rogers withdrew, leaving the guests to help themselves to what they wanted of the food and drink. Aveyard examined his crystal glass appreciatively, then replenished it with the delicious Pelure d'Oignon Rosé wine. Jim Bruton, standing beside him, was drinking a gin and tonic; more accurately it should be described as a tonic water with a little gin in it. Jim was out of place in these solidly elegant surroundings, lacked Aveyard's ability to blend into such a background. Colby, too, appeared ill at ease, and stood talking rapidly to Chief Superintendent Beasley. The Assistant Chief Constable and Chief Superintendent Batty stood together, each carrying a hefty drink, large and solid like men posing for the County Council portrait.

After ten minutes, Lord Mawsley came into the room.

"Thank you for coming," he said as he shook hands with each in turn, walking slowly and precisely from group to group. Aveyard noticed with some amusement that Colby and Bruton each wiped a hand nervously on his trousers before offering it for Lord Mawsley's handshake. When he had been the rounds, Lord Mawsley stood for a moment, waiting, and almost immediately the doors into the next room were opened from the other side, revealing Peabody and Rogers with a large table running down the centre of the room behind them, writing pads and pencils at each place.

"Shall we go in?" Lord Mawsley said to the nearest man to him at that moment, Sergeant Bruton. The sergeant looked around as if trapped into an impropriety, but then stepped forward bravely. Lord

Mawsley walked slowly to the head of the table, then beckoned to Aveyard. "Come sit here beside me, Superintendent," he said, "and your sergeant can sit at the other side of you. Perhaps the Assistant Chief Constable would like to sit here, at my right?" It was so deftly done, the protocol recognized and established, but the wishes of the Lord Lieutenant of the County made quite clear. Batty sat next to the ACC, with Beasley on the far side of him. Colby took his seat at the bottom of the table, leaving the chair next to Jim Bruton vacant since no pad or pencil had been placed there.

Peabody and Rogers closed the doors and withdrew.

Everyone was looking at Lord Mawsley.

He glanced round the table, a skilled "chairman" who'd handled many such meetings.

"You may all think it presumptuous of me," he began in a low mellow voice that flowed easily round the table, perfectly audible to each of them without stress, "to ask you here today to discuss the matter I am going to put before you, but I have often believed we can so encompass our minds with ritual that we are unable to think correctly. For that reason, I have chosen to ask you to come away from the formal atmosphere of the police headquarters, and now further ask you to take part in this meeting with unencumbered minds. Now I shall retire from the spotlight, so to speak, and ask Superintendent Aveyard to speak."

Aveyard looked round the table first. Was it possible for each of these men to achieve an "unencumbered" mind? So much of the ritual of police work is symbolic, a mere matter of form, a question of holding up the law in which few people still believe, maintaining a bulwark against the anarchy so many people seem to desire, upholding the traditional values of a legally ordered society against the many forces seeking to destroy it. Could these men participate in an experiment against their experience, their traditions, and prejudices?

"As we are all aware," he said, "I have recently been suspended from duty. I want to say immediately that I have no complaints. Even if I had, this would not be the place to express them."

The ACC looked at Lord Mawsley with concern. Was he to be exposed, in front of junior officers, to a breach of police tradition and etiquette?

Lord Mawsley smiled reassuringly at him, but didn't speak.

"As a result of my suspension," Aveyard said, "all communications with and from me are now channelled into certain directions. I am 'under investigation' and that fact, if you like, puts all communication into some sort of code. I believe that this 'codification' is detrimental to the efficient working of the police force; I mentioned this subject to Lord Mawsley and he kindly said he would be interested in provoking a discussion on it. He was also kind enough to suggest the meeting be held here and to provide the hospitality for which I'm certain you'll all want me to thank him. . . ."

There was a brief muted chorus of "Hear! Hear!" Lord Mawsley waved his hand deprecatingly.

"It boils down simply to this," Aveyard said. "I think I have learned much from what has happened to me recently. In this matter of the 'codification' of communications, I think, in a sense, that all our communications are becoming unnecessarily 'codified.' I don't think we talk to people any more. I think we interview or interrogate them. That may be all right with hardened criminals, with whom interviewing becomes a matter of skilled technique, but there are many occasions when we 'interview' or 'interrogate' unnecessarily. I have a particular chain of events in mind, and thought we might, informally here round this table, 'talk' about the events in that chain. Some of them concern me, and I have been suspended for my presumed part of them; some of them, however, concern Superintendent Colby. . . ."

Colby shifted uncomfortably on his chair. "I wondered why I had been invited," he said.

"You've been invited," Aveyard said crisply, "because I don't want, as a brother officer, the same thing to happen to you that has happened to me. I don't want you to be suspended 'pending investigation,' cut off from . . ."

Chief Superintendent Beasley interrupted. "If you have a complaint to make about a fellow officer, this is not the time or the place to make it."

The ACC spoke next. "Lord Mawsley, I'm certain your motives in calling this meeting were beyond reproach, but . . ."

"If you truly believe them to be 'beyond reproach,' Assistant Chief Constable, then you'll perhaps do me the honour of letting the meeting continue?"

Of all the senoir officers present, Batty knew Aveyard best. "All right, lad," he said. "You've had my trust and confidence for a long time. I don't think, from what I knew of you, that you'd wilfully hurt another officer to save your own skin. So, get on with it. No frills, no fancy stuff. Just get on with it. Perhaps we might all learn something!"

"On the night of the twenty-seventh of last month," Aveyard said, "somebody murdered Police Constable Baron. We've all been engaged in an investigation of that murder, with the exception of Chief Superintendent Beasley. I think, without realizing it, that he, too, has had a role to play in that investigation. But, if we may, let's go back beyond the murder. Let's go back to a time three months or more ago. Police Constable Baron, as we all know, was an enthusiastic and stubborn young man. He became passionately interested in the police force. Incidentally, unless you specifically want me to do so, I won't quote the source of any information I may use, though you'll have to trust me that I'll only say a thing positively if I can later substantiate it."

"We'd be here all night if we made you prove everything," Beasley said.

"Three months or more ago," Aveyard said, "I believe that Baron discovered that Herbert Wilson was operating an illegal roulette wheel. In a misguided attempt to obtain evidence, Baron 'accepted' a payment of two hundred pounds intended by Wilson to be a bribe. That two hundred pounds came from money drawn from the Herbert Wilson account in the NatWest Bank in Market Place, Birton. At the same time, I believe, Baron was told, rightly or wrongly, that 'a fix is in,' i.e., a senior officer is accepting the bribes to permit the wheel to continue to operate. Baron had no idea who this officer might be, and was too young, too inexperienced, to know what to do. He sat on the money and brooded for three months. Then, he decided he'd had enough, and asked Herbert Wilson to arrange a meeting between him and the senior officer. It was my belief that he intended to confront that senior officer, in the clubroom here at Mawsley Hall, and then, subsequently, disclose the name of the officer to Lord Mawsley, as Lord Lieutenant of the County and, more significantly, *the only man he knew absolutely that he could trust.*"

"What nonsense. He could have come to me," the ACC said.

"He could have come to me or my sergeant," Aveyard said, "but he didn't *know* that!"

A sudden light came to Chief Superintendent Batty's eye. "And that's why you have set up this meeting here, with Lord Mawsley's indulgence. Because you've taken a leaf out of Baron's book, and have realized that Lord Mawsley is the only man you can trust, too, to run the kind of meeting you want . . . ?"

Aveyard smiled at him, then nodded, happy to have resumed their relationship of understanding.

"Perhaps you'd like to get on with it, then?" the ACC said, not yet convinced of the propriety of the meeting but mollified by the presence of Lord Mawsley, the Lord Lieutenant of the County, on whom he could place the responsibility.

"On that night," Aveyard said, "the night of the murder, I believe a meeting did take place in the clubroom of the Hall. That meeting was concerned with this matter of bribery. Baron hoped that, as a result of that meeting, he would be able to expose this whole matter in a way that would, perhaps, mean promotion for himself."

"But you don't know who the other man at that meeting was," Superintendent Colby asked. All eyes turned to him and, suddenly aware that by speaking he had become the focus of attention, he licked his lips nervously and sat more upright in his chair.

"There are grounds for thinking," Aveyard said slowly, "that it might have been you."

The room became silent. Where, a moment before there had been voices, the normal shuffling of chair legs on carpets, the scratch of pencils on paper, the rhythmic intake and exhalation of breath, suddenly, there was nothing but silence. Colby's face turned white, pale-greenish white, as the blood fled from it.

Colby licked his lips again. "Am I accused?" he asked.

"This is not the correct way . . ." the ACC said, starting to rise in his chair.

Lord Mawsley extended his arm and pressed the ACC back down again. "You will all note the words that Superintendent Aveyard so carefully used," he said. "*There are grounds for thinking* . . . This does not constitute an accusation of any kind. Merely a statement of fact. Please proceed, Superintendent."

"That meeting was concluded," Aveyard said, "when Police Constable Baron was killed by means of an air pistol, or rather the lead pellet fired from an air pistol. That air pistol was later discovered in the pillow of a man, Ted Roper, and a quantity of ammunition was found. The man, Roper, has been arrested and charged with manslaughter. He has confessed to having killed Constable Baron and intends to plead self-defence at his trial."

Colby was shuffling nervously in his seat. "I don't think I want to stay here," he said, "to hear any more. I think I have certain rights as a police officer, and as a person, and I think those rights are being violated."

Aveyard turned to him. "Yes, you have rights," he said, "and had rights, too, and it's precisely because those rights were invoked by both sides that I find myself in my present position. If you want it that way, we can respect your rights, and the police force will respect its rights. I shall place certain facts at the disposal of the Chief and I am certain he will immediately suspend you from duty, just as I was suspended from duty. . . ."

"If you have such facts, Superintendent," the ACC said, his agitation revealing itself in his voice, "it's your duty to give them to me, now, and to permit me to proceed in the manner well established by police precedent and regulations. . . ."

"You're using the wrong words," Aveyard said. "It's not my *duty* to do anything. In fact, as Chief Superintendent Batty recently reminded me, it's my *duty*, according to *precedent* and *regulations*, to do *nothing*. Let's leave this matter of the meeting in the clubroom and the subsequent murder. Let's go to the matter of my involvement with the investigation of the crime. I believe that Herbert Wilson knew about the investigation of the murder of Baron through the newspapers, and suspected that, as Investigating Officer, I would discover his bribery and the reason for it, and therefore arranged the bank account, using a known criminal to whom I have talked, as a way of getting me off the investigation of the crime."

"The information of that 'criminal' should have been given to Chief Superintendent Beasley," the ACC said, his face suffused with anger. "Look, Aveyard, it seems to me that you have acquired knowledge which, if you won't accept the word *duty*, it is in your own *interest* to give to your Investigating Officer."

Beasley coughed. "With respect, sir, that information has already been given to me. . . ."

"Then why haven't you used it . . . ?"

"Because, sir, with respect, it was given to me in a manner that prevented me using it."

"You see where *duty* and *regulations* get us," Aveyard said. "Information isn't a solid piece of property that can be handed from one person to another according to regulations. Information comes from one person, yes, but that person is always involved in that information. A fact isn't made into a fact by being stated by a person. That person has to be prepared to hold himself ready to verify that fact. And if the verification involves that person in the disclosure of other information . . . why do you think that, in their wisdom, when framing the Constitution of the United States of America, for example, they made provisions to prevent a man being forced to declare information which might be detrimental to his own welfare . . . ?"

"But we don't have a 'Fifth Amendment' in British police procedures," the ACC triumphantly said.

"No, but we should have something much more potent. Individual responsibility. I will not be a party to coercing a man to give evidence against himself on my behalf, in my defence, in my own *interest,* as you said, merely to get myself off the hook. Anyway, let's pass from that matter of Herbert Wilson, to the matter of the clubroom, and the events in there after the murder. As we know, two people went into that clubroom after the murder. The first was Ted Roper. Ted Roper has stated that the body was in the clubroom when he arrived, already dead. Cedric Mawsley went to the clubroom, and we now have expert medical opinion that Cedric Mawsley was in no condition to fire that gun. Anyway, according to witnesses to the time of his arrival, Baron was already dead when Cedric Mawsley arrived, and fell unconscious into the chair next to the body, without, I suspect, being aware that the body was there."

Batty had been making notes on his pad. "So far, Aveyard, you've given us two suspects who didn't do it, and two suspects who might have. One of those suspects is Herbert Wilson, and the other the man who was taking bribes, the man Baron was hoping to meet that night and expose to Lord Mawsley. One question not yet answered is the matter of Roper and the gun and the ammunition. Do you want to say anything about them?"

"Yes. Forensic searched that house and found nothing. Later, Superintendent Colby and Sergeant Bruton found a pistol in a pillow, and a quantity of ammunition in a cigarette box."

"Which, the report says, carried Roper's fingerprints."

"That's right."

Once again, though all were listening to Aveyard, all were watching Superintendent Colby. "I discovered the gun," he whispered, "but Sergeant Bruton discovered the ammunition. I wasn't even in the house when the ammunition was discovered."

"I remind you," Lord Mawsley said in a kindly voice, "that no accusations have been made, Superintendent Colby."

"Nor will be, in my presence," the ACC said.

"I should think you're coming near to the end of things Aveyard, aren't you?" Batty said. He knew the dangers of carrying a thing on too long; he could sense that the ACC was being restless and soon would remember his official rank and status, and find his continued presence in this "discussion" incompatible with Police Procedures.

"Yes, I'm nearly finished. But now I come to the crux of the matter. From the matters I have so far raised, it becomes apparent that one should look for the murderer either at Herbert Wilson, or at the man reputed to be accepting bribes from Herbert Wilson. I can give you, a blueprint, if you like, of that man. He is obviously a member of the Birton police force, obviously a senior officer. I can give you a couple of pure speculations. Perhaps he possesses a tan-coloured gabardine coat, and on the left-side window of his car, at this moment, is a Point-to-Point sticker.

"Damn it, there's one of those on my car," Batty said. "I possess a tan-coloured gabardine coat, and I'm a senior officer of the Birton Police Force. Are you accusing me?"

Aveyard shook his head. "Let's approach this matter from another point of view. For the man to be a murderer, he has to have the opportunity to commit that murder. We have to say—where were you on the night of . . ."

"That lets me and the Assistant Chief Constable out." Batty said. "We were both together at that dreadful dinner, and then I came straight to Police Headquarters and into your office."

"This is intolerable," the ACC said. "We don't have to give alibis. I don't think I can tolerate any more of this. With your permission, Lord Mawsley . . ."

"Assistant Chief Constable, I urge you, in the strongest possible terms, to hear Superintendent Aveyard out."

Batty nodded to Aveyard. "Get on with it, lad," he said, "and be quick about it."

"Superintendent Colby has the qualifications we were talking about. He possesses a tan coat, a sticker on his car, he's a senior police officer of the Birton Force and, on the night of the murder, though he told his Incidents Officer he was going to interview a witness, *he had already interviewed that witness several hours earlier*. . . . He discovered the gun that implicated Ted Roper, after

Forensic had failed to find it, and he gave Roper cigarettes in his cell, from a packet." Now Colby's complexion had turned even greener as his face drained completely of blood. He looked at the ACC, at Lord Mawsley, at each man round the table, but finally his eyes settled on Aveyard and Bruton, both sitting silent. His shoulders slumped forwards, his spine hunched, his tongue licked his dry lips. He was a broken man. "All right," he said, "all right. You know, don't you? You know I did it."

★

Aveyard let out his breath in one long continuous sigh. "Yes," he said, "I know you did it."

Batty leaned forward, his eyes gleaming like those of a mountain bird. "Did what, Aveyard, did what?"

"He planted the evidence to try to get a quicker ending to the case. . . ."

"Not the gun," Colby whispered, "only the ammunition."

Aveyard turned to him in surprise. "Not the gun . . . ?"

"No, I swear it!"

"Will somebody please tell me what is going on?" the ACC said, irritated. Aveyard was deep in thought, half-looking at Sergeant Bruton, who was frowning with concentration.

"*Not* the gun?" Bruton asked.

"Lord Mawsley, I appeal to you . . ." the ACC said, his voice a mixture of anger and confusion.

Lord Mawsley had made no notes, but had followed every word of the conversations across the table. "I think I can understand," he said, "and perhaps the Assistant Chief Constable is right. Superintendent Aveyard has laid out the manner and nature of a crime for us, the crime of murdering Constable Baron. He's also indicated that evidence does exist to suspect Superintendent Colby of that crime. Motive—concealment of bribery. Occasion—a meeting that had been demanded by Constable Baron in the clubroom here at the Hall. Weapon—an air pistol. With such evidence as he possesses, admittedly much of it circumstantial, Aveyard would have been justified in reporting to a senior officer. Colby would have been suspended, just as Aveyard was suspended. But, and here Superintendent Aveyard must correct me if I'm wrong, he saw that such an accusation, though it conformed to the evidence in his possession, could not ultimately be justified."

"That's right, Lord Mawsley. I knew Superintendent Colby hadn't committed that crime. I knew he was involved—frankly I thought he had planted the gun and the ammunition to secure the conviction of Ted Roper. . . ."

"I thought Roper had done it, when the gun was found. I honestly thought he'd done it . . ." Colby whispered.

"But he hadn't. Any more than you had."

"You say you *know* Colby hadn't done it, you *know* Ted Roper hadn't done it," Chief Superintendent Batty said. "But how do you *know?*"

"Because I *know* who has done it."

"And that is . . . ?"

"Herbert Wilson."

CHAPTER 17

Colby was holding one end of the plank, Bruton the other, and Aveyard was bent beneath it fixing the last screw, when the Chief Superintendent walked into the office. "They've brought Herbert Wilson back from Mallorca," he said. "He should be here in a few minutes." He looked round what had been Aveyard's office, at the computer terminal newly fixed beneath the window on its own aluminium desk, the wall charts with their coloured flags and pins, the large map of the county which occupied one wall. "I think you'll be comfortable in here," he said, "with all your new toys."

Colby nodded vigorously. "I hope Bill will be as comfortable in my old office."

Bruton took hold of the chair behind the desk. "One thing is certain," he said, "he won't be if we don't give him his old chair."

"I have high hopes of this Crime Prevention Unit," the Chief said, "and now you're not going to Worcester, I think you're just the man to run it."

Colby seemed ill at ease. "It's very hard for me to say this," he said, "but I hope you all know how grateful I am. To all of you. To you, Sergeant Bruton, for persisting in making enquiries when I had closed my mind against Roper. To you, Chief, when you discovered I'd falsified the evidence about the ammunition, for interceding with the Chief Constable on my behalf. . . ."

"Lord Mawsley helped a bit there, lad. He accepted that you hadn't planted the gun but that, once you were convinced Roper had done the crime, you just wanted a tidy prosecution. If there'd been the slightest hint of self-interest, you know how we would have gone for you. But most of all, if you're grateful to anyone, you ought to be grateful to Bill Aveyard here. . . ."

"I am," Colby said. "I am. For 'talking the crime out,' rather than making accusations that would have meant my suspension and a departmental enquiry. . . ."

"I knew you'd never commit such a crime. I knew you'd never accept a bribe. It was as easy as that. Too many things smelled wrong to me. Cedric Mawsley sitting next to the corpse. Mumby being a 'fixer.' Ted Roper killing someone by means of an air pistol. And, of course, a senior officer of the Birton Police Force accepting bribes from someone like Herbert Wilson, for something he couldn't do anything about anyway. That was all a story, concocted by Herbert Wilson to throw Baron off the track. An experienced officer would have laughed right in Wilson's face and collared him."

"It's still a mystery who planted that gun in the pillowcase . . ." Colby said, musing.

"Not to me, it isn't. I don't know who actually did it, and perhaps we may never find out. But I'm certain we'll discover it was planted by somebody acting for Herbert Wilson, just as Wentworth was acting for Herbert Wilson when he forged my signature."

The telephone rang and Aveyard instinctively went to answer it, but then he stopped. "It's yours, now!" he said smiling. Colby picked up the phone and said his name. He listened and then turned to the Chief. "They've brought in Herbert Wilson," he said.

The Chief looked at Bill Aveyard. "Back to work?" he said.

"Yes," Bill Aveyard said, "back to work. One thing I'd like to do first." He picked up the telephone, dialled an internal number. "Claude," he said when the voice answered, "I think I've got one for you. Ted Roper. Lives in the village of Mawsley. We've had him in for suspicion of murder, but we've let him go. I think he's one of yours." He put down the telephone. "Ted Roper had to be going to that clubroom for a reason, didn't he? Cedric Mawsley had to have some strong incentive to get back as far as the clubroom, even though the alcohol/amphetamine mixture was killing him. I think they were going to meet each other. I think Ted Roper will turn out to be a pusher. Anyway, Claude and his Drugs Squad will find out. Now," he said "let's give Mr. Herbert Wilson a reception committee. Nailing him will be the best bit of Crime Prevention you'll ever do," he said, linking his arm with Colby's.

"You want me there?" Colby said.

"Yes, I do. And on the way down, you can answer a question that's been baffling me. Where exactly *were* you, at ten o'clock on the night of the twenty-seventh when you were supposed to be interviewing Mrs. Chase in No 4, Ormsby Villas, in the village of Wovenhoe . . . ?"

Jim Bruton went with them. After all, he was interested in the answer, too.

MYSTERY

Fraser, J.
Who steals my name?